SON OF TERROR

Frankenstein Continued

William A. Chanler

ISBN-13: 9781541343085

ISBN-10: 1541343085

William A. Chanler

Preface

The titan Prometheus made man out of clay and then stole fire to improve the quality of life for mankind. Victor Frankenstein, like Prometheus, created a man. Frankenstein achieved that groundbreaking milestone though scientific knowledge and unscrupulous acts with the purpose of creating a prototype of superior intelligence and gargantuan proportions. Both Prometheus and Frankenstein paid dearly for their ungodly acts.

This is the story of Frankenstein's immortal creature. It tells what happened to him after Victor's death in the Arctic. Would he be given an opportunity to redeem himself or shunned by mankind the rest of his life?

It is helpful to know the essence of Mary Shelley's story. Victor Frankenstein was repulsed by his creation's horrific looking face and gargantuan body. The creature aimlessly wandered the countryside, foraging for sustenance, mystified why people hated him. His sharp mind was his best asset. He learned to read and write, eventually fluent in several languages.

The monster blamed Frankenstein for his misery. He killed Victor's baby brother William and framed Justine, a member of the Frankenstein household for William's murder.

The eight-foot tall fiend met up with Frankenstein in the ice and snow covered mountains above Geneva, Switzerland. He persuaded an extremely reluctant Frankenstein to make a woman. After much procrastination, Victor set about the heinous task. Then, just before finishing his work, the creature witnessed Frankenstein destroy her. Furious, he began another killing spree, killing Frankenstein's best friend and bride.

After Victor recovered from a long illness and breakdown, he set out after the creature. The chase took them to the Arctic. The crew of an icebound ship saw the gigantic form of the creature on a dogsled. Sometime later, Victor stopped at the ship. He was taken aboard by Captain Walton and allowed time to rest before continuing his deadly pursuit.

Eventually Frankenstein told Walton his horrific story which the sea captain transcribed in a series of letters addressed to Walton's sister. After Frankenstein's death in Walton's cabin the captain encountered Victor's nemesis there. He allowed the giant to escape after announcing his intent to die in a funeral pyre.

Our story begins several days afterwards.

Chapter 1

The blizzard blew huge crystal-shaped snowflakes on his ugly, cold face. It was summer in the Arctic. The planet was in the midst of a mini Ice Age.

The gigantic man trudged onward, step by step into the gale as the snow lashed down and accumulated on the frozen terrain. Normal men would have hunkered down in a snow cave but he was not like other men.

* * *

A majestically antlered buck galloped through the forest, his face full of fear as he ran for his life. He was pursued by the eight-foot tall survivor of the Arctic journey. The man remarkably kept pace with his prey.

The distance between man and beast gradually lessened as they scampered over fallen branches and leafy, uneven terrain. The frantic animal, eyes bulging and tongue dangling, raced downhill, through a stream and then up a steep gravelly incline. Its hooves momentarily lost traction but managed to scamper up to the top. The buck accelerated on the level ground beyond.

* * *

A twenty-one year old woman drove a brown Ford Taurus on Maine State Route 90, a quiet two lane highway in rural Maine, less than ten miles from Penobscot Bay. A Neil Young song, "No More," played loudly on her mp3 player. She focused on the song's rhythm and Young's plaintive singing than on the road ahead. Her head and upper torso moved with the beat.

Less than a hundred feet ahead a large buck sprinted across the road, chased by what looked like an impossibly tall humanoid. Mary blinked, not believing what she saw. The gigantic being quickly looked left then right while never losing his stride. Their eyes locked on each other for a few seconds before he reached the far side of road and disappeared into the forest.

Mary slammed on the brakes, burning a trail of black rubber on the macadam highway. The vehicle came to a complete stop near where the man and deer crossed the highway. She breathed heavily while peering into the woods. Though the music on the audio system was loud she no longer heard it. Her mind already drifted to a different time and place.

* * *

The giant pursued the deer for a half mile. He sensed the animal's stamina weakening.

Now is the time to put him out of his misery.

He sprinted alongside his prey, angling closer. Then he leaped into the air with hands outstretched. The gigantic yellowish pale scarred hands grabbed the antlers and the buck crashed down. It struggled to get up but the hunter used his enormous brute strength to savagely twist the majestic antlers, breaking the buck's neck.

The giant, breathing heavily, stood up and gazed compassionately at his work. His two greatest physical attributes were his size and terrible face. His height was almost eight feet tall. His body was lean and hard. His pallor was almost a deathly white. Black, thin, uncombed hair mopped his forehead and covered his scarred neck.

He scanned the immediate area with a pair of intelligent, penetrating yellow eyes to make sure there were no human witnesses. Old scars lined his horrific face. The mouth was lined with pencil thin dark lips. He looked about forty-five years old but was in fact much older.

The slain buck lay with his tongue dangling out. The giant squatted down and peered into the beast's dead eyes, transfixed. Honoring the life of a slain animal was one of the hunter's rituals.

How many has it been? How many have I killed?

The prodigious quantity of deer, rabbits, and other species he slaughtered to sustain him. But he had killed dozens of men, too for a number of other reasons. Thankfully he has not been forced to being in almost a century.

Back in the closing decade of eighteenth century Europe, he murdered Victor Frankenstein's best friend, bride and brother among others. He blamed Victor for turning him into a monster. It was Victor who created the man with a gigantic frame, long arms, and a frightful face horror that made women faint or scream on sight, and men cringe.

Victor Frankenstein was the first to be repulsed by him. The young scientist fled the chamber adjoining the laboratory moments after watching the creature gaze down at him with a scary grin. The monster was ill-treated by practically everybody he met. Only a kindly blind man treated him fairly.

It wasn't his fault he looked like a monster but people treated him as one nevertheless. He was born with a healthy brain, one that helped him learn languages and understand who was to blame for his grave misfortune.

Over the seemingly endless decades since then, he has learned to diminish his horrific appearance with makeup and wear hats that cast shadows over his frightening face. He often wore shirts with the collars turned up to cover the scars on his neck. But not on this day. It was a warm day even in eastern Maine. He wore a size 6x large green t-shirt, a belt with scabbard, army style pants and size 22 EE brown boots.

He was an intimidating force of nature with a sharp intellect, a being to be respected, feared and yet had qualities to be admired. He was the epitome of the ultimate survivor. No living thing in the history of planet Earth had ever lived as long as this larger than life man. Would his lifespan be endured for additional centuries? Or would it finally end? He does not particularly care one way or the other.

The goliath was never christened by his creator, though he was called many names: monster, fiend, demon and creature. He adopted over the years several aliases starting with Sohn der Schrenken, German for "Son of Terror". That slowly evolved to a more Americanized Sohn (pronounced "zone") Schrenk.

Sohn often contemplated the beginning of the post Victor Frankenstein era, starting with when he floated on an ice float, drifting away from Walton's southbound ship. Fortune turned in his favor when he found himself within sight of his abandoned sled. He's let the remaining huskies free earlier. So he ended up pulling the sled, planning to use the wood to build his funeral pyre.

Then, some days later, deciding to go on living, he's roasted a walrus on the dying coals of his funeral fire. The beast was shot with the last remaining stolen gun in his possession. He was also armed a serrated long knife.

Sohn walked westward along the southern Arctic coast always keeping the ocean in sight to his left. He both hoped for and dreaded the prospect of seeing distant sails on the horizon. Sohn wanted to put as much distance as possible between himself and his native Europe. Perhaps North America held a better future.

I will be a new person there. Sohn laughed at himself angrily. *I have to keep walking. It's better than lying down and freezing to death or being burned alive on my funeral pyre. Damn Victor Frankenstein for creating me!*

Sohn trod onward in the bleak white wilderness while continuing to reflect on his violent solitary past. Positive contact with people was an extreme rarity as his physical appearance evoked fear and hostility. There was no wood for building a fire so he ate raw whatever wildlife he could slaughter. The warm blood and organs sustained him.

Can I blame people for reacting as they do? How many doors have closed in my face? How many people have turned their backs on me and fled for their lives? Who wants to spend time with a freak of nature, a monstrosity in dimension and ugliness?

The monster bitterly remembered the final time he saw Victor, laying lifeless in Captain Walton's cabin. Sohn, in despair, intended to incinerate his eight foot tall body in a bonfire at the very top of the world. But just as he was about to take a final leap into the flames, he thought Victor spoke to him from the underworld.

LIVE!

Sohn backed away, his eyes transfixed by the eerie blaze. *Did I really hear that?* He would wonder many time in the months and years ahead whether it was his own imagination or Victor communicating with him, life it was, miserable or not.

Sohn would always regret that he and Victor, his mentor and surrogate father, never bonded. But it never happened. Victor regretted his creation practically from the moment he encountered him. Sohn wanted acceptance, Victor chose denial. Sohn wanted Victor's help. Victor wanted nothing to do with him.

Sohn mourned Victor's death as he trod across the bleak, desolate tundra but came to realize that dwelling on the events of their time together was detrimental to his survival. In essence, Victor continued to be a negative influence by simply thinking about their failed relationship. Determined that better days lay ahead, Sohn sought to overcome challenges. He had a destiny to fulfill, whatever it might be.

As he stepped on to the hardened tundra Sohn contemplated what he would do should he encounter a wayward ship's crew. Verbal communication wouldn't be an issue as he was fluent in German and English. A ship's crew usually included men from diverse countries so there would be somebody he would understand. Sohn covered his face with fur from a wolverine he'd recently killed. He was still ferocious looking, but that couldn't be changed.

He kept walking with his sharp observant eyes scanning the distant horizon.

* * *

Mary awoke from her stark daydream of the giant. She seemed to be with him in a shadowy gray world from an earlier time. Was it in Europe? But the scene quickly receded from her consciousness.

Rap. Rap.

Mary looked to her left. A gray haired man in a plaid flannel shirt stood there, bent forward and looking at her anxiously. He circled his right hand, indicating that Mary should lower her window. Mary nodded and did so.

"You okay, miss?" he inquired.

Mary's eyes were a little glazed but she understood him clearly enough.

"Yes."

Pointing at the rubber marks on the highway, he said, "Where you testing your brakes or something?"

"I saw a deer and—"

"And you stopped to avoid it?" the man said, interrupting her.

Mary turned toward the slight opening in the woods where the man and deer had vanished before turning back to the stranger. She decided to agree with the Good Samaritan. Explaining what she saw wouldn't be smart.

"Yes."

"Well, hunting season is in a couple months, though that'll barely put a dent in their population. That's for sure," he said in his Maine accent. He regarded her curiously. "You okay to drive?"

"I'm fine." Mary smiled reassuringly. "I should be going. Thanks for asking."

Mary rolled up the window and eased down on the accelerator, backing the car slowly away from the man. He watched the Ford pick up speed, then shook his head and returned to his truck.

* * *

Meanwhile, back in 1798 Arctic, Sohn tried to devise a plan for what to do should he encounter another ship's crew.

Will they attack me at first sight? Should I skirt around them? I don't know. All I know is that I'm tired of trouble. I want to get along with people if they will allow it. Peaceful coexistence. Is it too much to expect? Am I like the Devil in Paradise Lost *with no hope for redemption?*

Where would he go? How could he interact with mankind without being detested and feared? The first question was easy to answer. Heading westward would eventually bring him to northern Canada. Once there, he would drift south. The population at the end of the 18th Century was concentrated in the southern region near the border with the recently independent young nation known as The United States. If he ran into anybody at all in northern or central Canada chances were they'd be fur traders.

During a week on the tundra, the only breathing beings he saw were birds, arctic hare, wolverines, seals and walruses. He ate them as needed trying not to waste the precious meat.

Then one morning he came upon a partially buried shipwreck. The vessel was mostly shrouded with snow and its bowels braced in thick ice. The giant stopped several hundred feet from the ship. He had perfect vision and hearing. He carefully scanned every inch for signs of habitation and strained his ears for any human sounds. There was no sign of life on board.

"Hello," he shouted.

He waited patiently for a few minutes. Then he sprang into action, taking long quick strides, narrowing the distance to the wreck rapidly before leaping onto the main deck. Sohn stopped instantaneously and looked all around him at his deserted surroundings. There were no recent footprints in the snow encrusted planking other than his own.

He looked down at his enormous footprints, slowly raised his eyes to the horizon and did a 360 degree turn seeing no life forms at all.

"Solitude sometimes is best society" he proclaimed with extended arms. He nodded with satisfaction. Perhaps it was just as well as he wasn't yet prepared to face anybody.

His stomach growled. Was there still food below deck or had the crew taken everything when they abandoned ship? Sohn expected they would have been unable to take everything with them by hand so he stepped across the deck and ducked his head below the hatch and went down a steep staircase.

* * *

Mary was bewildered as she drove down the highway hardly aware of the road ahead and her surroundings. She was essentially on mental auto pilot. The giant's eyes had been both hypnotic and disturbing. They were old eyes that had seen too much. Mary somehow knew that even though they had interfaced for only a few seconds. She lowered all of the windows to clear her thoughts and disperse the images. She smiled as her hair blew freely in the wind, forcing the recent disturbance into the recesses of her mind.

"It's a beautiful day and I'm going to make the most of it," she said aloud. Mind over matter and the power of positive thinking were two of her mottos. Mary needed to dig deep within herself to overcome her discomfort.

Chapter 2

Mary was born in New York City. Her family lived in a townhouse on the Upper East Side of Manhattan. Her father, William Godwin, came from old money. He was descended from Governor John Winthrop of The Massachusetts Bay Colony. Mary's mother, Mary died giving birth to her daughter. William remarried a year later. Jane, Mary's stepmother was a third generation American. Her grandparents emigrated from Russia during the civil war between The White Russians loyal to the Tsar and Red Russians following Lenin and his followers. Basically one side favored right wing totalitarianism and the other championed left wing totalitarianism.

Mary attended Hewitt School a private school for girls through the eighth grade. Her parents then followed the longstanding tradition of sending their child away to complete her secondary education at a prestigious boarding school. Mary spent the next four school years at Kent School in eastern Connecticut. She was initially homesick but gradually adapted to life away from home. She developed a few close friends but could never be considered overtly friendly. She was somewhat guarded. People had to earn her trust before she would open herself to them.

Her education was paid by a family trust and her father's earnings as publisher of *Manhattan*, a magazine devoted to covering all aspects of city living. Mary interned there during the summer following her junior year at Kent. She wrote a well-received article about the effects of global warming on the city, focusing on recent research into the rising sea level. The subject concerned Mary deeply as she believed the oceans of the world would gradually force mankind to retreat from low coastlines. Mary learned Manhattan wasn't the only borough that would be affected by the rising waters. But she adhered to the magazine's mission by concentrating on her native island.

The word Manhattan meant the island of many hills. Most of those hills were no longer part of the prodigiously populated island. They were razed over the past two centuries to allow construction of apartment buildings and commercial structures. To Mary that meant that more of the island would be susceptible to flooding. Also many office towers were constructed on landfill sites only a few feet above sea level. She foresaw the day, possibly in her lifetime, when much of the island would have to be abandoned.

That was the only summer of her young life Mary didn't spend with her parents at their island property in Maine. They had a fine summer cottage on Islesboro, located on the eastern section of Penobscot Bay. The property included several hundred feet of pebbled beachfront and a dock with granite piers. Mary loved the spectacular views of the island speckled azure bay and the pine scents.

Drivers customarily waved to each other on the narrow roads intersecting the long and narrow island. The customer waving in the city required one raised middle finger.

"It's awesome," she often told herself whenever gazing at the beautiful panoramic views. Schooners, lobster boats, pleasure cruisers and racing sloops often sailed past the house.

She sacrificed most of that summer to experience city living without her parents though her father flew down from Down East to check up on her and hold meetings at the magazine.

She did very little socializing as most of her friends shunned the city during the summer, preferring the Hamptons and other upper crust enclaves. Evenings generally found her at home reading her favorite authors such as Jane Austen, the Bronte sisters, Edgar Allan Poe and Thomas Hardy as well as several current authors including Stephen King, Joyce Carol Oates and Emma Donoghue. Mary enjoyed old movies though she'd see a new film occasionally with a friend.

The young men she saw outside of work were generally friends from school or sons of her parents' friends. She loved red wine. Mary risked her father's wrath in raiding the well-stocked wine cellar, choosing the least expensive bottles to keep her guilt in check. If caught, she'd own up to it. She always felt responsible for her actions even when sharing a drink with a date.

* * *

There wasn't a lot of levity in Sohn's life. He had his good and bad days like everyone. The day he discovered food and other supplies in the storeroom of the abandoned whaling ship was a good day. He gathered up a stack of provisions, bundling and strapping them like a backpack. He spent a comfortable night next to the vessel. Sohn used flint and steel to ignite some dried out planks. The fire-starting materials became his most prized

22

possessions. They would provide heat to keep him warm on cold nights and enable him to eat cooked meat on too many meals to count. They were essentially the instruments to his survival.

The only item he owned longer was Victor's wedding ring, given to him by Captain Walton. The ring barely fit on Sohn's pinkie but he intended to wear it for perpetuity in memory of his creator.

The ring gleamed in the firelight. The giant stared at it and spoke aloud. "Father, what do you think? How does your ring look?"

He laughed loudly. A distant howl replied. Sohn stopped laughing immediately. He turned his hideous face toward the sound.

"Come friends. Then you will sing no more. "

He lay down on a thick fur lined blanket and closed his eyes.

* * *

Mary lay asleep on a comfortable bed in the Islesboro house. Her bedroom was infinitely dark except for a thin thread of light from a clock radio on the night table to her right. It read 1:38 AM. Her eyes darted open. Did she hear something? Was someone standing outside the dark house looking up at her bedroom window?

That's crazy! I've never been scared!

Mary contemplated the possibility of a nearby malevolent presence. She was too scared to climb out of bed to find out. Scared stiff!

Suddenly there was a sharp KLUNK from somewhere in the house. *Was it downstairs?* She concentrated intently, trying to discern any more sounds.

Nothing.

"Oh hell!" She got some comfort from hearing her voice.

With a start she abruptly removed the covers and sat on the side of the double bed. She rose to her feet and turned her attention to the closed bedroom door. There was nothing there but the door itself. She tiptoed softly and lightly. A floorboard creaked. *Damn!* Mary kept moving, passing the open window, keeping her eyes looking straight ahead.

Mary stood in front of the door, taking a deep breathe in and out to calm herself. She fumbled for the knob then grabbed it firmly. *Here goes nothing.* She opened the door quietly and stepped into the hallway. There was nobody there; just an empty dark hall. She nevertheless strode forward cautiously barely seeing the walls to her left and right. She stopped at the top of a broad staircase. A shaft of light illuminates part of the first floor below. She dashed down the stairs, suddenly confident that a light implied no stranger was in the house.

Mary turned right at the bottom of the stairwell into a foyer. The marble floor cooled her feet as she veered right. She move into an ornate dining room. The light progressively brightens as she passed through the room. She pushed open a door at the near right and entered the butler's pantry and adjoining kitchen.

* * *

A tall bonfire burned brightly in the forest. Sohn sat a few feet away feeling content, stomach full, gazing peacefully at the hypnotic flames. The partially eaten carcass of the deer lay nearby. It was tough to beat venison charbroiled over a roaring fire. He intended to carry a sizable one hundred pound chunk home in the morning.

Sohn thought about the woman in the car. He normally didn't give such a fleeting encounter a second's thought but his intuitive mind insisted otherwise in that instance.

Who is she?

Sohn possessed a remarkable memory. If he's seen a person once, the memory was recorded permanently in his brain, enabling him to recall the time and place of the happenstance. He searched his memory banks without success.

"I don't know her," he told the carcass.

Why should I care who she is? He didn't have an answer. And that bothered him. He then engaged in a conversation with himself, half thought, half spoken aloud.

"I must find her."

Why should I?

"She means something."

Meaning what?

"I don't know."

How will I find the answer?

"Find her."

Sohn nodded. He felt better, knowing he's made the right decision. He lay down and continued thinking about the mysterious young woman in the car.

Who are you?

Where are you?

He still had no answer to either question. But there was no doubt in his mind the mystery wasn't permanent. His eyes closed. Sleep eluded him. His mind refused to shut down for the night. He can't stop wondering about the woman. Sohn wondered if he made an impression on her. Her eyes had widen in surprise on seeing him. Having a close encounter with a man of his dimensions and horrific face left quite an imprint on everybody.

Is she thinking about me? I hope so. If so, I'll find her.

Sohn has developed a unique ability. Just like his fine sense of danger, he used someone's thoughts of him as a diving rod. The more Mary Godwin thought about him the easier it was to locate her. Mental GPS!

Never fear. I'm coming.

He closed his eyes and slowly began the process of clearing his mind of all thoughts other than the woman. Let the search begin.

* * *

Mary entered the kitchen expecting to see one of her parents there. Someone else was in the room. Verna Gilkey, the family's housekeeper and cook, stood by the stove. She was a plain looking middle aged widow. Her husband Lew recently drowned after getting entangled in fishing lines on his trawler. The Godwins have allowed her to take a room in their spacious house while she dealt with Lew's untimely death.

Verna poured steaming water into a teacup, putting the pot back on the burner and turned to Mary, forcing a weak smile.

"I hope I didn't wake you," she said in a Maine accent.

"Not at all," Mary replied as she stops beside Verna. "I couldn't sleep."

Verna looked closely at Mary. "You look troubled."

"I guess that goes for both of us"

"But you're not usually like that, young lady." Mary smiled. "I guess not." She turned serious. "Verna, how are you doing?"

Verna walked to a nearby table and sat down, still holding the cup. Mary sat beside her.

"Oh, I'm managing. Night is the toughest time with nothing to do but watch the seconds ticking away on the clock and thinking about things. I can't stop thinking about my Lew. Her eyes misted. Mary placed a hand on Vera's free hand. *Should I tell Verna about the incident to distract her?* Mary has so far not told a soul partly because it seems too incredulous. She hated being doubted.

Verna looked at Mary. She frowned. "Will you tell me about it?"

Mary looked at Verna, and then averted her eyes. Perhaps she should say something.

"Something happened today. It was both incredible and scary. But nobody will believe me if I tell you what I saw."

"Try me."

"Are you sure?"

"I've heard a lot, my dear. Lew had quite a mouth. He'd exchanged a bunch of whoppers over the years with his old pals. So there's no need to hold back."

Should I or shouldn't I? What the hell! She sighed.

"Alright then," Mary began somewhat reluctantly to tell Verna about that afternoon's road crossing incident.

* * *

The giant suddenly stiffened. *She must be thinking of me at this very moment.* Sohn rose up, eyes still closed. He slowly rotated a full circle then reversed his motion. He stopped part way. His eyes opened to see which direction he faced. He peered up at the sky, noting the stars and planets. The night sky, though not as efficient as GPS is as good as any compass.

He nodded with satisfaction. *Well now, that's a start. I know the direction but not the distance. Keep thinking of me, my young one.*

* * *

Verna didn't know what to think or say. *Mary is as good a story teller as Lew. She even seemed to believe what she was saying as if it really happened. Was she drinking or taking drugs? Was that it/ I heard people can hallucinate from taking stuff. She really over exaggerated the man's size. And chasing down a buck was preposterous.* She didn't want to offend Mary especially as the young woman had been reluctant to discuss the matter.

"That's really something," she said neutrally.

"You don't believe me," Mary replied morosely. Verna sipped the tea and rested the cup on the table. She looked at Mary thoughtfully.

"How would you react if someone told you that same story? I mean doesn't it sound farfetched?" Verna asked.

Mary looked down, trying to hide the disappointment. She was upset at herself for broaching the subject. But Verna was right. Nobody would believe her story. She sighed again.

"You're right. Forget I said anything." She got up. "I'm tired. See you later, okay?"

Verna watched Mary step away. *Maybe I should have simply accepted Mary's anecdote as factual. B*ut she couldn't be anything but true to her stubborn New England Yankee self.

Verna nodded. "See you later, dear."

Mary turned and abruptly left the kitchen.

Chapter 3

The wolf pack liked the taste of human flesh and blood. They picked off two exhausted emaciated and half blind stragglers from the crew of the abandoned ship that Sohn recently explored.

The sun shone on the bleak arctic wilderness close to eighteen hours a day. As there was no such thing as dark glasses in that era the constant brightness damaged the retinas something fierce. And to boot there was a mini ice age. The shipping lane separating Canada from the Arctic was frozen solid most of the year. There were layers upon layers of massive snowcapped ice shelves covering thousands of square miles.

The crew survived their painstaking journey on half rations, then reduced by Captain Pounds to one quarter rations before the northern timberline was in their sight line. The wolves smelled the man before seeing them. The hungry animals watched the ragged procession slowly approach from the edge of the forest. They waited patiently for any opportunity to attack the interlopers.

Sohn covered his brutal looking face and much of his eyes with fur from an arctic fox. It partially shielded his eyes from the ever constant white light and cold. He made good time trekking through the snow and ice, slowly catching up to the crew of the abandoned ship.

Sohn discovered their trail when he saw discarded empty food tins. Then he noticed the faint imprints of boots in the snow.

Frankenstein's Creature squatted and peered at the prints etched in the snow. Sohn stood next to them, faintly amused at how small theirs were compared to his. He peered ahead with a hand shielding his eyes, trying to make out movement ahead, but the landscape was empty. He shook his head before continuing the odyssey in a southwestern direction, his eyes alternating between the overlapping prints, strewn garbage and horizon. The view changed an hour later when he noticed trees for the first time. His pace quickened from the steady six miles an hour to ten miles an hour.

What will I do when I catch up with them?

Up ahead, less than a mile from the desolate Arctic wilderness, the wolf pack decided that trailing their intended victims through the trees was a waste of time.

The savage beasts sprang into action and assaulted the men all together. The attack surprised the depleted men. Several throats were ripped out before the first gunshot rang out. Ammunition was low as most of it had been used in shooting wild game the past two days. The snow was deep making speed difficult for the weakened men especially for those with frostbitten toes and feet.

Two of the men became separated in the desperate scramble away from the vicious carnivores. They were caught by the leaping wolves. The impact knocked both men off their feet. Sharp canine teeth savagely ripping open throats. Blood streamed from the lacerated throats as the pack temporarily turned attention away from the other men.

It took several long minutes for Captain Pounds to assemble his crew together and organize a suitable defensive position. He ordered his crew to gather nearby branches and twigs to start a large fire. They kept the fire going all night. Guards were rotated every three hours. Sleep came sparingly to the hungry and exhausted men. They were frequently awakened by the dreadful howling through the night.

* * *

The next morning, a giant was in the forest. Sohn smelled the acrid aroma of a distant campfire. He stopped momentarily, unsure whether to skirt the smoke or head directly for it. He decided on the direct approach, wanting to ascertain the crew's strength and condition.

Minutes later Sohn der Schrenken came across the remains of the two slaughtered men. He'd seen corpses before. But that day was the first time he'd seen half eaten human bodies. A normal person would have been sickened by the horrific sight. But he was hardened by man's hatred of him and handled the sight differently.

His eyes and hyperactive mind surveyed the intermingled animal and human tracks. They led south deeper into the evergreen forest. He recognized the wolves' footprints as he'd seen them in northern Europe. Sohn realized the animals would pursue their prey until their appetites were sated or the men had escaped beyond their territory.

Death is my eternal companion.

The behemoth made a decision. He would try to save men's' lives that day and await the consequences. Would he still be the damnable monster?

He trod on with a new purpose, scanning the ground carefully. He noted the wolves generally stayed together but as he moved further two wolves apparently veered away. Should he follow them or the rest of the pack? He made the right decision, remaining steadfastly on the main cluster of tracks, but occasionally glancing to his right to prevent being outflanked.

The wind was calm and the air still. Did the wolves have his scent yet? They'd hear him soon enough. He stopped, inhaled deeply and unleashed a long and loud blood curdling shriek.

The forest was still for an instant before becoming full of a chorus of distant howling. He guessed the pack was a mile in front of him. He had their attention and expected a visit a few minutes later from them.

Sohn was exhilarated. It was either kill or be killed. Primal at its purest! He would use his enormous deadly hands and perhaps a knife to kill off the pack. He listen keenly and scanned the forest for evidence of the imminent onslaught.

The men reacted to the awful scream with mixed emotions. They spoke quietly among themselves while huddling together.

"What was that?"

"Should we be afraid of what made that horrendous sound or thankful it has drawn the attention of the wolves?"

The distressed sailors kept their scared eyes on the wolves until the predators vanished. They argued among themselves about whether they should sit tight behind an outcrop of boulders or hurry away. They decided to hold their position there as they didn't want to being exposed out in the open again. The men sharpened the ends of several stout branches into spears while waiting restively for the wolves' return.

The pack galloped through the forest toward the unknown source of the primal scream. The scent was very similar to those from the men behind them but it was somehow different. They wanted to identify the potential threat. It was a combination of curiosity and survival of the fittest. A few minutes later they stopped to sniff and stare at the huge man facing them a hundred yards away in a small clearing.

Sohn sneered menacingly at the pack. He counted eight wolves but there could be others in the immediate vicinity.

The standoff did not last very long as Sohn wanted to get the confrontation over quickly and continue on, assuming he was still alive. He feinted a retreat by turning his back on the animals. They seized the opportunity and lunged forward toward the solitary man.

Suddenly he spun around and sprinted forward, screaming bloody murder. The charging wolves instantly lost some resolve. They slowed. He surged through the frontrunners, knocking them off their feet and slamming their heads with his boots.

The raging man moved gracefully in spite of his size, evading wide open jaws, and driving his fists down into their sculls. A few wolves scampered away, whining, tails between their legs. It was over in seconds.

Sohn stood, chest heaving, throat sore, lungs working overtime and surveyed his latest victims. He regretted having to kill so many beautiful animals. He sacrificed their lives to ingratiate himself with the nearby men from the ship. Would they tolerate his presence?

The men were tense when they heard the fierce screams. But the ensuing silence was worse. What happened?

They waited silently, staring into the forest, waiting for the return of the wolves or whatever had drawn away the beasts. They glanced at each other occasionally for support before anxiously then peering back into the woodland.

At last, their vista changed as a huge man slowly walked toward them. The tension mounted as the horrific being approached them. He stopped fifty feet away and scrutinized them silently. The crew looked warily back at him. More than one man shuddered involuntarily after the giant removed the fur covering from his face. They noticed blood dripping from his hands as proof of the recent battle.

"I come in peace," he said.

"What of the wolves?" a crewman asked.

"They are not a threat to you anymore," the behemoth replied.

"You did that for us?" the captain inquired.

The giant shrugged. "It needed to be done or you'd be dead soon."

"That is kind of you. Do you live nearby?"

"I have no home. Like you I was stranded. My father recently died on a ship stuck in the ice. I am all you see."

The captain conferred quietly with his crew as the giant waited. There was considerable disagreement with Captain Pounds who wanted to invite the man into their midst. He felt obliged to the man who saved so many lives. Most of the crewmen were vehement about turning the newcomer away. He was just too scary looking.

Sohn's excellent ears allowed him to hear every word in hushed or excited tones. He expected to be turned away. It was nothing new. Then the captain spoke to him.

"You may join our sad company until we reach civilization if you like."

"Thank you. I accept your offer, "the giant replied with a bow.

The giant and sailors stepped forward, meeting in middle ground. They reluctantly introduce themselves. The big man introduced himself as Sohn der Schrenken in a thick German accent. He learned Captain Josiah Pounds and his meager crew hailed from England. *He must know Walton. I better not inquire. It is best to leave that part of my life behind.*

The sea captain used his people skills to relax his crew and Sohn. A genuine smile did much of it though there was little he could do to reduce the crew's fear of the man who was almost two and a half feet taller than them.

Sohn gratefully accepted the strained crew's hospitality seemingly genuine kindness of Captain Pounds.

They continued the long walk southward without mishap for a week. The newcomer won points in bagging small game. The men gawked when observing him run over twenty miles an hour after deer, rabbits and other prey.

The men gradually relax a little around Sohn though they refused to turn their backs to him. They could barely keep their thoughts to themselves about his superhuman speed.

How is that humanly possible?

He's a freak of nature, that one.

Going out on his own to hunt was essential to the German. He had spent so much of his existence alone. Traveling with the sailors took some getting used to. The adjustment was quite difficult for him, especially when he overheard the ill-concealed whispers of the crew as they speculated about him. Hearing their remarks and seeing their fear and distrust grated away at him.

The good captain was a different matter. Pounds proved to be an intelligent, articulate and educated man who read extensively. The two men devoted many hours on the journey discussing books and authors. Time flew by whenever they debated literary and philosophy.

If only Victor had been more like this good man I walk beside. I would never have had to kill.

Sohn learned the sea captain commanded merchant ships crossing the Atlantic between England and the United States for more than ten years. Like

Walton, he was a voyage of exploration in search of the elusive Northwest Passage.

It was rumored there was a sea route connecting the Atlantic Ocean and Pacific Ocean. The sea lane known as the Northwest Passage was through the Arctic Ocean. There were as yet no successful voyage through the northern ocean due to impenetrable ice cover most of the year. The passage was partially navigable only during the summer months. The explorer Henry Hudson had made it as far as Hudson Bay before his crew mutinied and cast him adrift in a row boat; never be heard from again.

Pounds' ship *The Navigator* most recently joined the growing ranks of stranded icebound vessels.

The remnants of that particular crew continued their constant vigil of their captain's unlikely new friend. The crewman wondered if the eight food monstrosity would turn do unto them as had been done to the wolves.

Would they be next?

Chapter 4

Mary couldn't face her parents or Verna the next morning. She was too tired to see anybody. Sleep usually came easily to her but not last night. After leaving Verna alone in the kitchen she'd gone back to bed. Mary burned a few calories tossing and turning, but she couldn't sleep.

She found an empty journal on her desk that had been given to her on her sixteenth birthday. It had been gathering dust ever since as Mary had no inclination to write a diary about her life. But now there was a personal experience that was better left unsaid. She saw no harm in writing about it in a private journal. She discovered it to be rather cathartic.

Mary tried to focus her mind on pleasant activities such as sailing on the bay and watching the sunset but those images were inadvertently replaced by her moment with the terrible hulk. Her pleasant moments after finishing the first diary entry didn't last very long.

She shivered.

This is bullshit! Why should I be afraid of some nightmare guy I'll never ever see again!

Mary jumped to her feet, stripped, and stepped into her bathroom. A few moments later she showered with hot water spraying her lithe body. She lathered herself thoroughly with hot water and rinsed. Then Mary reduced the temperature by fifty degrees. Mary stood, enduring the cold jets of water as long as she could. Her skin glowed. As her shivering intensified, she turned off the water and stepped out of the stall. Mary grabbed a bath towel from the towel rack and dried off quickly. All of her tension was gone, replaced by an infusion of energy.

A few minutes later Mary walked out the front door onto a circular gravel driveway. She wore a sweatshirt, running shorts and shoes. She limbered up a few minutes before jogging toward the end of the driveway. She turned right onto West Shore Road, a narrow two-lane road without any lined lane markers.

The scenic road was bordered by woods. She enjoyed the fresh aroma of fern and evergreen trees abutting the road. Mary passed driveways every few hundred yards. The properties were owned by other summer residents. Most of them had docks and small fleets of motor yachts and day racing sloops moored nearby.

Whenever a car passed by the drivers followed the customary practice of waving. Mary smiled and waved back as she continued her running rhythm, careful to avoid the occasional pothole.

After a mile the road surface become blacktop. She approached downtown Dark Harbor on Pendleton Point Road. The tiny commercial district included The Dark Harbor Shop that served an excellent malt shake, an art gallery, book store, and a few other small businesses.

Her running sessions were usually opportunities for reflection and planning. Today, however, she forced her mind to focus on her motion. She intuited that her mind has tricked her into actions that were best not done.

She continued past a large calm tidal pool and followed by a steep hill. She slowed to a walk, as her breathed harder.

Mary stopped at the top near the intersection with Jetty Road, her hands holding her sides, elbows extended. She felt old and out of shape. Her track days at school seem a lifetime ago although it's only been a few years.

The young woman turned back toward the village after deciding she doesn't have the energy and stamina to make it all the way to the southern tip of the island.

Perhaps I'll stop in the store and get some breakfast. Put it on the tab.

Mary nodded to herself and walked back down the hill.

Seven miles to her west, Sohn stood in a meadow gazing across the bay toward distant islands. *Somewhere out there is a young woman I must see again.*

He peered left toward a ferry loaded with a couple dozen cars, bikers, and passengers voyaging from the Lincolnville Beach terminal to Islesboro.

Sohn contemplated whether he should risk purchasing a ticket and exposing himself to the usual horrified expressions. He's never quite gotten used to being abominated and spurned but has managed to endure the negativity.

He has earned respect at Pine Tree State Lumber, using his extraordinary size and strength sawing down more trees and hauling more sections than his fellow lumberjacks.

Sohn, like workers everywhere, deposited his salary in a bank to spend on such living expenses as utilities for his free and clear small house in a rural community in addition to groceries, gas and oil on his

150,000 mile pick-up truck and other sundry items. He was frugal to a fault, wanting to make every dollar last. He combined store bought food with venison and other fresh meats from his hunts. The man never entertained or went to the movies.

He preferred reading more than anything. He was a fixture at local libraries, taking out five books at a time and returning them a week later. He'd just finished the latest book Lee Child's Jack Reacher series. He identified with Reacher. Both were outsiders, ugly and big men. But Reacher had nothing on Sohn. Child's protagonist was far easier on the eyes. Reacher would win a beauty contest hands down 24/7. In any case, Sohn admired the strong literary character and wished they were friends in real life.

Was he lonely? Yes!

Perhaps the woman on the island could fill part of the emptiness that dominated him so much. He wanted to find out.

Is today my luck day? Sohn wondered, watching the ferry motor across the bay at 12 knots, plowing a wake behind her.

He decided to catch the next ferry.

Mary sat at a picnic table outside The Dark Harbor Shop reading the early edition of The New York

Times. Like everything else, the newspaper was transported from the mainland on the ferry. Mary was of a devoted reader of the daily due to her constant interest in all things Manhattan and global warming. The latter issue consistently commanded more space every year as scientific data about the damages to planet Earth became direr.

That morning's most interesting article was about Hurricane Isabella. The storm was tracking toward the city with a prediction of heavy rain and wind. Mayor Michael A. Bloomberg coordinated preparation by the city's agencies to gear up for potential flooding and power outages.

I should be there to see for myself what a hurricane propelled surge will do. It will be an experience that will help me decide my future.

Mary thought it over while scanning the rest of the newspaper. Was there enough time to catch the next ferry and book a flight to Boston and New York before Isabella entered the city? She has her press credentials from the Godwin's magazine that would get her into news conferences and get interviews at the MTA, FEMA and other agencies. Or she could sit tight on the island and watch The Weather Channel's on the scene intense coverage which usually put their reporters in the middle of the severe conditions.

With her mind a few hundred miles away, Mary was oblivious to the approach of a handsome 26 year old man wearing khaki shorts, a navy blue golf shirt and leather sandals. He stopped beside her and looked down at Mary with amused eyes.

He cleared his throat.

Mary was startled. She shuddered involuntarily, gazing up at him.

"Mary, I'm sorry to have taken you from your thoughts. Where were you?"

"Hi Perce. That's okay. I was just thinking about Hurricane Isabella."

Perce sat across from Mary. "I think we'll be safe enough up here, don't you?"

"Yes, but I was thinking of getting down to New York to face the hurricane and see how the city and storm handle each other.

"That's crazy, Mary. Why not stay up here on the island? Better safe than sorry! Right?"

"I agree Perce but being down there in harm's way may be a job requirement I can't pass up."

"Ah! You mean your father's magazine, right."

Mary frowned. "There's more to it than that," she said with an edge. "I have a real need to see for myself what a surge of water will do to the city, especially lower Manhattan. Will it impact Ground Zero? This may be a precursor to the city of the future" she finished with evident intensity.

"You said that with such passion," Perce commented with a wry smile.

"It's something I am passionate about" Mary said, looking at Perce without blinking.

"Then go for it Mary."

"I will," she replied adamantly.

"Though I was hoping we could hang out." His eyes searched hers to see if there was any hope.

Mary was curious. "What do you have in mind?"

Perce smiled brilliantly. "We could go over to Seven Hundred Acre Island and hike around the island. I heard there's an old one room schoolhouse from around 1900 over there. And perhaps we could pick raspberries," he said hopefully.

Mary laughed. "That sounds fun but what about my little trip?"

"There will be bigger hurricanes hitting the city, perhaps even next year."

Mary looked at Perce closely. They knew each other since she was a little girl. But due to their five year age difference they traveled in different circles. Perce was engaged to be married two years ago. But the wedding was called off some reason Mary did not yet know. Then Perce suddenly started taking an active interest in her. Mary thought it may have been a rebound reflex but was nevertheless flattered by his attention.

Perce's excursion was tempting. She loved hiking on dirt roads and traipsing through the woods looking for abandoned buildings. Spending time alone with the handsome man could be exciting and a welcome development.

"Sure let's do it," she said happily. *The city can wait. CNN and The Weather Channel should suffice this time around.*

"Great! When should we go?" Perce asked.

The ticket lady's eyes widened with fright and repulsion. She tried not to look directly at Sohn's face.

Sohn nodded agreeably. "Morning, ma'am. I'd like a round trip car and driver for the next ferry."

The middle aged, plain looking woman inadvertently zeroed in on the awful face a few feet away before tearing away her eyes from the man. *Why does this ugly monster have to be here? This job's not worth it.*

Sohn stood stoically. He resisted the urge to reach out and grab her. He'd endured thousands of similar reactions from people who were unable to overcome the shock of seeing him for the first time. Sohn was no feast for the eyes for sure.

"Did you understand me?" he inquired.

"Ayuh," the woman replied after mustering enough courage and determination to get him out of the ticket office as soon as possible.

While the ticket was punched out, Sohn contemplated Maine lingo. He wasn't sure if he'd heard more Mainers say ayuh or yes. They meant the same thing. He seemed to think that Maine residents with the thickest accents usually preferred ayuh. He grinned at the woman.

She glanced up, thinking *he's even worse when he grins. Usually a smile beautifies a person but there's no hope for this bastard.*

"Mister, that's $27.50."

Sohn handed over a twenty and a ten in his enormous hand. She stared at it, eyes narrowed and visibly perspiring now. She breathed out before taking the offered bills. She made change and slid over the balance and the ferry ticket.

Sohn scowled. He grabbed the bills, coins and tickets then turned away and stepped to the open door. He gazed back, smiling as best he could.

"Be seeing you," he said.

I need some time off she told herself, trembling uncontrollably.

Sohn shook his head and walked to his pickup. It was parked in a line of other vehicles waiting for the arrival of the "Margaret Chase Smith" from Islesboro. He ignored the stares of drivers and passengers. Sohn looked at the stretch watch on his right wrist. It was 10:40 am. The boat would arrive in ten or eleven minutes.

He opened the truck's driver's door and sat down behind the wheel. He put the tickets in a side panel to his left and peered out at the bay.

A coastal tanker was steaming up bay in the wide channel a mile from shore. Seeing the ship reminded him of his distant exploits in the Arctic, the first on board the stranded ship on which Victor Frankenstein died and then the wreck he later discovered captained by his friend Josiah Pounds.

Sohn avoided boats of any kind for at least a century after his ordeal in the Arctic. Since moving close to Penobscot Bay in the 20th Century he managed to overcome his aversion to boats. Earlier that summer he went out on a lobster boat to help haul up crustaceans from the rocky bay bed. It was an invigorating experience. After making the rounds at the lobster pots, he was able to enjoy the serenity of the calm water and the beauty of the fir tree lined rocky coastline as the boat motored back to port.

A car horn blared nearby. Sohn noticed the car procession was moving away from him toward the docked ferry. Sohn turned over the ignition and stepped gently on the accelerator. The vehicle eased up on the car ahead. He carefully kept pace, alternating braking and accelerating during his approach to the docked vessel.

A man dressed in a khaki shirt and khaki trousers scanned tickets handed by the car drivers.

Sohn pulled up next to the crewman and extended the two part round drip ticket.

The crewman glanced at Sohn as he took the offered ticket. He smirked at Sohn.

"Hello, "Sohn offered, mystified by the man's expression.

The crewman just nodded as he stamped and returned the ticket into the gigantic scarred pale hand.

"Be seeing you," Sohn added as his foot put minimum pressure on the gas.

The ticket taker glared in Sohn's direction briefly before turning to the driver of the car behind the big man.

The truck moved down a metal grated incline onto the ferry. He followed the hand signals of another crewman pointing him to the rightmost line of cars parked on the boat. The vehicle crept toward the back of a silver Volkswagen Passat station wagon. The crewman signaled for Sohn to stop just inches behind the Passat. Sohn turned off the engine.

The three mile ride would take about twenty minutes. His target was getting very close. He smiled at the small cluster of islands across the channel where the unknown woman apparently was located.

I'm almost there. Keep me in your thoughts and you'll see me before you know it.

A frightful smile lit up his face.

Chapter 5

Mary and Perce Shelley scheduled their hike for the following morning. They wanted to make it a daylong outing. Perce planned to pick up Mary at the Godwin's dock in his efficient Fortier 30 cabin cruiser. The investment banker promised to bring a picnic lunch for their enjoyment.

He offered to drive her home from the store but Mary declined. She felt like walking back to the house. They kissed briefly and exchanged smiles when Mary stood to hit the road.

She checked her watch a few minutes into the walk. It read 11:18. She was surprised. *Where has the time gone?* Was she so mesmerized by Perce that time sped up around him? She smiled to herself. Perhaps that was good.

She accelerated to a steady jog.

Sohn sat in the pick-up truck, daydreaming about his long life. He'd lived through the beginning of the great Industrial Revolution. He witnessed enormous improvements in quality of life that allowed mankind to have greater comfort and live longer, though nowhere close to his lifespan. Sohn clearly remembered driving a car for the first time a century ago, listening to a radio for the first time a decade later, watching black and white television and his first experiences with many other technological advances.

He was very surprised to become a fan of rock music. He'd grown up with classical music and mid European funky music popular in the late 18th century. He'd endured music since then but nothing quite moved him as rock.

His favorite song was *Who Are You* by The Who. He loved the lyrics and beat equally. The insightful message sung by Pete Townsend was close to home for the big man. A few people knew something of his of his recent history but nobody really knew who he was. He couldn't risk it. Sohn changed his address every decade or two since arriving in North America. The fact that he never visibly aged would be noticeable.

Sohn discovered that after a few brave souls who dared speak their mind commented to Sohn.

"You look the same as you did fifteen years ago."

"What's the secret to staying young?"

"Did you find the fountain of youth?"

These remarks set off a preservation alarm in him. *It's time to move again.*

He'd be on the road the next morning before dawn with only a few possessions, heading for another province or state. Sohn was the eternal nomad having to start over in a new community time and time again. Happiness was an unknown emotion to Victor's creation.

He was spurned from the day of his creation. Sohn was essentially a newborn with an oversized body when he first got off the long examination table in Victor Frankenstein's laboratory. He could only mumble incoherently. But Frankenstein thankfully endowed him with a superb mind that eagerly and rapidly absorbed knowledge. By the time Victor met him in the ice cave high in the mountains some months later, they were peers intellectually.

Sohn learned the hard way that intelligence did not guarantee contentment. The misanthrope spent much longer than an average human lifetime living by himself. He lodged in a prodigious amount of temporary homes as nobody would tolerate cohabiting with him.

The loner stoically endured his situation. The best moments of his evenings were spent reading amusing passages from his beloved books. Levity brightened the darkness that enveloped his essence like a shroud. Sohn despaired, although he hated feeling that way. Was he damned to eternal melancholy?

Sohn identified with Dante. He believed hell on Earth had been a reality for part of his existence. Only a long term friendship could help fill the emptiness within him and bring a semblance of happiness. Would that ever happen? Was there that special person alive at that moment and would they ever meet? How would it happen?

Sohn realized he just couldn't drive to the young woman's island home, ring the doorbell and say "Hi, it's me, the man you saw chasing down that fully antlered buck. Let's take a walk on the wild side and then go dancing in the moonlight."

Sohn smiled. The young woman made him lighthearted for the first time in years. Then he turned serious, as he planned how to approach her. His thoughts were interrupted when he sensed being observed. He casually looked toward the ship's bow. The ticket-taking crewman stood there, staring contemptuously at him.

Look all you want with those sharp hateful eyes. It won't do you any good.

Reacting to provocation, especially in a finite space, was unwise. Sohn created too much attention on himself just by being there. He was the outsider and had to take the high road whenever possible.

Sohn averted his eyes away from the unfriendly crew member. He noticed the ferry was then passing a green navigation buoy rocking gently in a rolling ground swell. The buoy marked the east perimeter of the shipping channel. The ship approached a narrow channel between Islesboro on the port side and Warren Island and Seven Hundred Acre Island on the starboard side.

He was tempted to get a better view of the panoramic seascape from the ferry's observation deck but time was short and he preferred to be as inconspicuous as possible.

Sohn stifled a yawn after a side glance at the crewman determined he was still the focus of the man's attention. If the guy lived on Islesboro there could be a chance encounter. Hopefully not. His appetite for violence and mayhem had greatly abated.

The ferry decreased speed as the captain turned the helm aport. The ship seemed to glide into its wide berth. There was a gentle bump when the bow slowly hit the dock. Sohn watched with interest the ship being secured with heavy rope.

Car engines turned over throughout the ship. Sohn's admirer started signaling the front vehicles forward. When it was his turn Sohn pulled up to the man. "Be seeing you," Sunny said and then eased the truck up the metal grating and onto a roadway.

The crewman softly cursed and glared as the giant drove away.

The pickup motored past a small lighthouse and a few other structures before leaving the water view behind. He turned on the radio. "The Future Is Too Late" by Richard Rowlands had just started. He listened to the song and badly accompanied the singer on vocals.

I've been waiting for the day
When change will turn around fate
And sometimes it turns to gray
And the future is too late.

When you get old you just don't know
How your health will turn out
In your mind you may grow
But your body is left behind.

You see the people around you
Not in a place you want to be
There's nothing you can do

But show support for whoever you see.

You hope one day there'll be a cure
You read the papers every day
Some good news will be in store
Memory won't be far away.

You wish you can turn back the clock
Set a course that has some hope
You pretend you are a rock
But in reality you can't cope.

You see the people around you
Not in a place you want to be
There's nothing you can do
But show support for whoever you see.

His singing was no treat to one's ears but he didn't care. He was in a rare good mood.

"Where are you, little darling?" Sohn asked as the pickup truck headed down a narrow two lane road in a procession of other vehicles that had been on the ferry.

He applied the brakes at a stop sign, looking left and tight. He shrugged, unable to decide the correct direction. It shouldn't matter too much on a 69 square mile island. The right signal blinked and the truck turned in the general direction of the Godwin house. It felt right.

Mary was only two miles away, within sight of her driveway as she slowed to a walk. She felt a little disoriented for some reason. There was a pressure feeling in her head for the first time in her life. She stumbled forward toward the driveway.

The pickup truck moved along at 30 miles an hour. The driver of an approaching car started to wave but stopped in mid motion, somehow discouraged by Sohn's face. Sohn waved back more demonstratively, amused by the driver's demeanor.

He came to another stop sign and veered right onto Pendleton Point Road. He was about one mile from Mary.

There was a slight tingling in the back of his head. He could use the sensation like a diving rod from here on in.

Almost there.

Mary's vision blurred as she inched forward. The driveway was only a few yards further.

What is wrong with me?

That was as much thinking Mary could do coherently as she struggled to the edge of the driveway.

Two hundred feet away, the front door of her house opened unbeknownst to her. Jane Godwin, 48, an attractive slender woman, stepped outside in her tennis whites carrying two racquets. She had a noon court time at the Tarratine Club.

As Mary's mother stepped briskly to her 2012 Jaguar XF to speed off, she stopped abruptly. Was that Mary lurching about the head of the driveway?

God, I hope she's not drunk at this hour!

"Darling, what's wrong?" she asked.

Mary barely heard her mother talking. The voice seemed like a million miles away. Mary dropped to her knees and held her arms out as she had done as a little girl when she needed help.

Jane dropped the racquets on the driveway and ran to Mary. She was shocked by Mary's apparent collapse, paleness and dilated eyes. The island had an on-call doctor but the nearest hospital was more than an hour's drive in Rockland, accessible in a roundabout, ferry trip or a speedboat. There was a tiny airport with a single runway that could fly them to the Owls Head airport.

What should I do? Jane wondered anxiously.

She helped Mary up and led her slowly toward the house.

"Are you feeling any better, darling?"

Mary nodded her head very slightly.

Jane looked up as a pickup truck driven by a scary looking big man slowed and stared at Jane and Mary. Mary turned to look at him.

"Who is that hideous man?" Jane asked quietly.

Mary couldn't reply. She was too shocked to speak. *Oh no! Why is he here?*

Sohn drove the pickup into the driveway and parked next to the terrified women. He opened the door, ducked his head, and stepped onto the gravel surface. He looked from one to the other. *The older woman must be her mother. She looks horrified. Nothing new there.*

The young woman he'd pursued and found so easily looked at him with glazed eyes. She was 5'8", slender, with shoulder length auburn hair. Her green eyes held his watery yellow eyes. She seemed scared, curious and in shock. Sohn thought that combination was better than outright fear and rejection.

Jane seemed to muster some courage. Craning her neck up at him, she spoke. "You have no business here. Please leave now."

Sohn admired the woman's spirit. But he didn't intend to turn away and make a hasty retreat. He focused on Mary, who had kept her eyes on him.

"If you don't leave immediately, I'll have call the police. They don't take kindly to trespassing around here," Jane said resolutely.

"There is no need for that ma'am. I won't stay long. I am not a total stranger to your daughter." Sohn looked then at Mary." Are you all right? Do you want me to leave now?

"It's you, isn't it?" Mary whispered.

He nodded.

Jane looked at Mary. "You know him?"

"I saw him yesterday on the road but no I do not know him."

Jane didn't like the having the terrible looking giant on her property. She didn't feel safe. Still, having Mary nearby gave her strength. She wished her husband would come out of the house.

"And you just happened to be on Islesboro today?" Jane said.

His thin dark lips barely covered his teeth when he smiled then.

Mary broke away from her mothers' grasp. Jane Godwin regarded her anxiously.

"Go in the house and lay down," her mother cautioned.

"I am quite all right. Thank you mother."

Not knowing why, Mary stepped slowly toward the giant. She noted his pensive expression as he gazed down at her. She stopped in front of him.

"I am Mary Godwin."

"I am Sohn Schrenk."

"I hear a trace of a German accent."

"That is surprising. It's been several years since I was last there."

Mary nodded. She thought Sohn implied more than he'd admitted but this wasn't the time to ask. "Why are here?"

"To see you."

This was more than Jane could tolerate. How could a monstrous looking being have any business with her lovely daughter? Beauty and the beast! She stormed over to Mary and grabbed her by the hand. Mary barely glanced at her.

"You and I go need to go into the house right now," Jane said, averting her eyes from the hideous man towering over them. He made her think about death and graveyards.

"I want to stay out here," Mary replied testily.

Sohn stood still. He studied the dynamics of the mother daughter relationship. Sohn was fascinated as the never had a mother nor was ever a child. His life began in a laboratory where he was orphaned on day one. He was the hollow man created without love, never nurtured and made to suffer for it.

"I will leave," he announced.

"You needn't," Mary replied. Mary turned to her mother. "Does he, mother?"

Very clever, Sohn thought.

Jane looked at her stonily.

"Since when, mother, is it right to turn away a guest?"

"Mary, I've never told a guest to leave. You know that. This man is not a guest."

Jane tried to avoid looking at the man, but he took up so much space. He was massive. She thought the scariest part of him were his yellow penetrating eyes. They could reel you in like a fish caught on a hook. His skin was horrific. It seemed almost translucent. His veins and arteries were quite visible, in fact too much so. And those thin black lips! *They are evil lips.* She shuddered at the thought of being kissed by them.

* * *

Sohn had morphed into a much more primal and violent being in the year after awakening in Victor Frankenstein's laboratory.

Sohn remembered standing at Victor's bedside in a dark room adjacent to the laboratory. He tried communicating with the sleeping young scientist. The newborn man was happy and hopeful at that time. But the mood lasted only seconds, erased by the shock in Victor's eyes and more so when the young man fled. Sohn was confused, disappointed and lost.

What did I do wrong to deserve being cast out into the world? It's not my fault I look the way I do. I'm stuck with it and have paid the price of Victor's ungodly act ever since by being scorned everywhere I go.

Victor considered him a monster from the moment his yellow eyes were open. What had the Creature done to cause it? He was stunned. It was only when he'd seen his reflection in a smooth pond that the answer became apparent.

Seeing and knowing what he looked like triggered a fresh set of hostility and resentment. Why had the Victor made him as he was? If Victor had been created in God's image, in whose image had the monster been created?

He was destined to never get the answer from his creator.

Back in Sohn's distant past, he would have reacted very much differently to being asked to move on. But his bad temper moderated over the years.

Chapter 6

William Godwin, 55, sat at a desk in a plush study. The walls were lined with full bookshelves. He was watching the Weather Channel report the latest prediction on Hurricane Isabella. The storm was still expected to make landfall in the New York City metropolitan area.

The patriarch was a handsome, distinguished man with silver streaked brown hair. His cell phone rang. He put the television on mute and picked up the telephone immediately.

"Godwin."

He listened attentively. His eyes absentmindedly regarded a framed picture displayed on the desk of Mary, Jane and him on board a forty foot sailboat.

"Make sure we get some direct quotes from Mayor Bloomberg at the news conference this afternoon and have every angle of the hurricane's impact on Manhattan covered. Jack, you don't need me to tell you any of this."

Godwin listened to his editor tell him what to expect for the next issue. He felt a little guilty about not being at the magazine during the hurricane. Jack would make sure all angles would be covered by the experienced staff. The next issue would feature in depth articles about the city's preparations to the weather maker and what Isabella did to the city.

William knew his daughter was antsy as hell about riding out the storm on Islesboro instead of being in the city working on her own contribution to the magazine. He watched her blossom into a good investigative reporter and proficient writer. Journalism may not become her career but it would provide a solid foundation for the young woman.

"Sounds good, Jack. Keep me posted." He ended the call and rested the phone on the desk.

Now where is Mary?

They had had an argument last night over her ardent desire to fly down to the city to witness to experience Isabella's fury. He had talked her out of it for her own safety. As fathers and daughters often saw a picture differently, so did they differ on what impact global warming would impact the eroding coastlines. He was somewhat skeptical that the city was in danger of a tidal surge which would flood Manhattan. He recalled a recent discussion with Mary.

"What about the calving Antarctic ice sheets?" Mary asked heatedly.

"What about them?" Godwin asked calmly.

"The melting is accelerating, father."

"So?"

"Come on, father. Isn't it obvious?" She stared incredulously at her father.

Godwin raised his eyebrows, waiting for her to continue. He tried not to display the pride he had for her intelligence and passion on the subject. Perhaps she was right. He hoped she was dead wrong, as the magazine would cease to function if and when the borough was abandoned.

Mary waited out her father, sensing he was holding back on her. A minute later, William smiled at her.

"Well Mary, I expect if you are correct, there will be more and more dire reports made available to us."

"And we'll educate the public, right?"

Godwin hesitated. He wasn't in business to scare away his readers.

"We have the duty to enlighten our subscribers. They must know the truth, "Mary added in a slightly louder voice.

"We'll see, Mary."

"Yes we will,"

William frowned. Recalling their discussion was not all that pleasant. He stood up, stretched, and walked out of the study to see what Mary was doing.

Mary's mind drifted to another time and place. She sat in a large stonewalled chamber. She heard the wind howl outside. Rain pelted the dark windows. It was night. She was all alone in a dark room. The blackness around her was scary. Her heart fluttered and heaviness settled on her. Was she alone?

"Hello," she called out.

Silence.

"Is there anyone there?" she shouted.

Silence.

She strained her ears. She only heard the windows rattle and wind outside howl.

Where am I? Where are my parents?

Only minutes ago she stood in broad daylight outside the Islesboro home. She had been with her mother. And there was somebody else there, too.

Him. It was him. He put me here. How is that possible?

"Where are you?" Mary yelled. She waited and listened.

"I know you hear me."

A large old oak door creaked open. She looked toward the sound but saw nothing.

Mary's pulse quickened. Her chest heaved with each breathe.

"Who is there?" she asked in a quivering voice.

"You know," a man's voice answered in a slight German accent.

"Why am I here?" she asked.

"We are alone here. Nobody can interrupt us."

Heavy footsteps came closer and closer. Her heart pounded even more. "I want to go home. Please."

Mary blinked and discovered the giant had granted her wish. She looked at up at him in the driveway. He looked at her with a knowing expression that troubled her. She trembled slightly as she brought herself back under control.

"Look at me, Mary, not at him," her mother urged. Jane turned to the man responsible for her daughter's distress.

"See what you've done to my daughter? If you have a heart you will get in your truck, drive away and never set foot on this property again."

Sohn's eyes sparked heat. *If I have a heart! My heart has been pumping blood for a hell of a lifetime or is it a lifetime of hell? Though that's not what this woman implied, is it? She thinks I'm a monster, a fiend, a man without a soul.*

Sohn contemplated whether he possessed a soul. Did Victor ever consider that important essence? Sohn doubted it ever crossed Victor's mind. Religion was not part of Sohn's life though he had read both the Old and New Testament more than once from cover to cover looking for answers about why and what he was. The answers remained out of his reach. Paradise Lost was more illuminating to him.

William walked rapidly across the driveway. What happened to his daughter? He was surprised Jane was still there. Anything to keep her from her beloved tennis spoke volumes.

"What is going on here?" he demanded. "Are you ill?" he asked Mary.

Sohn watched the proceedings quietly.

"I felt faint, father, but I'm better now," Mary said with a faint smile.

"It is his fault," Jane exclaimed, pointing at Sohn.

Godwin gave Sohn a hard look. "Who are you?"

"I am Sohn Schrenk," the giant replied with a slight bow. "I mean you and your family no harm."

"Why are you here?"

"Hah, that is the question!" Sohn said with mirth.

"I demand a serious answer. This is not an amusing situation Sohn Schrenk."

"All right then. You shall have it." Sohn paused a few seconds before continuing as the question was a tricky one. Total honesty could create much trouble. And frankly, he didn't truly know the complete reasons why he felt so compelled to seek out Mary Godwin. He as yet hadn't determined why he had to find her and what role she would or could play in his life.

Mary waited expectantly. She felt a connection with this stranger. It seemed illogical but right. Sohn gave his inquisitor a cold stare. Then he spoke.

"You will not be pleased by what I have to tell you all." He then looked benignly at Mary. She regarded him anxiously.

"Mary, where do I begin?"

"At the beginning," she suggested.

"No, that will not do."

Godwin was getting impatient with the interloper. He believed the man was being too evasive. And what did his daughter know about this unique individual? He was tempted to excuse himself and call the constable. He decided to give the man another minute to spit it out.

"When you saw me yesterday on Route 90 I sensed our short encounter was not accidental. I still do not know why but I know it to be true. This has happened to me once before but that was ages ago" he concluded with a long look.

"That is a lot of baloney," Godwin said.

"No it isn't father."

"You believe him then?"

"Yes I do because I saw something yesterday."

Sohn listened hopefully.

"What did you see?" Jane asked.

"I cannot say."

Her father grimaced. "Now you are speaking in riddles like this this man. What is it you are hesitant to tell us?"

"You'll laugh at me," she told her parents. She looked questionably at the big man. He nodded slightly.

"Mary, we have never laughed at you. You know that," her mother said.

"That's not our way, is it?" her father added.

"No, I suppose not, but then we've never discussed what Sohn and I have alluded to."

"I'm confused. What am I missing here?" Godwin asked, looking from the newcomer to his daughter.

"Go ahead," Sohn told Mary. "I'm curious what you intend to say."

Here goes nothing.

"When our eyes locked yesterday, I seemed to have been transported into the distant past for an instant. I know that sounds crazy," she told her parents, "but that is what I experienced."

Her parents glanced doubtfully at one another. Was Mary in need of a psychiatric evaluation?

Mary didn't like her parents' expressions. She had been honest. Obviously they couldn't handle anything out of the ordinary. Supernatural or paranormal activity weren't comfortable subjects for them, especially involving their one and only child.

Sohn, on the other hand, was perfectly satisfied with Mary's statement. It made his pursuit of her to the island worthwhile. He tried to temper his attraction to her. It was more than physical. He was impressed with her young mind and her extrasensory perception. Her ability, possibly considered as a gift, would make it easier for him to be acceptable to her.

He needed to be patient with Mary. He'd already pushed the envelope by suddenly appearing at her home. It was a risky move on his part. He had not used his customary caution.

"I'll know better from now on to keep certain things to myself, "Mary said hotly.

"Perhaps that's best," her mother replied. Her father shook his head with dismay. He didn't know who to side with nor did he know what to believe. He respected Mary's passion about global warming and using that zeal and writing ability to contribute coherent articles at the magazine. But looking into some heinous being's eyes and seeing some other time and place was another matter entirely.

I should have stayed in the damn house. He glanced at the stranger. *How do I make this lurking hulk vanish? I don't like the way he's looking at Mary. He sees something that he wants from her. There's nothing good there in those yellow eyes.*

Godwin turned to his daughter. He was especially disturbed about her fascination with Sohn Schrenk. He had a sudden idea which could hasten the man's departure.

"Mary, I almost forgot. There's news on the hurricane. Let's go inside to watch together."

Mary felt like a deer hypnotized by headlights when looking at her new admirer. She barely discerned her father's wistful words.

"Mary, listen to your father," Jane urged plaintively.

Mary turned her eyes to her father. "Did you say something, father?"

"I was just on the phone with the office. Let's go inside and get the latest reports on the hurricane. Perhaps you can make a contribution from up here," he suggested with a hopeful look and bright smile.

"Maybe," she replied vaguely."

Godwin pushed the matter. "You've told me countless times about your interest in how Manhattan will be impacted by global warming. Have I misunderstood you?"

"Of course not!"

Sohn decided it was time to go. Getting the family into a squabble would not help him see Mary again.

The Godwins were startled by Sohn's sudden movement toward the pickup truck.

Sohn knew where to find Mary. As Sohn opened the driver's side door, he turned to his audience.

"I'm sorry to have caused a disturbance."

"Do you have a phone number?" Mary asked, surprising everybody, including herself.

Sohn laughed. "Yes, even someone like me has one of those. It's a land-line as my fingers are too big for a cell phone." He gave her the number. She entered it on her i-Pod.

"Be seeing you, Mary Godwin," he told her. He nodded amiably at her parents.

Sohn climbed in bending his impossibly tall frame in the drivers seat, closed the door, and turned over the ignition. He nodded once more as the vehicle turned right on the road. The others silently watched until it moved out of sight.

Chapter 7

The yellow-eyed driver couldn't focus on the road. Traffic was light and the speed limit generally fluctuated between 25 and 40 miles per hour on Islesboro so he could get away driving on auto pilot. His mind did not completely leave the Godwin house. He was captivated by Mary and that could be dangerous to all concerned.

He could count the fingers on one hand the number of occasions a woman captured his mind and monopolized his life. None had lived up to his expectations or satisfied him. They never fully shared his infatuations with him. He always left feeling more alone and bitter when he'd reached the ultimate decision to leave them behind and travel to another continent by himself. Unfortunately he could never forget any of them, especially the loveliest of them all, Helga Meyer.

"Du bist schön," he muttered under his breath in his old native language. "You are beautiful indeed, fräulein Helga."

He hid behind a stone pillar, his head spinning from simply looking at the lovely German immigrant hoisting a bucket of water from a village well. He had to sit down on the dirt and allow his heart rate to slow. Does she hear it beating for her? Did she see me? Do I dare take another peek? He dared.

Fräulein Helga was a pretty 19 year old with a long blonde pigtail, blue eyes and long lashes.

Sohn watched the voluptuous woman, taller than most women of the nineteenth century, as she worked the winch to raise the wooden bucket.

She stopped suddenly and turned her head toward him. He ducked out of sight as she laughed. It was a pleasing sound and made him smile.

Sohn wondered what he should do. Do I show myself to her or continue to hide like a scared rat? He was used to people cowering at the sight of him, not the other way around. This was a new and unwanted sensation.

He took a deep breath and stood again. He stepped away from the pillar and looked at the well. She was gone!

He took a few long strides toward the well, furtively looking left and right. He caught sight of her bouncing along gracefully, holding the heavy bucket in her hand. She was walking to the center of the village, toward the front door of a small cottage. Helga must have had eyes in the back of her head as she turned and glanced at him with a smile before entering her home.

She must be nearsighted. How else could he explain her smiling at a man as repugnant as him? At the time Sohn lived on the outskirts of Rhinebeck, New York located on the west bank of the Hudson River. A fair amount of German settlers lived in the verdant Hudson River Valley. Views of the nearby Catskills reminded many residents of Germany, especially where the wide river cut around the perimeter of the mountain range. It was local legend that the sound of thunder really was Rip Van Winkle bowling a strike in the scenic mountains.

Sohn worked at a mill on Landsman Kill cutting logs into boards, a profession he worked at for the better part of two centuries. He enjoyed the hard work and knew he was benefiting homeowners. His experience could get him work all over the young and growing nation.

But looks often deterred employers from hiring him. So the big man told prospective employers he would work free for a day and the mill owner had assessed his output. Sohn almost always landed the job.

Sohn's accent was more pronounced in the early years of the 19th century than today. He fit in easily with the other immigrants, many from Holland or Germany or whose parents or grandparents had braved the dangerous Atlantic in pursuit of religious freedom and a new life.

That night he lay on his grass-stuffed bed wondering how to pursue Greta. Sohn figured rejection was almost guaranteed but that did not stop him from plunging ahead. Sunday was his one day off. *Tomorrow it is! Will she go to church?*

Sohn had never attended a church service of any kind. At that time he didn't believe in God. He felt damned as a misanthrope and atheist since being turned away from humanity beginning with Victor himself in the laboratory.

Two years after taking his first breathe, he used his superior intellect, immense height and ferocity to force his creator's hand. In the ice cave high above Geneva an agreement was made to create a woman companion for him. Victor reluctantly agreed after Sohn promised to travel to the far side of the planet with his mate. Frankenstein procrastinated in starting the heinous project but finally got the job done. Almost immediately, as Sohn watched through a window in horror, Victor destroyed the female. Victor's act possibly extinguished any hope of the monster turning to religion. His feverish mind instead turned to revenge and evil deeds.

Those terrible memories were still all too fresh in his sharp mind. He seemed destined to suffer from the sacrilege of his maker, his father figure, the man he initially looked to for comfort and guidance. Sohn at one time wondered if Victor was God. If so, was Sohn supposed to be the new and improved Adam? He laughed bitterly.

Life improved for the new Adam in North America. He remained with Captain Pound for several months after their arrival in Boston. Their company was a little smaller by then because Sohn had to break a neck or two along the way. Who wouldn't, he reasoned, after having to endure the glares and whispers day and night of the two crew members who wanted him dead.

It was kill or be killed, wasn't it? They have no right to be so rude to me.. Who'd killed the wolves that would have eaten alive those ingrates? Damn them to hell!

Perhaps the two dead men would welcome him when he arrived one day at the pearly gates. He expected to see other acquaintances in Hell including Victor Frankenstein.

Sohn rose before dawn after an unusually restless night. His mind had been unusually active. He dreamed about being run out of Rhinebeck. Being chased by angry citizens carrying pitchforks and other sharp weapons pointed at his retreating body vexed him. *Please don't let that happen again!*

Sohn sat alone at the table he'd hewn from wood cut at the mill. There were four chairs around the table but that was really three more than were needed. A few men once shared a meal with him in the cabin. This morning, he ate a loaf of bread with cheese and half dozen apples. It was washed down with a tankard of beer. He wiped his mouth with an arm and stood on the rough planked floorboards wondering what to do next.

Just then there was a knock on the door. Was he hearing things? Who on earth would be seeking him out? *What have I done?*

Sohn strode swiftly to the door and opened it. Nobody was there. He stepped outside and looked around and cocked his head. His astute hearing picked up heard running feet. He started to chase them, but stopped after only a few paces. He didn't want anybody to see him racing around the town at more than double the speed of other men.

Too exposed, too risky!

It was probably some teenager who'd been dared to knock on the door and then run away before the big, scary man could show himself.

Teenagers!

Sohn couldn't relate to them at all. He had no firsthand knowledge of being a teenager, of his natural parents, siblings and childhood at all. Was he a good son? Did he have loving parents? These were among the unanswerable questions that periodically haunted the eternal man.

Sohn angrily slammed the door behind him after reentering his modest home. The incident ruined the beginning of such a promising day. He was too rattled to make introductions with the blonde woman. He needed to be calm and have a positive mindset. He laughed aloud at himself. It was ludicrous to think there was any way for a monstrosity to make a positive impression with a pretty young woman. He'd just embarrass himself and her, too.

Who am I fooling?

Venting his frustration made him feel better. He would see Helga another day. *I will instead go for a long walk, perhaps head west to the beautiful river.*

Several estates were being built along the Hudson on land owned by the powerful Livingstons. The family owned about a hundred thousand acres at one time. He read that Robert Livingston was one of the central signers of the Declaration of Independence. Sohn grinned. *We're both big men, aren't we!*

Sohn looked around the one room cabin absentmindedly. He was too claustrophobic to remain there another minute. The man exited immediately. He avoided the commercial district as best as possible. A few minutes later he crossed The Albany Post Road not far from The Beekman Arms, America's oldest inn. He dodged a stagecoach. One of the horses neighed fearfully. Sohn felt badly for the horse. It was a noble, handsome creature. Sohn recalled the wonderful, carefree sensation of galloping through a field with the energy of the animal pulsating through him.

His mind was totally focused on horses when he heard someone call out to him. "Excuse me, sir." He didn't actually think the person was speaking to him, but just in case it was best to stop walking and see for himself. With some effort he stopped moving and looked to his right and downward. His heart raced. It was her! Sohn bowed deeply and looked at Helga nervously from his hunched position. Looking up at people from their level was a unique experience for the towering man.

She laughed with sparkling eyes and curtsied gracefully.

Oh how his spirits lifted from the depths of despair. He completely forgot what brought him to this unexpected and surprising encounter. His planned jaunt through the scenic countryside had completely disappeared from his consciousness, at least for the time being as Helga became his world. He then straightened his posture and gazed down at her from his customary height.

"Fraulein, we haven't been introduced. I am . . . "

"Herr Sohn der Schrenken, I presume," she interrupted.

"Why yes, but how did you know?"

"That would be telling," Helga replied teasingly.

They were unaware that two elderly men watched them with disdain from across the street.

"You have an interesting name," Helga said seriously.

Sohn nodded, hesitant to respond.

"Son of Terror."

He nodded again.

"Why?" she asked.

"Does it not seem appropriate to you? Look at me and tell me I am wrong."

"Well, I think it could be a proper name under certain circumstances but right now I do not see or feel terrified. Was your father, um, a terror?"

Sohn had never been asked these questions and was reluctant to tell anybody about Victor. It would only create trouble for him and whoever he answered truthfully.

To lie or not to lie.

Helga rescued him. "I see that I have asked a sensitive question. It is no matter, Sohn der Schrenken." Sohn nodded. He'd disappointed her but that couldn't be helped. Would he ever reveal his identity?

Helga regarded Sohn expectantly. When he continued to stand there mutely, she became uncomfortable.

"Well, nice to meet you," she said. "Perhaps we'll talk some more again?"

"I'm sure we will."

"That is good. Bye."

She smiled and then started walking down the hard packed dirt sidewalk.

Sohn followed her with his dull yellow eyes. He suddenly felt watched and turned his gaze on the two elderly men. They gave him a cold stare. He turned away, not wanting to cause a stir in the town. Their attention troubled him.

I wish I know what those old codgers are thinking.

Sohn picked up his pace and walked westward toward the river.

"Are you sure?" Franz asked as he and his old friend Dieter regarded Sohn walking out of sight.

"Well, it's been more than twenty years since I left Germany. I only got saw the monster that one time. That sure looked like him, all right," Dieter said, squinting into the distance.

"But how could a monster travel in broad daylight across the ocean in a boatload of people?" Franz inquired.

"You must be right. He never would have been allowed on board a ship. But still, I think that man bears watching."

"I think he works at one of the mills on Landsman Kill."

"That's good to know. I don't like his interest in young Helga."

"She seemed as much interested in him for some reason."

"I have a mind to have a talk with her father Hans Meyer. He needs to know the danger she may be in. We all may be in danger if my eyes and memory are not playing tricks."

Both men looked in the direction the monster had walked.

Dieter shivered.

It's him! Or is it? He looked the same as he did all those years ago. How is that possible? Then again, I don't see so good anymore.

The countryside west of the village was dotted with farms. Several had Dutch barns made from saw cut and ax hewn wood from the richly forested region. Sohn vigilantly kept his eyes alert for any human movement that would necessitate slowing from twenty miles an hour to a moderate speed. He raced around a cornfield, jumped over a stone wall and came upon a small herd of cows. The grazing animals were startled when he hurdled over a few of them.

"Hey," yelled a man who couldn't believe what he was seeing.

Sohn kept up the pace without stopping to exchange pleasantries. Every property was lined with stonewalls. The steeple chasing continued for some time. As he ran and jumped, his mind went back to the two old men who in fact were probably older than himself. Sohn thought he recognized one of them but couldn't remember any details. Was it in Rhinebeck? Or was it in some earlier town or village he'd either passed through in the old country? He expected the answer would come to him sooner or later. Something would jog the memory. Sohn slowed at a dirt road that ran parallel with the river. The Hudson lay another mile west of the road. The estates under construction were situated between the river and the road.

He was curious to see what kind of ingenuity was being put into the mansions of The New World and how they compared to the old structures he'd seen in his travels through Europe, England and Scotland.

The man turned right, walking north, with Manhattan nearly one hundred miles southward and Albany about fifty miles upriver. His destination was La Bergerie, (French for The Sheep Hold), a seven hundred acre property owned by former United States Ambassador to France. General John Armstrong was a veteran of the recent American Revolution. Sohn heard that Napoleon had gifted Armstrong with a herd of sheep that would now be grazing on the property's pastures. Sohn loved the taste of freshly slaughtered lamb. Perhaps he'd feast on a succulent lamb this afternoon.

A wagon pulled by two oxen approached Sohn from the north. It was likely on its way to Rhinebeck to load up with building materials and household supplies for the crew living at La Bergerie. The four husky men on board the wagon scowled at Sohn. The wagon stopped abreast of the tall man. Sohn decided to play the part of the friendly local out for a Sunday walk.

"Good day to you," he greeted.

"What's good about it, Mister? We have work to do seven days a week" the driver holding the whip said.

"Where are you coming from?"

"What business is it of yours?"

"I'm just wondering what lies ahead," Sohn said indifferently.

The men on the wagon glanced at each other then back at the giant warily. He was too big and scary looking to be trifled.

"Well there's the general's place up the road a couple of miles. You looking for work?"

Sohn was surprised by the comment. Not many jobs landed in his lap out of the blue.

It must be my good looks.

"That's kind of you but I got a job."

"Well there's plenty of work to go around up there."

"All right."

There was nothing more to say. The driver nodded, cracked the whip and the oxen started moving forward. Sonny strode up the road as the men looked over their shoulders now and then.

"That's somebody I wouldn't want to cross the wrong way," said the driver.

"Amen to that," one of the others replied.

"Then why did you offer him work?" asked a third man.

"Just being neighborly," replied the driver. "To hell with that! I'll quit if that happens."

Sohn heard the fading dialogue despite the growing distance he put between them. It was typical behavior. He would have felt the same if he was one of them. His face could crack a million mirrors. He could have the distinction of being the ugliest man in the world. However he had superior strength, intelligence and stamina to partially offset his horrid looks.

He continued up the road, occasionally passing small modest homes. At one house, he saw a mother clipping flowers and her daughter holding a rag doll watching her. When the woman observed the behemoth walking along, she stood, grabbed the girl and ran inside the house. The woman looked over her right shoulder to make sure he wasn't in hot pursuit. The door slammed as he walked briskly past the house.

"Just typical," he said aloud.

Two visitors sat in the living room of the Meyer home speaking to Helga's father. Hans Meyer, 45, owned

Meyer & Sons, a Hudson River shipping company. He was also an elder at St. Peter's Lutheran Church. The widower was in a bad mood because Helga failed to attend this morning's service. She had sneaked out of the house. Meyer was forced to tell fellow parishioners that she was too ill to leave the house.

"So what is it you have to tell me?" he asked Dieter and Franz.

Dieter cleared his throat and spoke nervously. "Herr Meyer, we have something to tell you that may be upsetting."

Meyer's eyebrows rose in quiet response. His ears picked up the front door opening and closing quietly as Helga returned as quiet as a church mouse. He would deal with her later.

"Go on," he demanded.

"Well, it concerns your daughter."

"Helga?" he called out loudly.

Helga assumed her father was calling her, not realizing he was only reacting to Dieter's comment. She nervously walked, aware he was angry at her for skipping that dreadfully boring, long church service. She stepped into the living room. Dieter and Franz jumped up from their seats politely but her father remained seated. He looked at her sharply.

"Helga, these men have something to tell me. It involves you. Let's find out together what it is." To Dieter, he said "Go on quickly. I don't have all day."

"Yes, Herr Meyer. Well, as you may know I emigrated from the old country some years ago." He paused for Meyer's acknowledgment but none was made so he continued. "Anyway, before I left my village there was a terrible tragedy."

"I don't see what your tragedy has to do with Rhinebeck and my daughter," Meyer interrupted.

"I'm getting to that, sir. There was this horrible monster, a heinous giant of a man who'd caused trouble."

Helga's breathing quickened. *Oh no!*

Dieter continued. "This man stole my neighbors' food and threatened to kill them. The whole village was terrified."

"That is terrible but I still don't see the connection."

"Here's the kicker. I think I saw that monstrosity today talking to Helga." The visitors looked at the master of the house and his daughter.

Meyer turned to Helga. "Do you know who they are referring to?"

Helga regarded her father carefully and spoke. "I spoke earlier today to Sohn der Schrenken. He is very tall but not a monster."

"Describe him to me, Helga."

"Well he's at least two feet taller than you and very ugly. I guess he can be scary, but he is nice to me."

"I don't like it. Why was he talking to you?"

"I've seen him around town and was just being friendly, father. There's nothing to be concerned about."

"How can you say that after hearing this man's report? You must stay away from him, at least until I know more about the man. Do you understand?"

"Of course." She paused. "I'm not a child to order around but I'll stay away from Sohn for now. And I don't think you should make him the monster until you've at least spoken to him."

"Now who's being bossy," Meyer said.

"Is there anything else?" he asked Dieter and Franz.

They all looked at one another doubtfully. Meyer stood.

"Thank you for stopping by. I'll look into this matter. If you are right, then the village will have him apprehended and locked up at The Old Stone Prison."

"Guilty until proven innocent," Helga muttered.

"What's that, daughter?" he asked sharply.

"Nothing," she replied demurely.

Meyer led the two men to the front door and opened it. They bowed while leaving. He nodded curtly before closing the door quickly. He turned to Helga angrily.

"Never talk back to me, especially in front of others. Do you understand?"

Helga nodded moodily. She wondered if it a good idea to warn Sohn or just let events take their natural course. She needed time to think it over and let her father think she was deferring to his parental advice.

"You were missed at church," he said pointedly.

"Father, I'm sorry if you were embarrassed. I've never not attended a service without you. I should have told you that I didn't want to go."

"Why wouldn't you?" He couldn't understand the concept of skipping a Sunday service.

"You wouldn't understand. There's no point discussing it."

Helga walked out of the room, leaving her father to gawk incredulously at her back. *If only her mother was alive.* He realized immediately Gertrude, who was a devout Lutheran, would have been extremely upset. Gertrude even went the day before she died giving birth to Helga's brother. The mother hemorrhaged after the baby came out stillborn. She died hours later, leaving Hans alone to raise young Helga.

Chapter 8

Sohn stopped in mid stride. Something was wrong. He didn't yet have the fully developed sensory perception that would be used two centuries in the future, but he still sensed danger. He slowly turned around. It seemed to be coming from the village. Not one to shirk danger, he started retracing his steps at a fast trot. He took a Swiss timepiece from a trouser pocket. It was 1:18. He figured on crossing the Post Road at 1:30, taking slowing down in traffic to a moderate 12 miles per hour, just a tad faster than top human speed.

He wondered what had gone wrong. It could be anything. He was innocent of any crime, at least in Rhinebeck. His stomach churned. Did it have something to do with a prior location? He seemed to think so. But where? The answer lay beyond his scope. He continued onward, increasingly vigilant to any telltale sign of elevated animosity.

Should I take the main road into the village or try to sneak around and enter on the Post Road itself. His mind worked it out. If he'd been seen leaving the village, then it was possible there could be a lookout posted, expecting him to return the same route. Then again, perhaps he was over thinking the situation and his imagination was playing tricks. Perhaps there was nothing wrong.

Yes, there is.

He made a left onto a side road that he knew would eventually take him to the highway, perhaps a quarter mile above the road he's taken after leaving Helga. He slowed to a fast walk, passing homes every now and then. There was minimal foot traffic and the occasional horseman or horse and buggy. He raised a hand to the brim of his hat and nodded in a customary greeting. His gestures were nervously reciprocated.

His alabaster skin had a fine sheen of sweat as he walked steadily onward. Would he be expelled from Rhinebeck soon? He hoped not. It was a fine community and certain views reminded him of Europe. And when he listened to his native language spoken, he sometimes imagined himself in that distant land where his life began.

He didn't know where to go. Should he go home and wait for a knock on the door? Should he walk down the Albany Post Road to the spot he had been with

Helga? Should he go to her house? No, he suspected immediately that was improper. Her father was a respected figure and known to be stern and puritanical. Meyer would never welcome him into his home or accept the big man as an acquaintance of his daughter.

Going back to his house could be risky. If the house was being watched, his approach would be monitored. Entering the structure could trap him there with nowhere to turn. Still, he had some possessions there to retrieve should he be forced to flee.

He wanted to see Helga again. She made his large heart beat faster. If she felt the same way perhaps he'd take her away with him. The spirited young woman was not too young to marry. Sohn seemed to recollect most young women of her age were already married. Why hadn't Helga tied the knot? Was she waiting for the right man? Was that him? He grinned at the thought of Helga being his wife. He'd make their wedding night one never to forget.

Sohn grew edgy as the memory of another wedding night was recalled. It was the night he'd broken the neck of Elizabeth Frankenstein. The neck had snapped like a twig. It was Victor's fault, wasn't it? He promised Victor that evil would happen on the night of

Victor and Elizabeth's nuptial unless Victor created a
mate for him.

Sohn shook his head angrily as he passed a man
and woman strolling leisurely on the edge of the main
road.

"He is a menace," the man whispered.

"He is a monster," the woman replied, looking
over her shoulder with an ashen face.

"I have a good mind to report him to the
constable."

"Honey, take me home if you would and let's lock
the door."

They walked faster, eager to put as much distance
from the impassioned monster.

Helga sat on her bed thinking. This is stupid. I
feel like a prisoner. I'm going to leave this house for
good. I'm sick and tired of father having to know my
every move in this place and wanting me to go to church
every week. I need a place of my own and nobody
looking over my shoulder.

Helga taught at a village school. She could use her
experience teaching anywhere. Perhaps she could teach at
a school in the city. There were plenty of teaching
opportunities there.

Do I tell father? No, he would put his foot down and tell me my place is at home with him until I marry a local man. I need to get out now! This place is suffocating! I'll go out of my mind if I stay a day longer. Yah, it's time to pack up a few clothes and catch a southbound coach.

Helga felt newly confident and energized. She started packing.

Hans Meyer strode away from his home toward the jailhouse, determined to find out if there were any complaints or suspicions about the mill worker. Sohn appeared from around a corner. He stopped and gazed at Helga's father. His heart beat faster. His feeling of dread magnified while staring at the man who seemed to be walking with purpose away from him. Sohn looked around, taking in everything around him. He looked at the nearby Meyer house. The house seemed safe enough. Was Helga inside? Was it safe to pay her a visit? No answer came. He looked toward her father, but he had walked out of his view.

Sohn stepped over to the house and knocked on the door. He turned around again, wondering if he was being watched. No prying eyes were seen. He waited a minute; then he knocked louder. After several seconds he heard fast footsteps inside the home approaching the door. I don't need someone here now. I need to get away from here.

"Who is there," Helga asked, her hand an inch from the door handle.

"Sohn."

Helga hesitated. Did she want to see him? Was he really a monster? Would opening the door result in her death? She trusted her instincts, opened the door and looked up expectantly at her caller.

Sohn scrutinized her. She seemed conflicted and anxious, yet she had opened the door.

"I do not mean to intrude, Helga, but I fear my life may be in danger."

He watched for a reaction and would gave her words and body language carefully.

Helga nodded. "It is true. There were men here talking to my father about you." She frowned.

Do I dare ask why?

"What did they say about me?"

Helga's discomfort grew. "I heard tell that you caused trouble in Germany." She dared not ask if it was true as she looked at his yellow eyes. She saw a brief shadow in them. What did that mean? She feared nothing good. Still she must remain as composed as possible.

"I see." He paused then continued. "Did your father and these men leave together?"

"No. He departed some time afterward. I was not even aware he'd left the house until you knocked on the door."

Sohn turned around, surveying the street. He didn't see anybody at the moment. Helga looked, too, unsure what or who he was searching for.

Is he guilty?

"What will you do?" She asked.

"I don't know." He looked at the pretty young woman intently. "Do you believe them?"

Helga hesitated before answering. "Should I believe them? Is it true?"

He laughed bitterly. "Those questions have two meanings. In any case you only have my promise I will be your white knight. I mean you no harm nor do I plan any violence against anybody at this time. You should know however I will do everything necessary to be a free man. I will not be shackled."

Seconds later he added, "I have perhaps said too much".

"Nobody wants to be imprisoned whether deserving or not."

"Do you think I should be locked up?"

"If you did something bad," Helga replied bravely.

Sohn remained silent. He preferred honesty whenever possible. Silence was preferable to admitting guilt. He knew that silence would keep the issue unresolved. He felt that it was safe to do so with Helga as she seemed to like him. But he had to be careful and ever vigilant as the danger was still imminent.

Hans Meyer stood before Constable Schot in the jailhouse on West Market Street. Schot sat at his desk with arms folded across his chest.

"I can't do anything about it without proof."

"It's for the safety of Rhinebeck," Meyer replied. "Perhaps and perhaps not. I'm more suspicious of your source than the alleged criminal, this Sohn der Schrenk." "Have you seen this man or had any complaints about him?"

"That's none of your business, Mr. Meyer."

"I strongly disagree, Constable. It's your job to keep us safe."

"Don't tell me my business. I know damn well what to do," Schot said. His eyes bored angrily through Meyer.

"Is that all or may I get back to my other duties?"

"I expect you will at least investigate."

Meyer turned around. He exited Schot's small office without saying farewell. The law officer stared at the back of his head.

"Bastard," he muttered under his breathe.

Schot made it his business to keep track of the whereabouts of all suspected criminals in the village as well as persons of interest. The giant mill worker fell into the latter category. It wasn't due to any particular criminal behavior. It more had to do with the giant's physique and demonic look. A few citizens complained to his assistants about feeling threatened and scared of the man. But the German immigrant had done nothing illegal in Rhinebeck as far as the lawman knew. What he'd done in Germany was old news but still worth his looking closer at the man. He stood up and left the room.

The constable, armed with a pistol, stepped out of the stone jailhouse. Schot was alone, thinking he wouldn't need any of his deputies. He walked along the streets, exchanging greetings with its citizens. Schot took pride in the respect shown to him. He had just been promoted to the rank of a lieutenant in George Washington's army shortly before the U.S. victory at Yorktown and enjoyed his roles as a war veteran and senior law enforcement official. Perhaps only General Montgomery and General Armstrong were esteemed more than Schot in Rhinebeck. So his confidence in handling any potential adversary was very high.

The constable arrived at Sohn's home. He stood on the doorstep and knocked firmly on the oak door. The house felt empty to him. There was no sense of movement within. He contemplated leaving a note but decided against it.

Schot turned and started back toward the jail. A block away, he decided to make a thorough walk through the village. The lawman wanted to maintain a thorough familiarity of each street. Knowing the homes and commercial buildings would help in future investigations. The man grunted with satisfaction as he began his first grid.

Helga's view of the outside world was obstructed by the hulk standing in front of the door. Sohn was too captivated by Helga to care if there were people on the street watching him.

Helga was troubled by her visitor's constant gaze on her. She started to feel trapped. She was wasting her window of opportunity to escape Rhinebeck.

Sohn looked at Helga's troubled face.

"What is troubling you? Is it I?"

"I was in the middle of doing something when I heard your knocking. I must get back to it while I can. It will soon be too late, I fear."

"I will leave you to it. I am sorry to have intruded."

Helga smiled beautifully at Sohn. He inhaled and held his breath. Helga laughed.

"Please breathe."

Sohn felt his face redden from embarrassment. He exhaled more air than was held, making him cough. It was very loud. He bent over from the exertion. The forward movement of his head brought him in contact with the dumbstruck young women as his head brushed against her breasts.

Several pedestrians witnessed what appeared as a lewd public act and one that certainly prohibited in that era.

"How dare you!" Hans Meyer shouted as he strode rapidly toward them.

Sohn's head jerked up and he turned to face the irate man.

"Oh no," Helga cried. Her time to leave was suddenly gone.

Meyer clearly heard his daughter's distress. Meyer assumed the giant was the cause as he did not know about her plans to leave. His temper boiled.

Helga struggled to move around the behemoth. She lost her balance and fell.

"Ouch!" she cried as her nose hit the top landing. Her nose crunched and started bleeding profusely. Her father ran. "What have you done to my daughter, you fiend!?"

This can't be happening again? I have done nothing wrong.

Sohn looked from the charging man to the injured young woman.

What should I do?

Should he keep her father away? Sohn clenched his fists. His eyes glared menacingly at Meyer. In reaction, Helga's father stopped and looked up at the horrific creature.

How dare he call me a fiend! Sohn was sorely conscious of his appearance. He had never forgiven Victor for giving him his horrible, ugly face. Reminding him how he looked never worked out. His partly dormant penchant toward aggressive behavior came bubbling up to the surface. His body shook under the supreme effort of preventing an explosion of violence.

Constable Schot's vigilant walk brought him at that time to the Meyer house. His right hand drifted briefly to his gun. Shooting was the last resort. He listened to Meyer yell at the mill worker.

"You back away from Helga right now. Do you hear me?" he shouted.

"I am not deaf," Sohn replied, looking at Meyer with his cold yellow eyes.

Schot stepped forward.

"What is going on here?" he demanded.

Meyer turned to the constable.

"Arrest him instantly."

Sohn turned to Helga. She moaned. He reached down to pick her up. Her father objected immediately.

"I told you to back away. You've done enough already."

Sohn ignored him and lifted Helga easily, cradling her in his powerful arms. Her broken, bloody nose was a mess. Her eyes flickered open. She felt lightheaded and disoriented. Her father moved closer. Schot followed.

"Are you all right?" he inquired.

"Yes, father." She touched her nose gingerly and moaned again.

"You need to see a doctor. Your nose looks busted," Schot said.

"How did it happen?"

"I'll tell you how it happened. It was the, this man who struck her down," Hans Meyer said forcefully.

"That is a lie," Sohn said.

114

"Tell me what happened, Miss Meyer."

"I tripped and fell. It was my own fault. I don't think Sohn would do anything harmful to me, would you?" she asked him.

"Surely not!"

"Well then Mr. der Schreken, while you have the injured Miss Meyer secured safely in your arms, why don't we all get her to Dr. Monroe? Any objections?" he asked Helga's father. Meyer's cheeks were flushed and his eyes glared at both men. He reluctantly agreed with the recommendation as his daughter's well-being was his primary concern.

Meyer nodded quickly He opened his right hand and extended it outward and in a forward motion, signaling the men to start the short walk to the doctor's home.

A few minutes later, Schot and Sohn stood outside the doctor's home while Helga and her father were inside with Doctor Monroe.

"This is the first time I've had the honor of conversing with you since you moved to Rhinebeck. How do you like our little community?" Schot asked.

"I like it fine, Captain. It reminds me of Germany in many respects." Sohn said calmly.

"Ah yes, Germany and you seem to know more about me then me about you. We should rectify that, don't you think?" the constable inquired, examining the giant closely for any evident signs of deceit or nerves.

"So be it," Sohn replied.

"Were you a mill worker in the old country, too?"

"No."

"What was your line of work there?"

Sohn hesitated. He couldn't very well admit to being a vagrant. That could get him in trouble.

Schot realized he'd asked a sensitive question as no answer was provided. The constable anticipated a dishonest response was forthcoming. He would then decide either to play along with Sohn or press him for details.

Sohn finally replied, trying to keep his voice calm. "I did many things including working in a laboratory under the auspices of a scientist, but mostly I did odd jobs for people like cutting firewood and fetching water for a kindly old man and his family and the like. Oh, I was involved in grave digging, too."

"How nice. And where were you educated?"

"I am basically self-taught. I've had the benefit of being in the homes of well-read men. I've enjoyed the benefits of reading."

"Yes, indeed."

The constable sensed he was missing something. But what? The man was leaving something out intentionally." He looked around, one finger idly rubbing his chin.

You're not getting too much useful information from me, Sohn told himself with satisfaction.

"Who was the scientist and what was his specialization? Perhaps I've heard of him," Schot said suddenly.

Again there was hesitation. Schot knew he was getting closer to the moment of truth.

"His name is Frankenstein. He was a physiologist."

"Was?" Schot asked quickly.

Sohn's black thin lips squeezed together, making them almost a narrow line. The constable felt uncharacteristically edgy. "Well he was also a chemist."

"Again you use the past tense."

"It's been some years since I saw Frankenstein. I can't say what has happened to him."

"I suppose not."

Constable Schot decided to stop the informal interrogation. Whatever the giant had done in Germany was beyond his jurisdiction and besides there was no indication of any malevolent behavior since the man moved to Rhinebeck. He was just about to thank Sohn for his time when Dieter walked up the street with wide eyes, staring at Sohn. The big man's back was turned away so he was unaware of Dieter's approach until he observed the constable looking fixedly past him. Sohn turned around to see what Schot was looking at.

"That's him!" Dieter said excitedly. "That's the monster! Thank God you have him!"

"We are only having an amicable discussion here Dieter. And stop using that terminology here. It is inappropriate."

Sohn's blood pressure skyrocketed. He was ready to make a run for it if Schot took Dieter's allegation seriously. Had his cursed past caught up with him? Would he be a hunted man on two continents? He knew that violence would follow him forever unless he used restraint here and now. Otherwise he would be hunted down from town to town, state to state until he ended up lost in the wilderness and forced to live in territory inhabited by Native Americans and a few hardy mountain men.

"Captain Schot, I don't know what this man is ranting about. Do you?"

"Something about a monster terrorizing villagers in Germany. Do you know anything about it, sir?"

"No, I do not."

"Liar!" Dieter shouted.

Sohn took a threatening step toward his accuser. Dieter backed off. Schot put a restraining hand on the giant's arm. Sohn looked inquiringly at the constable.

"Don't do anything foolish. Do you understand?"

Sohn clearly pictured himself ripping apart the meddlesome old German. He got some satisfaction from the mental image. It made him feel better. He nodded to Schot.

"Good." He continued, speaking to both men. "There will be no accusations made on the streets where fellow citizens can overhear. This is a private matter. I have already heard all I need to know and I will not tolerate any more outbursts. If I learn about another outburst one or both of you will be spending time in jail. Any questions?" he said looking earnestly at each man.

Dieter sulked but did not reply.

Sohn directed his next remarks to Schot as speaking to Dieter would come to no good end. "I insist that Dieter stop harassing me. If he violates his agreement, I will notify you directly."

"Rat," Dieter muttered under his breathe.

"What did you say? Sohn seethed.

"Dieter, one more derogatory word from you," Schot told Dieter, "will mean an immediate arrest."

"What about freedom of speech? It's in the Constitution, ain't it?"

"That's not funny. Now go home or wherever it was you were going to before making a scene," Schot said sternly.

"Alright already!"

Dieter trod away. He briefly looked back over his shoulder, glaring at the giant. Sohn sneered and spoke quietly to the lawman. "I don't think he'll quit."

Schot warned "Don't put the law in those large calloused hands of yours. Stay away from him."

Sohn nodded.

We shall see.

All was quiet in the village. It was well past midnight. The dormant Grim Reaper lay inside the gargantuan reposing body.

It had been such a long time before being permitted to put a human to death. The Reaper had hijacked Frankenstein's Creature just before going on a killing spree. The strength, size and stamina of its new host were ideal but the Creature's advanced brain fought to evict the Reaper. Since slaughtering the wolves in northern Canada, Sohn had forced the Reaper into remission, hoping eventually it would vacate the premises and take over someone else or perhaps go off on its own.

The Reaper awakened.

Dieter had drunk more than his share of Schnapps. After being kicked out of the tavern he'd continued his binge elsewhere. His friends told him enough was enough but the man was too worked up to stop. He kept on ranting about a monster on the loose and nobody was doing anything about it, not even the constable. His drinking companions thought he was making it all up so they just nodded and offered sympathetic comments. Then when everyone called it a night, Dieter walked home.

He was too sloshed to walk straight home, let alone walk straight period. Dieter carried a sheathed knife attached to his old, worn Prussian Army belt. His muddled mind decided it was a good time to use the knife. He staggered toward his new destination with a steely crooked grin.

The Reaper awakened his host just as their uninvited guest stopped outside the dwelling. The yellow eyes darted open. They peered intensely at the infinite darkness and saw nothing, nothing at all. It was too black even for shadows. There were no streetlamps to provide any greyness, and an overcast night sky hid the moon.

The man outside the home stood and listened. He swayed slightly.

The man inside the home stood and listened, his senses on high alert. He would not make the first move. He would allow the other to have that honor. He anticipated how it would come about and what he would do to the assailant. Planning ahead was essential. Sohn did not want the constable to be forced to apprehend him.

Perhaps self-defense would work for him. Being captured and caged was out of the question. It would drive him insane and bring out the monster in the man. And that never particularly ended well for his victims.

Dieter stepped over to a window. It was partly open. He squinted and attempted to look inside the house. "It's too damn dark in there," he murmured. He hoped to see his quarry lying asleep. But he couldn't see anything. Sohn stood to the side of the window. He barely heard Dieter.

Come to me, his mind beckoned wickedly. Dieter wondered if he should try the door or use the open window to get inside.

"I'm right here," he reasoned. "I just need to open the window some more and I'll place my house call." He grinned at his choice of words. He was a regular wit though the alcohol perhaps made him more of a dimwit. The window was pulled up with some effort. He grunted but was unaware of the noise he made. He paused to look inside. There was still nothing to see. He pulled himself up and forward and propelled himself inside, landing heavily on the floor.

Suddenly an enormous hand grabbed his throat and yanked him to his feet. The other hand reached for the window and closed it. A closed window reduced any light to moderate noise transmission. Awakening the neighbors was absolutely unwanted.

Dieter was forced up to his tiptoes and his head raised up to the invisible ashen face looking down at him. I'm going to die.

"Welcome to my humble abode," Sohn said through gritted teeth. "What do you have to say for yourself?"

Dieter couldn't say anything with his larynx constricted by the powerful hand.

"Speak up man as you have done nothing than run your mouth about me. Well?"

Dieter's eyes bulged then he felt his sore throat being released. He fell on the floor landing with his hands and feet. Sohn bent down, his hands ready to snap the man's neck should he scream out.

"So tell me Dieter about Germany.

I'm going to die.

"Cat got your tongue?"

Dieter felt lightheaded and nauseous.

"I'm not going to wait much longer. Speak up!"

Dieter urinated in his pants. He didn't care.

Sohn's nostrils flared.

"That is crude but I should have known better from the likes of you. You had to start blabbing about me, didn't you? I've been a good citizen in this little hamlet. I was starting to feel at home until you decided to end it for me. Well, Dieter, perhaps I'll end it for you. What do you have to say? Should I let you go?"

Was there hope? Dieter saw a glimmer, but the only source of light was inside his head.

"Do you mind if I stand?" he croaked. His throat hurt.

"Be my guest."

The Creature took a step back cautiously while Dieter slowly stood, Unlike Dieter, the alabaster man had excellent night vision. It was another of the gifts Victor had given him.

"What will you do to me?" Dieter asked meekly.

"That depends on you."

"What do you want from me?"

"I want your retraction. You will stop making trouble for me by stop talking about me. If someone asks, then say you were mistaken. Can and will you do it?"

"Do I have a choice?"

"No, you do not. Consider what could have happened to you tonight. I am giving you a reprieve." Dieter relaxed just a little bit.

"You are not the monster."

The monster laughed.

The unholy sound made Dieter shiver. He'd promise to do whatever was asked of him in order to live another day.

"You have my word."

"I truly hope so. It is for both of us, you know. Do you understand me?"

"Yes, I do."

The Reaper was furious with Sohn as the opportunity for a fresh kill was passing by. The giant's heart was softening just a bit as the years flowed along. The Reaper was sickened. He'd have to find another host soon to quench his thirst, someone more eager to bring death, somebody like his favorite death machine from a village some fifty miles south in Sleepy Hollow. But that being was as dead to the world as this pathetic Dieter ought to be.

It growled angrily inside the Creature. He was angry enough to inflict pain.

Sohn winced. He spoke urgently to Dieter. "You better leave while you can and do it fast."

Dieter nodded. Sohn opened the door. Dieter stumbled out and ran all the way home.

He stood in the middle of the room with outstretch arms. He closed his eyes and slowed down his heart rate. His mind opened communications with his tormentor.

"It is time for you to leave, Reaper. You are no longer needed or wanted. I am a changed man."

"You have become soft as jelly," the Reaper sneered. "I have lost my respect for you."

"I accept that and release you," the Creature replied.

"You will always be a monster," Reaper derided.

"Perhaps but perhaps not. We have come to a cross road and we will now go in separate directions."

"You are leaving this place then?"

"Yes."

"What about that delicious treat, that Helga? She wants to leave, too."

Sohn was stupefied.

126

Reaper sensed that his host was clueless. "You didn't know, but that should be no surprise. It seems you know so little about people. That may be your undoing."

"Helga is leaving Rhinebeck? Alone?"

Reaper refused to reply. He was done. It was time to leave.

"Prepare yourself," Reaper announced.

Sohn's body started to vibrate. He shook all over. A searing pain past through him as the other slowly oozed out of his pores. He lost consciousness. The next sound he heard was a crowing cock.

A new day dawned on another chapter of his life. He left Rhinebeck that day.

Chapter 9

Sohn sat in the pickup truck parked by a deserted rocky beach. He remembered the yesteryear time in Rhinebeck like it was only yesterday. Sohn recalled the frantic last day in the village.

He purchased a horse and cart and then packed essentials. His destination was unknown. The only known was that remaining in the village was suddenly too risky.

He was on the radar of too many people.

One person dominated his mind that morning. *Is Helga really leaving, too? Should I take her with me?* Sohn decided to drive past her home on the way out of Rhinebeck. He did not intend to knock on the front door at her home. But if she was seen outdoors he would stop and question her. It was a long shot but well worth a slight detour. The thought of never seeing the fair young woman was too depressing for the big guy. His life would be miserable evermore.

Around midday the German immigrant drove the loaded horse drawn cart past the Meyer home. His heart grew heavy as he left the building behind without any sign of the lovely Helga. He was angry at himself for getting emotionally attached to her. He daydreamed about carrying her in his arms the previous day. Those few moments were the highlight of his life, though he was sorry about her discomfort.

"Whoa horse!" a voice commanded. The oversized driver forced himself from his pleasant reverie.

There she is!

Helga held a rein in one hand and a loaded basket in the other. She smiled up at him. Helga looked as pretty as ever despite the bandaged nose.

"Are you going somewhere?"

"Helga, I am so happy to see you. But sadly, I am leaving Rhinebeck now," he said both happily and sadly. "I was afraid I would never see you again."

"You were going to leave without saying farewell?"

"Your father does not particularly like me."
"I know that. My father likes very few people. He has very high standards, so is often disappointed. Take me for example," Helga said sadly.
"You are the opposite of disappointing."

"Truly?" she asked. Her eyes sparkled.

"You should leave with me," he said urgently.

"I tried to leave once," Helga said dejectedly, "but I am still here."

"It's now with me or some other time with another" Sohn said. He didn't want to put much hope she would accept his offer.

"I can drop you off someplace if you like."

Helga contemplated Sohn's proposal. It was providential that only a day ago she planned to escape her overbearing father and now she could have a traveling companion. But what a traveling companion! Nobody would dare harm or otherwise take advantage of her with Sohn at her side. The big question was whether she would need protection from him. Those rumors about monstrous doings in Germany were nerve racking. She glanced up at him to gauge his expression and saw only hope and affection.

"I will go with you, Sohn. Will you wait here?"

He scanned his surroundings and looked back at her. "I can't wait out on the street. Someone will wonder why I am here. You should meet me a few blocks away. It wouldn't be wise to be seen by many people leaving town with me."

"How clever of you."

Sohn beamed in his own way.

"I'll pack a small trunk and meet you by the cemetery."

He looked at her earnestly to determine if she was serious or pulling him along.

"Good. Please make it fast."

"I will." She smiled and then walked quickly toward her father's house.

Sohn flicked the reins and the horse moved forward.

Sohn waited at the graveyard. He did not feel comfortable being there because he knew Victor had stolen body parts from at least one graveyard. Being there really made his skin crawl.

Every few minutes he looked at his stopwatch. He looked to his left in the direction Helga would be approaching the cemetery. Each time he decided to look, his heart jumped an iota followed by disappointment.

An hour passed. His mood soured.

What has happened? Has her father stopped her? Has someone else in the village stopped Helga?

He would give it another few minutes.

Sohn jumped down to the ground and stood forlornly and restlessly gazing at the marked gravestones. He stood slightly hunched over as the minutes passed. He almost missed the approaching sound of boots. Sohn turned. His expression hardened.

"Herr Meyer."

Meyer stood with his hands behind him. He laughed. "And you were expecting my foolish daughter. She is in her bedroom consoling herself."

Sohn took a step closer to Meyer. Helga's father lowered his arms to his side. A pistol dangled in his right hand. Sohn stopped.

"Are you here to shoot me with that?"

"Not if I don't have to."

"Meyer, you have no right to stop Helga from leaving Rhinebeck. She is an adult."

"True, but she will not be going anywhere with the likes of you. I made an effort to come here and give you the news. Now you can go on your journey while I go home. Farewell."

Meyer bowed and turned. Sohn stood there watching the man until he was out of view.

* * *

Sohn sighed deeply. He stood on the beach looking out at the island dotted bay. He shivered, not from the temperature, but from the bitter memory of leaving Rhinebeck without Helga.

His was a solitary existence. He was used to living alone and being deprived of a friend but he nevertheless still envied most of humanity who was fortunate to have family and friends. Did the loner give up hope that he could ever live a so called normal life? Almost, but not quite!

He planned to camp out that evening on the beach. Sohn would burn dried driftwood, perhaps gather a bushel of mussels from the boulders below the high water line and dig some clams from the low tide line. He would make the most of a night under the stars and hopefully fall asleep listening to the soothing sound of the small waves lapping on the beach.

Sohn sat down on a grassy outcropping over the beach and closed his eyes. He blocked out the sounds of crying seagulls, a gentle breeze and the waves hitting the shoreline.

He withdrew from the world around him until he found himself back in a spacious stone walled chamber. Mary Godwin stood watching with wide eyes as the impossibly tall man stepped closer to her.

What does he want? I don't want to be here. How do I get out?

"It's all right, Mary. You are safe here. It is our sanctuary."

Sohn stopped a few paces from her. He noticed her quick breaths as her breasts moved up and down rapidly.

"I'm here against my will. What do you want?" Mary asked although she was hesitant to hear the answer.

"I want you to be my friend."

Mary shivered. The stone walls kept any warmth outside.

"By putting me in this dreary place?" She replied.

"It is where I was born."

She looked around. "It looks very old. Where is this place?"

"It is in Germany."

"I don't see anything modern in here."

"That is true, Mary."

"I don't understand."

"I am older than I look. That is all I will say about it for now."

Mary was confused. What was he saying? There was innuendo that was beyond her understanding. All she could piece together was that he was born in this depressing room. She took a few steps around the man to inspect the room. It appeared to be some sort of laboratory. There was a very long table in the center, perhaps more than eight feet in length with straps. There were glass jars with body parts. There was a separate operating table with medical instruments. Medical journals were stacked on shelves. She had seen enough and turned back.

"What is this place?"

He gazed down at me shrewdly.

Sohn looked from the man to the eight foot operating tables and back again. *That's impossible!*

"It is?" he asked though Mary had not spoken aloud.

Sohn was amused by her disbelieving expression.

"Nothing is impossible. We're in the 21st Century."

"No, this is another era," Mary replied. "Do I dare ask what century I've been transported to?"

Sohn considered. He was afraid to say too much. "No, I don't think so. But Mary looked at the man next to me with a new awareness and awe. She was too stunned and horrified to speak.

Victor's creation stood patiently waiting for Mary to absorb the inferred knowledge. Most people would be unable to grasp and accept the reality that he was brought to life on one of the neighboring tables.

Thankfully her youth and open mind enabled Mary to think it over, incredible as it seemed. Mary's demeanor seemed to change.

"How old were you when you were, um, born here?

"I do not know. How old do I look to you?" Mary looked at his face as long as she could, not an enjoyable thing to do.

"You look to be in your early to middle forties." "Then that could have been my age when I was created here."

Mary's jaws dropped. He implied something else extraordinary. He was apparently created in the gloomy, dank laboratory by some genius and could be immortal. She shook her head.

"You do not believe me, Mary Godwin?"

"If what you are telling me is true then you are one of a kind, unless your creator made others like you." Sohn's head sagged. Mary guessed she had struck a nerve. He finally look up sadly.

"I am one of a kind," he said glumly.

"That is too bad. I mean it is unfortunate for you."

"Yes it is."

Sohn didn't see any point continuing the session. So he brought himself back to the beach, more depressed than ever. In just a few hours he had reflected on losing Helga and the female companion Victor had promised him. Sohn really needed something good to happen to bring him out of the despair that overwhelmed him.

* * *

Mary opened her eyes. She was seated outside watching a fleet of sloops racing in the channel near her house when she suddenly fell asleep. That perplexed her as she wasn't tired when her eyes seemed to close on their own accord. While asleep Mary dreamed about being in the cold room with the giant.

She didn't know what to believe about the man. Was the dream reality or something imagined? She wasn't sure.

Suddenly there was a degree of clarity. The giant must have a connection with her. But how was that possible? She reflected on their chance encounter on the highway.

Is it fate?

She was ambivalent about the man's desire to be in her life. He was apparently drawn to her like a magnet. That made Mary nervous. Did she really want this man in her life? She knew her parents abhorred that possibility. They were accustomed to being around attractive people. Sohn was the total opposite.

The only self-evident redeeming qualities of this man was has apparent intelligence and his vulnerability. Sohn would have been pleased to know Mary felt sympathy for him. He'd consider that a start, but a start to what?

He had a roaring fire going in a pit on the beach. It was surrounded by pebbles, smashed seashells and damp sand to contain the fire. The parked truck usually carried a few essentials just in case he stopped spur of the moment at campsites or other spots in the countryside and seashore.

A steaming pot of fresh mussels and clams cooked on the fire.

The German also had a couple of bottles of ale, the beverage of choice for him the past several centuries. Sohn rarely drank out of a can or bottle, preferring to pour the contents into a one liter wood stein. He painstakingly carved it from an oak tree trunk. He enjoyed the oaken flavor as the amber liquid was greedily swallowed.

"Aah," he said aloud after draining the stein. Nobody was nearby as far as he knew to hear him. He put the stein down carefully next to him on the sand, and leaned back with his arms propping up his head. He watched the red sparks dance in the night sky. It was a wondrous form of entertainment as the sparks moved in every conceivable direction.

"It's beautiful."

"More than I can say about you, asshole!" a gruff voice said.

Sohn started to get up until a sharp object dug into his upper back.

"Stay on your ass!" a man's voice said. "That's a 12 gauge shotgun pointed at your innards."

"What do you want?" Sohn asked calmly.

He heard idiotic laughter. His right hand inched closer to the scabbard. The shotgun was no longer against his back but he heard the scrunch of shoes walking from behind to his left. He jerked his head around and looked into the eyes of the ferry crewman who had taunted him that day. The man held the shotgun in front of him with only one arm.

He's either very confident or very foolish.

"If you stopped by here for beer to wash away your sins, help yourself. You can put down the rifle and join me for a drink."

"That'll be the day. Now shut up. You'll answer my questions only. Understand?"

Sohn gave his unwanted visitor a cold stare. The man held the weapon with both hands very tightly.

"Why are you on my island?" the crewman demanded.

"You own the island, do you?"

"Shut the fuck up!"

"But you told me to answer your questions."

"You're a smart ass, ain't you?"

"If you say so."

Sohn wanted to taunt his persecutor a bit for fun to see what effect it would have on the man. He wanted to avoid getting shot and having to hurt the crewman if possible. The gunman's face darkened in the firelight and his jaw grated.

The ferry worker quickly looked at the discarded pot of food and beer stein then focused his attention on the giant's horrid face. He removed his left hand from the trigger and pulled a flask from his pants. The man looked at the flask with frustration.

"How do I unscrew the top with one hand with my other hand still on the trigger?"

Sohn used that free second to grab hold of his scabbard while carefully observing the gunman. The man didn't seem to notice anything wrong because he was busy unscrewing the flask top with his teeth.

Sohn was an expert with several weapons. There was plenty of free time to practice his marksmanship during the past centuries with knives, pistols, rifles, bayonets and others using boards, trees, and walls of abandoned building as his target. He was deadly accurate from a variety of positions including standing, kneeling and sitting. He calculated it would take four seconds to yank out the knife and hurl it at the center of the target.

"You should leave now," he warned.

The empty flask went into a pocket. The gun wavered slightly. Sohn remained patient.

"I think not," the man replied. "You'll be sorry you ever set foot on Islesboro."

"Why me?" Sohn asked coolly, his eyes locked on the crewman's eyes.

His reply was given with a shrug. "You don't fit in here, Mister. You should have gone back to Lincolnville on the return ferry. You have to pay the ultimate price." The shotgun was pointed at Sohn's head, then his heart, then his testicles and back to the heart again. All the while the tormentor kept his eyes glued to Sohn with an evil grin.

Sohn decided to disrupt the man's attention.

"I think I hear a car. It's getting louder," Sohn said.

The shotgun stopped moving, as its owner strained his ears. Sohn hurled the knife at the hand holding the gun. The aim and trajectory was perfect. Sohn lurched to his feet and sprinted forward.

The ferryman was in sudden agony. The shotgun fell on the beach. Both men lunged for it. They fell on the weapon simultaneously. Sohn struggled to keep it aimed at neither of them as he wanted to avoid further harm and death. But the other man proved he was no weakling. Sohn was somewhat surprised he couldn't pry the gun loose. So he forced the end of the barrel into the sand, driving it forward with all of his might.

There was a muffled explosion as the crewman's finger pressed down on the trigger. Sohn had noticed the gun was a pump shotgun instead of a semi-automatic. That was good news. It would not fire another round without pushing back the pump to load another cartridge in the chamber.

"There's no way in hell that's going to happen," Sohn said harshly. He drove the man's head down into the sand, applying steady pressure as the man thrashed his legs about urgently. Sohn waited until the movements eased. Then he released his grip. He leaned down and yanked the deadly weapon out of the partially unconscious man's grip and tossed the rifle out of reach.

Sohn stood and backed up a few paces until he found his hunting knife. He cleaned the blade with sand, rubbed it clean against his pants and put it back in the scabbard.

The prostrate man stirred. Sohn used restraint to make sure neither man was seriously injured. He was upset nevertheless about the incident. If released, he expected the man to press charges against him. The whole island would turn on him, even Mary Godwin.

Everyone would be convinced the stabbing was unprovoked when Sohn was doing what he could to not get shot. He had seen murder in the other man's eyes as sure as it is dark at night and bright in the day.

There was only one thing to do. He sighed.

Damnation! I have to do it again!

The giant stepped over to the man and did what he had done too many times in his elongated life.

He snapped the islander's neck.

Chapter 10

The sound of silence echoed through his head as he blocked out the waves, tweeting birds and buzzing insects. He had a grim task to perform and little time to perform the burial. Sweat beaded on his forehead and occasionally flowed into his eyes. He blinked away the discomfort as the hole was excavated above the high tide line with a shovel taken from the pickup truck.

He selected a large boulder as an ideal location. With maximum effort, he swiftly dug the hole about a foot from the rock. The going was slow and rough as the shovel constantly scraped against small stones and beach debris. His right shoulder ached but he kept up the assault on the beach. He didn't want a beach goer to show up unexpectedly. There'd be hell to pay again for somebody.

The corpse lay on its back. The moonlight illuminated the dead eyes looking at nothing at all. A surprised expression on the pale face showed the man was conscious when receiving the coup de grace.

A flock of interested seagull stood nearby looking intently with blinking eyes at the possible meal lying on the beach. The prospect of nipping away at a pair of eyeballs and other body parts was too good to pass up.

The gravedigger ignored them as he stove to deepen the pit to a depth of five or six feet. But the shovel hit a limestone shelf about four feet down. He probed the rock with is shovel and knife but there were no openings to dig around.

It'll have to do, he thought. He didn't have the patience to try another site. He wiped his brow with a sandy arm and looked at the dead man.

Are you ready?

Sohn nodded to himself. He stepped over to the body, vaguely noticing the scavengers running away a few yards. Sohn picked up the shotgun and removed his fingerprints with his shirt. He flung it into the hole. Then he hauled the still warm corpse into the grave and dropped it on top of the gun. The head hit the limestone. Blood started oozing across the rock.

The hole partially went under the boulder making it possible for Sohn to use every ounce of his power to leverage it a foot until it eased on top of the crewman's final resting place. Then Sohn filled in to make the ground around the rock level. Then he tamped it down with the shovel. Finally he spread some dried seaweed for good measure.

The gulls still congregated nearby. Sohn smacked his callused hands together, scaring the birds and sending them soaring into the night air. It was time for him to flee the scene, too. He picked up his belongings and tossed them in the truck.

His enormous shoe prints would attract attention He tore off a pine tree branch and used it to erase his footsteps on the beach. Before getting behind the driver's seat he stood looking at the beach wondering if there was anything left to do.

The shells!

Sohn took the discard tree branch to the campsite, picked up the empty mussel and clam shells and tossed them into the water. He expected the seawater would erase any fingerprints on them. Then Sohn strode back up the beach, spraying the beach with the branch until he reached the vehicle again. He tossed the branch into the woods, hopped onto the front seat, closed the door and started the engine.

The car!

What was he supposed to do with the bastard's car? The headlights of the pickup illuminated a dented, rusty old sedan. Sohn stared at the car, wondering what to do with it. Should he hide it in the woods? Or should he leave it parked in its current location?

The first option was not likely as the island was very narrow. The car would be discovered in a matter of days at the most. That left leaving the car where it was. The crewman would be missed after failing to report to work the next day. His boss would reach out to his emergency contacts. Eventually the island's constable would get a call and file a missing person report. It could take days before his car was discovered parked by the beach. Sohn figured a possible outcome would be the supposition he drowned. That was good enough for the man's murderer.

In the end, he decided to push Herston's car into the wood a short distance. He tried screening it with pine branches from nearby trees. Then he jogged back to the black pickup truck.

He stepped gently on the accelerator and drove slowly down a dirt road some two hundred yards until it merged with a macadam road and continued onward with no destination in mind. His mind skirted around the dirty deed.

Mary fell asleep after writing five pages in her journal. The entire content was about the giant. Her most recent dream revealed something of his origins. She considered it Gothic horror and science faction. A man created and brought to life in a laboratory and still alive centuries later. It was unbelievable! Impossible?

She had been there, at least she thought so. It seemed so real. She had smelled the lab and had been chilled by the cool, damp air. Was that possible in a dream?

The investigative reporter in her saw a challenge. She needed to get more of the man's back story as well as what she could dig up about his life in the present time. The honest and direct approach was getting his permission. Would he be willing to be interviewed? What would she do with the finished project? Would he allow her to get it published? How would that exposure affect his life?

She knew none of the answers. Plus she did not have any way of contacting him.

No, that's not exactly true.

He had taken the ferry from the mainland and driven right up to the house with little difficulty. How did he know where to find her? The answer was just out of reach. She sensed it would come to her.

The next morning Mary got the latest update on Hurricane Isabella. It was hurtling through New York

City in a northerly direction. Waves smashed over innumerable shorelines in the metropolitan area. Trees fell on power lines, cars and buildings. There were massive power outages. Mary was both sad and glad about staying in Maine. She would make more of an effort the next time a hurricane hits the city.

She looked forward to her outing with Perce. The weather was perfect, promising a relaxing boat ride to Seven Hundred Acre Island and the potential for a good hike on the small island. Her feelings about the handsome man were mixed. His reputation for being a womanizer gave her low expectations for any romance. He probably wanted to seduce her. She would allow it if she wanted him. Right then she didn't know what she wanted.

Sohn was tempted to park at the ferry landing and wait for the first boat to the mainland. But he didn't want any potential witnesses to see him. Instead, he drove around looking for a safe, inconspicuous location where he and the pickup truck wouldn't be noticed.

He discovered a small airstrip with a single runway. A few small airplanes were parked to the side. There were several sheds but not a controller tower. The place looked little used. The largest aircraft was a small jet owned by a famous actor. Sohn felt it was safe enough to stay where he was for the rest of the night.

Falling asleep was a tall order. Dismissing the killing was impossible. In Sohn's mind there was no alternative. The dead man held an incurable grudge against Sohn that would only be sated by killing Sohn. Sohn attempted to shake the depressing situation. He closed his tired eyes again.

He awakened a few hours later. His mouth was dry and he was very hungry. There was nothing left to eat or drink in the cab. He got out of the truck to look around for a vending machine. Perhaps there was one next to a storage shed. The big man walked in the dawn's early light to each building. There wasn't a vending machine in sight. He did locate a spigot. At least thirst was no longer an issue.

It was time to get over to the ferry landing. There had to be a source of food there as people congregated at the tiny terminal at least eight hours a day. Grabbing a bite while waiting for the next ride seemed like a good idea.

A few minutes later, he pulled into a parking spot at the small harbor. Sure enough, there was a takeout stand off to the side of the ticket office. A few early birds sat at picnic tables having breakfast. They stopped chewing and drinking at the sight of the unnaturally rangy ugly guy sauntering over to place an order. One man forgot to swallow and started choking. Snot fell into a steaming Styrofoam cup of coffee. Sohn grinned at the diners.

"Morning," he greeted the heavy set woman standing inside the takeout establishment.

"Morning," she replied halfheartedly. "Frickin' aye!" she muttered faintly.

Sohn hopefully examined the menu stationed next to the closed screen door. He then favored the woman with his attention.

"Two large black coffees and three bacon, egg and cheese sandwiches on a hard roll."

The woman nodded and set to work. Sohn felt eyes staring at him. He quickly spun around. The people dropped their eyes and looked away. He walked over to an empty table. He was too tall to sit on a bench so the table served as his seat. The diners couldn't refrain from gawking some more. Sohn decided it was safer to ignore them as he wanted to be low key.

His breakfast of champions was ready. He paid for the meal and carried it back in two trips to the table. By then, he had his choice of tables as the others customers went their own way.

A car pulled up, but the prospective patrons decided to wait out the lone eater before leaving the relative security of the vehicle. The takeout woman shook her head, hoping the stranger would eat and run instead of frightening away her customers.

Sohn was a typical German in many ways. He was methodical, very neat and businesslike. The man liked getting to the point in conversations much more than beating around the bush. He still considered himself more German than American despite the two hundred and twelve years in The United States. During World War One he even considered returning to Germany to enlist. He remained in the USA and was thankful he did not put himself in German trenches against the U.S Expeditionary Force that joined the terrible front lines in 1917. In later years he joined American opposition to The Third Reich. Sohn worked in the shipyard at Newport News, Virginia building warships.

During breakfast Sohn Schrenk concentrated how he would spend the day. The smart course of action was catching the first ferry to Lincolnville Beach. He was curious to find out the morale of the ship's crew. Was he missed yet? They could be expecting their missing comrade to show up at any time assuming he was scheduled to work that day. Sohn guessed it was still way too early for them to be concerned about their former coworker.

Sohn was not absolutely convinced that going home was what he wanted to do. He still hoped to see Mary again. She seemed interested in him, especially since showing her the laboratory. Perhaps he should drive back to the Godwin cottage. Perhaps parking the truck in the woods to watching her comings and goings would be useful. Another option entailed renting a small boat to do surveillance.

By the time the empty wrappers and one of the cups were dumped into the trash can his mind was made up. Schrenk sat behind the steering wheel and placed the other coffee cup in a beverage holder. He turned over the ignition and eased the truck ahead toward the back of the line of vehicles waiting to board the ferry. His visit to Islesboro was over.

Mary's cell phone rang. She glanced at the caller ID and smiled. It was Perce.

"Hi."

"Mary, I'm approaching your dock."

"I'll be right there."

She ended the call and walked toward the back door.

"See you later," she called out to her parents.

"Have fun dear," her mother replied.

Her father didn't say anything as he was in his study coordinating the magazine's coverage of the hurricane as it shot north.

Mary thought about running down to the dock but she didn't want to seem overly eager to see Perce. She walked fast instead. Mary wore a short sleeve shirt, jeans and walking shoes and carried a small backpack.

The sleek motorboat docked as Mary stepped down to the float. She exchanged smiles with Perce. He held out a free hand to help her step from the dock onto the boat. She stepped onto the narrow side and then jumped down to the main deck of the boat.

"Welcome aboard," he greeted warmly.

"Thanks."

Mary noticed a large canvas bag.

"That's our lunch," Perce commented.

Mary nodded.

"Where to? The boatyard?" she inquired.

"It's a little too busy there. I thought we'd hop over to the Edgerton's place. They're away now and wouldn't have a problem with using their dock."

"Okay."

Perce pushed the boat off the dock. The engine had been idling. He put it in forward and the boat moved into open water. He looked around to make sure there were no boats or other obstructions in his way and pushed the handle forward. The boat accelerated up to twenty knots. Mary stood next to Perce, watching the boat speed through the calm waters. The waves were little more than a slight chop.

Her hair blew in the speed induced wind. Mary aimed her face directly into the wind and closed her eyes. Being out on the water was exhilarating. It made her happy.

Perce enjoyed seeing her making the most of the experience. He hoped the rest of their outing would be satisfying for both of them. Hiking was not one of his usual recreational activities. The man preferred golf and reading poetry. He'd even started writing poems and managed to get a few published by New Yorker magazine. He heard Mary enjoyed the occasional hike from mutual friends so it seemed a good way to spend the better part of a day with the attractive young woman.

"Fun in the sun," he said.

Mary looked over at him, eyebrows raised. It was difficult to hear above the loud twin engines.

"Excuse me?" she said.

He recovered quickly.

"I brought some sunscreen along," Perce replied.

"I'm glad one of us remembered."

The boat sped along the channel between Islesboro and Seven Hundred Acre Island. They past an estate on the latter. A picturesque brick chapel was located on the grounds. Mary half expected to see a monk leading a knight and lady outside the dilapidated structure.

She noticed two docks up island. The bow seemed to be aiming for the nearer one. A minute later, Perce lowered the throttle and allowed the boat to slow in its approach to an empty dock. A sloop and skiff were moored a hundred feet from their destination.

"Can I do anything to help?" Mary asked.

Perce glanced at her and replied "You can take the stern line and secure it if you'd like."

"Sure."

Mary turned to the stern and walked back. She saw the stern line looped neatly to a hook. She bent down, picked it up, and waited to step onto the starboard side deck. They were coming up fast on the dock. Perce put the throttle in reverse, allowing a smooth cocking. Mary hopped quickly onto the float and secured the rope to a cleat with three efficient half hitches. Perce turned off the engine, scrambled up to the bow, grabbed a looped rope from the forward deck and stepped onto the dock.

He applied a couple of half hitches and a bowline knot for good measure.

Perce and Mary nearly collided in the boat when bending down to pick up the picnic basket and backpack. Perce reached out defensively to prevent their heads from crashing and cracking.

"Wow!" Perce said. "Sorry about that," he added with a hand on each of her upper arms.

Their faces almost touched. Their eyes locked and their minds wondered what would happen next. Perce, behaved as a gentleman, thinking it was too soon to kiss. He allowed the heat of the moment to pass. He would have taken full advantage if it was another woman.

Mary blinked as she straightened herself. For a second she wanted to kiss him. But Perce backed off. Perhaps he wasn't attracted to her. She felt a little self-conscious. Maybe the outing was a bad idea. She discovered Perce looking at her quizzically.

"Are you okay?" he asked, wondering if he'd blown it with her.

Mary smiled politely. "Sure."

"Good."

He leaned down and picked up the closed wicker basket with his right hand. He laughed. Mary managed to pick up her backpack without incident. Perce carried the bundle up to the float and reached his left arm out gallantly to Mary. She grabbed his hand and stepped up beside him.

"Well then, shall we be off, Mary?"

"Absolutely, please lead the way."

Perce nodded, smiled and started up the gangplank to the pier. Mary followed a couple of steps behind. She looked around as they approached an embankment. They climbed up the wood railed stairs to the top. A flag pole stood next to the top of the landing. Old Glory blew gently in a soft breeze.

"I thought you said the Edgertons are away," Mary said, glancing up at the Stars and Stripes.

"They are, but I suspect they made arrangements for someone at the boatyard to watch the house, mow the lawn, raise the flag in the morning, etc."

"Makes sense, just like it's done by the other summer families on Islesboro, I guess."

"That's right. Are you thirsty?"

"No thanks. Not right now."

She looked at the house. It was a small, gray Cape Cod house with a large picture window facing the water. A slate deck was situated on the bay side, too.

"You wouldn't know it but that's a prefab house."

"It looks really nice."

"Shall we hit the road?" Perce inquired.

"Let's go."

They went. The only road on the island was dirt. It ran from the boatyard on the northeast corner and meandered around a couple of miles past a few summer homes to the southwest corner. The narrow road was bordered by pine woods and meadows. Traffic was very light with the occasional weathered light truck or SUV. A former summer resident was known to drive his family around in an old McCormick tractor and trailer. The prodigious potholes made it a bouncy ride for all, regardless of the vehicle.

Mary and Perce turned left at the end of the Edgerton's dirt and grass driveway. Mary looked left and right for any approaching cars. The road was deserted.

"It's peaceful, isn't it," she commented.

"It sure is."

"I love getting away from it all. Far from the madding crowd," she said conversationally as they strolled along a couple of feet apart.

"I don't mind it once in a while," Perce said, glancing at Mary.

"But you prefer the bustle of the city or knowing there are people nearby on Islesboro."

"That's right Mary. I like being around people."

"I do too, but having spent so much time in New York makes me want to be by myself sometimes. Perce, can you understand that?"

"Of course! I guess my version is being on the golf course. It's a pastoral setting supplemented with other people a few yards away."

They walked down the road a few minutes silently, keeping their thoughts to themselves. Mary noticed a patch of wild blueberry growing beside a large bed of moss. She wondered if deer ever swam to the island. She asked Perce.

"I'm not too sure about deer but I've heard a story about a moose on this island. I think it was back in the 1930s. Apparently some guy shot it in the face. One of the poor beast's eyes was dangling out of its socket from the gunshot. Somehow the moose lived long enough to swim four or five miles to the mainland where it was put out of its misery."

"My God! That's horrible! "

"I agree," Perce said.

"I mean shooting a moose is crazy. They're herbivores. I think they eat roots and stuff like that."

"Could be," he said casually.

Mary wasn't thrilled with Perce's lack of empathy.

"Perce, doesn't it bother you about what happened to that poor moose?"

Perce realized he'd got himself in a situation from which there was no ready answer.

"Well, sure it does," he said complacently.

Mary stopped and looked at him heatedly. Perce stopped a couple of paces down the road, turned and stepped back to her.

"Mary, I wasn't the one shooting that moose and I have no plans to ever do so. I don't hunt period. I don't know why the moose was shot. Perhaps the man had a reason. He could have been starving or felt threatened by it. Moose are enormous for God's sake."

Mary continued staring at Perce. Gradually her demeanor softened.

Perce was surprised by her quick temper and passion. She was definitely a principled woman with strong convictions. He was impressed by her spirit and wondered fleetingly if that carried over to the bedroom.

Mary caught his wry grin.

"What?" she asked, hands on her narrow hips.

Perce laughed then suddenly stopped, seeing she was taking his glee the wrong way.

"Mary, you really impress me. No really, I wasn't laughing at you."

She thought it over a moment, gradually realizing she may have been a little tough on the guy. Mary lowered her hands much like a boxer lowering his guard. She didn't know why her temper had gotten out of hand so quickly. Did she dislike Perce? Was that it? Time would tell.

"I'm sorry for behaving so bratty."

"Let's forget it ever happened," Perce replied.

"Sounds good to me," she said with a smile.

"You ready yet for a snack or beverage?" he asked.
"What do you have?"

Perce walked to the side of the road, put the basket down on top of some overgrown grass, turned a latch and opened the lid. Mary moved next to Perce and looked down at the contents. There were pears, oranges, sandwiches, tortes, bottled water, two plastic cups, napkins and a bottle of red wine. No wonder Perce carried the basket like it was an effort. The longer he held it, the heavier it would seem. She turned to the man. "That's a nice spread."

"Thanks, Mary. Help yourself."

She reached down and picked up a pear. She put some pressure on the fruit and squeezed. It was definitely ripe. Mary took a bite. It was sweet. She chewed and swallowed as Perce watched for her reaction.

"Delicious," she said ripping another chunk with her teeth.

Perce nodded happily and retrieved an orange. He closed the lid and stood over removing the rind. He threw it into the meadow grass.

"It's biodegradable, right?"

"Absolutely," Mary replied. A drop of pear juice oozed toward her chin.

Perce stuffed orange slices in his mouth and chomped them down. He noticed the pear juice on Mary's face. He fetched a napkin from the basket, closed the lid and carefully dried Mary's chin. She stopped chewing and looked into his eyes. Perce kissed her briefly and stepped back. Mary took a step toward him and kissed him. Perce dropped the partially eaten orange and Mary reciprocated with the pear as they caressed.

Mary broke their embrace and looked for a comfortable spot to lay down.

"There," she managed to say, a little out of breath, her head pointing at a lush spread of moss.

Perce nodded happily. They pulled one another toward nature's bed and then eased themselves onto the soft ground cover, lying side by side facing one another. Perce raise himself on an elbow looked hungrily at Mary.

Her mouth was slightly open. She wanted to taste him. Perce smiled and lowered his mouth onto hers. Their fruit scented breathes were intoxicating.

Perce didn't want to push Mary too far on their first outing.

"Take me," she urged in a husky voice.

He rolled over and quickly removed her trousers and boxers as Mary slipped out of her pants and panties.

Five miles away, Sohn walked on the rocky shore. He had stayed within sight of the bay after the ferry docked in Lincolnville Beach. For some reason he had to keep the islands in view. Now his eyes looked at a smaller island southwest of Islesboro. Sohn knew it was called Seven Hundred Acre Island. He had never been there but had seen it on charts and from a distance on boat trips.

Something is happening there I should stop. What is it?

Sohn jogged to the passenger side of his pickup truck, yanked open the door and retrieved a foldout map of Islesboro from the glove compartment. It included the ferry schedule. He glanced at his trusty old time piece and scanned the ferry schedule. The next ferry left in ten minutes. But it would not take him to the small island.

164

He would need another boat. Sohn noticed a small advertisement for a private boat that made scheduled stops at both ferry landings. The boat also made special stops to people's homes and other destinations.

That's it!

He would charter the water taxi and have her drop him off on the island. Once there, he's take the next step to find out what was happening there.

"You wiped me out."

"Literally," Mary replied wryly. "Me, too," she continued.

"I need to eat something before we continue our walk."

"I'm starving," Mary admitted. Making love with Perce was spontaneous, something natural. She had no regrets and no false hopes that their intimacy would deepen their relationship much further. She was too pragmatic to confuse physical attraction for love. The two together was wonderful but wonderful could be an illusion.

They ate quietly.

"What are you think about?" he asked.

"That we've had a special time here but neither of us should feel pressured to rush into anything."

Perce arched his eyebrows and studied her face. "What does that mean?"

"It's too soon to know."

"You've lost me, Mary."

"Forget it."

Perce frowned. "I know I have a reputation as a man who likes the ladies. But when I tell you that I consider you special, I mean it."

Mary looked up from the food in her hand, looking intently at Perce. She smiled. "I'll take that as a compliment."

They finished their meal. Mary stood. She stretched. Perce looked at her curves and liked what he saw. But it was more than that. She had intelligence and spirit, attributes he loved in others and tried to exemplify. He wanted to spend more time with Mary Godwin.

The Quicksilver was a handsome, seaworthy 34 foot long boat. Captain Samuel Woodsby gripped the helm with both hands in the pilot house. There was seating for up to 28 passengers on board the broad beamed vessel. At the moment there was only one passenger. Woodsby, a respected was veteran, felt uneasy being alone on the boat with the giant.

The man hadn't threatened him but there was something lurking behind his severe face and huge physique that was ready to erupt into violence. Woodsby had served in the Gulf War as a First Lieutenant. He saw action in Kuwait. After the war, he remained with the Corp until mustering out as a Captain. He moved to Saco, Maine a few years ago where he landed a job with a military contractor. The veteran managed to save nearly two hundred thousand dollars. When he discovered a listing for the Quicksilver on a local yacht broker's web site, he immediately fell in love with the boat He wanted to make her all she could be with her classic Maine broadness and modern navigation system.

During his years on active duty he had developed an ability to size up the men under his command. He recognized what moral traits they possessed and those that were lacking. The foremost to Woodsby was using sound judgment at all time. In looking at his passenger and reflected on the brief communication they'd so far exchanged the skipped concluded that the big guy needed be handled very carefully and with utmost respect.

Woodsby stood at the helm steering the boat past the ferry. He spoke over the engine to the passenger. "Have you served?"

"Excuse me?" Sohn asked from the stern deck.

He stepped into the cabin, trying to appear calm, though anxiety churned his psyche.

"Were you in the military?"

Sohn decided to lie.

"No," he said looking at Woodsby eyes without blinking.

Woodsby caught the lie but pretended he hadn't caught on. He nodded.

"You have military bearing in your walk and mannerisms."

"I'll take that as a compliment, Captain." What about you?"

"Yeah, I did my duty."

"Which branch?"

"The Marines."

"Semper fi," Sohn said.

"Hoo-rah," Woodsby replied evenly. He wondered if the man was possibly a dishonorably discharged Marine. He sure looked like one.

Woodsby wanted to ask his passenger about his plans at the boatyard situated at the southern tip of Seven Hundred Acre Island. But he decided the lesser he know the better. He guesses that prying would likely antagonize the giant. Still, it would serve to be as observant as possible. He had spent his final year on active duty working as a liaison with MPs. The time had been very instructive in learning criminal behavior.

When Woodsby moved up the coast he had checked in with the Waldo County Sheriff in Belfast. The Sheriff used Woodsby periodically for consultations of infrequent criminal investigations on Islesboro. Sohn felt a little guilty about deceiving Woodsby regarding his military experience. The captain seemed to be a straight shooter and a respectable guy. Acknowledging he was a war veteran would be telling Woodsby too much.

Chapter 11

For many, many years Schrenk had no interest at all in fighting for a cause; he felt betrayed and abused by mankind. That feeling of alienation was altered by reading *Uncle Tom's Cabin.* He was fascinated by the Underground Railroad. Sohn understood very well about escaping from persecution. Fettered by his looks, he wished he had been tolerated in the towns and villages of Europe.

Schrenk lived on a farm near Gettysburg, Pennsylvania during the 1850s and 1860s. He cleared the rocks from the soil, built stonewalls, plowed the fields and milked the cows. Even the farm animals were nervous around him.

There was a deer trail in the woods. He occasionally climbed an oak tree before daybreak to wait for the next meal. When the unaware buck or doe trod below him, Sohn leaped down, made a quick kill and carried the carcass back to the farmhouse.

Early one morning, while in the tree, he heard footsteps and hushed voices approaching from the south. He listened attentively, trying to catch their words but the murmuring was too indistinct to understand. Were the people planning to steal eggs from the hen house? Sohn needed to get closer and get their attention. He waited for them to come within a few yards of the tree then jumped to the ground.

The small group of people dressed in cloaks were terrified by the large apparition in front of them. "God help me, it's the devil!" a woman moaned.

"Please don't hurt us, Mister," a child said plaintively.

"What do you want here?" Sohn said harshly. A man stepped closer to Sohn. "You live on the farm?"

"That's right."

"We were just walking through."

Sohn could see the faces better in the brightening light of day. The leader was the only white person. There were four Negros behind him. They looked afraid and vulnerable. Sohn's suddenly thought about the Underground Railroad. He wanted to help.

"Anybody thirsty and hungry?" The travelers glanced at one another anxiously. The white man looked at them and then back at the huge man.

"That's kind of you, sir. We could use some nourishment."

"Well come along with me. We can talk on the way."

So the largest farmer in the world escorted the group of escaped slaves and their protector to the farmhouse. The guide spoke more readily than the others.

They weren't used to speaking to whites and were particularly reluctant to speak to the towering farmer. He reminded them of a scarecrow.

They couldn't stop looking at him spellbound by his monstrous appearance, both in size, pallor and face. It didn't bother Sohn in the least as he learned firsthand of their flight north from one helping hand to another like rungs in a ladder.

Sohn passed around heaping plates of fresh ham, venison, eggs and thick slices of buttered bread. There were mugs of buttermilk, water and coffee. Everything except the coffee came from the farm. He felt satisfaction in seeing the newly free former slaves stuffing themselves contentedly. Their smiles seemingly widened after each bite and swallow. Sohn was pleased to play a part on their freedom trail.

The group told their host about their hard lives, their escape from a plantation in western Virginia and close call in evading a posse led by their former owner. One fellow fugitive was caught and put in irons after getting stuck in a bear trap. The long suffering woman struggled to cut off her foot to prevent capture. But she lost too much blood and lost consciousness.

"I feel your pain," Sohn told them shortly after breakfast while the party prepared to continue their journey. "I know what it is like to be hunted down."

The travelers exchanged questioning and nervous looks.

"Why was that?" he was asked.

"Because of how I look."

Nobody replied. What could they say anyway! They understood. There was an uncomfortable silence. Then their guide stood up to tell them it was time to hit the road. They departed a few minutes later, waving farewell to Sohn as he stood in front of the farmhouse. He kept his gaze on them as they walked through a field to the woods and disappeared from sight. Sohn was sad to see them leave. Companionship of any kind was cruelly rare for Victor's creation.

Oh well. He sighed and went back into the house to tidy up and clean the dishes only to discover his guests had already done those chores.

Sohn maintained the farm without incident until one day in late June 1863. Plowing was traditionally done with the assistance of horse or oxen. Sohn didn't need a beast of burden to drive the plow forward through the furrowed soil. He could do it himself.

One afternoon, while plowing, a column of several hundred Union cavalry galloped onto the field. Sohn stopped and stared as the soldiers rode up to him led by a senior officer with brown hair and a thick mustache.

Sohn recognized the handlebars on the officer's uniform.

"A general, for God's sake," he said to himself as the man called a halt.

"Mister, you say something?" General John Buford inquired.

"Sorry, General. I'm just surprised to see a man of your stature here on my farm."

"You know who I am?"

"No sir."

"This your place?" Buford asked, surveying the farm and distant buildings.

"Yes sir, it is."

"What's an able body man of your stature doing on the sidelines instead of serving your nation, son?" Buford asked sharply.

"I'm being useful here, General," Sohn relied sharply.

An aide took exception to the farmer's tone and raised a saber. Buford shook his head and looked critically at the civilian.

"The Confederates will be here soon. I hope you will be as uncooperative with them as you are with us."

"I shall." He looked down at the ground and then at the farm. He didn't want it to become a battlefield. If that happened, the place would be destroyed. He needed to make a decision.

"General, I'd hate to lose this place. Can you spare some men and help me defend it from the enemy?" Buford looked at the man thoughtfully. Perhaps the farmer would be an asset after all.

"Can a big man like you ride?"

"Yes, sir."

"I'd like you enlisted as a PFC for the duration of hostilities in the region. You will serve Captain Renwick's troop which will be posted here. I can't say for how long. He may receive orders to move. I need to use my men wisely to beat our southern brothers back to Virginia."

"All right, sir. I'm your man," Sohn replied grimly. *What am I doing?*

"What is your name?"

"Sohn Schrenk, General."

"Good luck, Private Schrenk."

Buford saluted the new conscript. Private Schrenk returned the salute awkwardly. Buford raised his hand and pointed forward. He led the cavalry forward. Sohn watched as the column trotted through the farmland.

Sohn walked slowly back to his house to gather some possessions in a sack. A few minutes later, he heard approaching horses. The new private went to the front door. A troop of one hundred men entered the farmyard led by Captain Renwick, a 30-year old man with long blond hair and a goatee. Renwick stopped in front of Sohn, saluted smartly and looked down bemusedly at the hulking figure.

"My God, I think we have our secret weapon. You'll scare the pants off the Rebs. I'm Captain Renwick and you're Schrenk, if I'm not mistaken.

"Yes, Captain."

"Private, you should salute me in greeting."

Schrenk saluted. Renwick smiled.

"That's enough. Now we don't have a uniform your size but we'll come up with something for you."

Renwick turned his body around to face his troops. He ordered them to dismount. The cavalrymen stood beside their army mounts staring with mixed expressions at their new newcomer. Renwick alighted and pointed to the front door.

"Shall we, Private?"

Sohn nodded and let his commander inside the farmhouse followed by junior and noncommissioned officers.

Renwick politely requested Private Schrenk's consent for the horses to graze and be given any hay that could be stored in the barn. Permission was reluctantly given.

Sohn was asked if he could share his food supplies. Schrenk told him about the salted venison and other provisions and explained game was usually abundant. The farm had a deep well that would be tapped for the men and horses and there was a stream in the nearby woods.

The soldiers each carried carbine, saber, pistol, belt set, saddle, blanket, and other equipment for their horses. They pitched tents near the house and set about feeding and watering the horses. Renwick ordered a rotating patrol to scout the countryside for signs of the Confederate vanguard. General Robert E Lee's army recently passed through western Maryland and entered southern Pennsylvania. Renwick was under orders to report enemy strength to General Buford.

Meanwhile a patchwork uniform was put together for the new trooper. It had to be configured from two sets. Sohn never kept a mirror in his homes as looking at his reflection caused heartache. But he was curious how he looked in his uniform. One of the men let him use a portable mirror. Wearing a cap stretched tightly over his scalp, he was astounded by the transformation. Perhaps enlisting wasn't such a bad thing to do after all.

I do look good.

The peaceful anxiety on the farm lasted until the next morning. A messenger notified Captain Renwick of the Confederate Army's position around Gettysburg. Renwick was ordered to ride swiftly to Seminary Ridge situated west of the town. There they were expected to take a defensive posture against Confederate infantry. Sohn was given the largest available horse. He swung easily onto the saddle, held the reins and nudged his mount forward in line with the advancing column. He glanced over his shoulder once at the receding view of his farm, sighed, and looked forward. Would he ever return?

He was close to a century old at the time and perhaps death lay ahead from a bayonet, cannon ball or bullet.

Buford's 1st Division, Cavalry Corps of the Army of the Potomac staked out McPherson Ridge late on June 30. The goal was to hold the heights at all costs against a superior numbered enemy.

The dismounted cavalry was put to work building breastworks and other defensive positions to stop a charge up the hill. It was tough work in the sultry weather. Sohn performed the work of two men. He became respected and appreciated quickly as he cut down trees, heaved logs and piled dirt. Sohn forgot he was ever alone as he saw thousands of men around him.

That night they peered at the distant campfires of the enemy.

The Battle of Gettysburg began the next morning around 8am. The date was July 1, 1863. Buford's 3,200 observed the advance of 7,000 Confederate infantrymen.

Private Schrenk felt the tension escalating with each step they made closer to him. He sucked in morning air and tried not to think too much. He allowed his mind to drift away.

He became alert some minutes later to gunfire. The battle raged as the advancing Confederate 3rd Corps exchanged fire with Buford's dug in cavalry. Despite being outnumbered, wave after wave was repelled by the well positioned northerners. At times it was like a duck shoot as the attackers were exposed in the open.

But hundreds of brave southerners managed to continue their uphill run. Soon the gap between both armies was nonexistent. The front lines engaged in close fighting. Private Schrenk found himself in close quarters defending himself from pistol shots and lunging bayonets.

This is hell on earth!

He fought to stay alive and kill off the soldiers trying to kill him. Sohn glanced sideways briefly and saw a blade pierce a comrade's eyeball. While his attention was diverted, the butt of a carbine smashed Sohn's nose spraying blood in all directions. That infuriated the giant, turning him into a savage beast. He yelled and surged forward, swatting, kicking, twisting necks, stabbing and shooting the enemy.

The Confederates backed away from the monster. The ridge was held for two and a half hours, buying time until the thankful arrival of 1 Corps infantry to take over possession of the ridge.

Sohn's broken nose throbbed and he had a wicked headache. He rested in the rear line sometime later, gazing into oblivion.

He pressed a handkerchief against his nostrils to stem the blood flow.

"Welcome to the war," a neighbor said, grinning up at him.

"Does it get any better?" he replied.

"Just wait and see."

Soon he listened to orders to move out. It was back in the saddle.

Buford's cavalrymen served their purpose and were reassigned to protect supply lines in Maryland while The Battle of Gettysburg was continued for two more climactic days.

* * *

"Hey buddy! We're here!"

Sohn's Civil War memories were abruptly interrupted by a man shouting at him. He blinked as the boat captain looking at him and pointed to his right. Sohn followed the outstretched arm and noticed they were docked.

I'm here.

"Sorry Captain. I was daydreaming," he explained. His nose was sore for some reason.

"I suppose you were. I had a hell of a time getting your attention. Are you okay? You look a bit out of it," Woodsby said with real concern.

Sohn nodded. "I'm fine. Thanks for the ride, Captain."

"You're welcome. You want me to pick you up at a certain time?" the boatman asked calmly. He intended to memorize the cadence and body language of the passenger's response.

"No, I'm good to go," Sohn replied evenly, noticing the other man's sharp scrutiny.

Sohn stepped onto the narrow side deck and then the outer float that the sea taxi had tied up. He kept walking, careful not to look back at the captain. There was something about the man that bothered him but he couldn't quite identify it.

Woodsby watched the big man cross from the outer to the inner floats and up the gangplank to a concrete pier. He wondered why his passenger refused to discuss his purpose in going to the island. The guy was up to something.

What should I do? Follow him? Wait at the dock?

He stepped into the pilot house and sat down on a passenger seat to be screened from view. He could still see his target walking off the end of the pier onto the dirt surface of the shipyard. The tall guy rounded a large storage shed and disappeared from view.

Sohn strode to the end of the shed, stopped, and eased his head partly around the corner toward the dock. He could see the top of the sea taxi. He was annoyed it was still there. Perhaps Woodsby had business at the yard?

In any case, Sohn ducked back and continued walking through the complex. He targeted a narrow dirt road that traversed up a long hill at the far end of the facility. He kept scanning left, right and straight ahead continuously, ever vigilant to movement of any kind. His ears were tuned to listen for any human sound. The stalker moved up the road.

Mary and Perce followed the meandering dirt road past a log cabin on the right. A few hundred feet later they sauntered past a long grassy driveway to their left. The road meandered up and down some hills for a mile before coming out next to a flat grassy meadow. A large raspberry bush stood near the road. Dozens of red ripe fruit hung on slender prickly branches ready to be picked.

"Shall we? Mary suggested with a bright smile. She walked over without waiting for a reply.

"Why not," Perce answered, putting down the mostly empty picnic basket on the grass.

They spent a few minutes plucking and eating the savory berries. Their lips and fingers were soon berry red.

"They're nice and sweet," Perce commented between chews.

"Yum."

When their dessert was done, Perce and Mary looked at each other expectantly.

"Where to?" Perce asked. He wanted to get back to Islesboro. The hike was getting tiresome. He'd seen enough of the little island.

Mary observed his demeanor and body language. She would have been happy to walk to the end of the road and hang out on the wide beach of Philbrook Cove. But Perce disappointingly seemed ready to turn back "I suppose we can head back now if you want?"

"I can tell you want to press on."

"Well that's true but I wouldn't mind walking back to the boat." She tried to look content.

"Let's walk a few more minutes, find a spot to finish off the contents of the basket and then retrace our footsteps. Would that work for you?" he asked courteously.

Mary smiled. She liked him more and more. She appreciated his gesture.

"Sounds fine by me," she said cheerfully, kissing him on the mouth.

He kissed her, forgetting momentarily about the walk.

They were locked in their own bliss when Sohn stopped on the road, watching them. He recognized Mary instantly but not the man she embraced and kissed. His heart ached and his blood pressure spiked.

Perce noticed they were not alone. He breathed in involuntarily and held his breath at the shock of the frightful man staring at them with cold pale eyes. Mary turned from Perce to see what upset him. Her brain and body froze.

Sohn was disappointed by her reaction. He naively misjudged Mary, thinking they had bonded in their dreams as well as yesterday's encounter at her house. What was he supposed to do now? Sohn remained quiet and refrained from moving closer.

"Who are you?" Perce said. "Why are you watching us?"

Sohn didn't reply, his eyes moving from Perce to Mary.

Perce grew irritated. "I asked you two questions, Mister."

Sohn looked at Mary's friend scornfully.

Perce diverted his eyes from the unfriendly gaze and looked at Mary anxiously. She seemed to be in shock. What was wrong with her? He put his arms on her shoulders.

Sohn took half a step forward before forcing himself to stop. He didn't want Mary to see what he could do to a throat. Why did he hate to see her touched by another man?

"Mary, can you hear me?" Perce asked.

Mary ignored Perce. She stared blankly at the big man.

"Mary, please!"

She blinked. Her mind unclogged. Her attention turned to Perce.

"Did you say something?" she asked.

"You've been in la la land since this man showed up. Do you know him?"

Mary glanced at Sohn then looked at Perce.

"He was at the house yesterday."

Perce was confused. What business could someone of the intruder's stature and ugliness have at the Godwin's upscale home? Then the answer came. He must be some local islander who worked for the family in some capacity. A contractor perhaps? Or maybe he was a lobster man delivering fresh out of the cage shellfish.

"I understand," Perce commented.

Sohn and Mary looked at Perce questioningly. How could Perce know?

"You know nothing of the sort," Sohn said.

"I don't? Then explain yourself."

"Perce, it's really nothing that should concern you," Mary said.

Was she right? He cared about her to want to know how the lurking terror knew Mary.

Mary saw the raw emotions in his eyes and face. She was touched by his feelings for her and implicit desire to get involved in her life but rehashing the disturbing event might reveal too much about her and their intruder.

Her parents would have a fit of she confided in anybody about it. They wanted the tall, light skinned stranger to vanish forever.

Sohn had no intention to grant their fervent wish. He was frankly at a loss what to do. For perhaps the first time in an extraordinarily long life, he was stymied. Sohn looked down at the ground, his shoulders drooping and long sinewy arms dangling at his sides. He took a step to turn around. And then another.

"Wait."

He stopped and looked over his shoulder. Mary peered up at him.

Perce frowned, looking alternately at Mary and Sohn uncertainly.

"Why are you following me?" she asked Sohn. He shook his head.

"You don't know what you want from me?"

Sohn's pulse quickened. He was afraid to tell her the truth. She would taunt him. Her friend would laugh at him. The combination would be unbearable. It would be better not to risk either action. He turned away and retreated back toward the boatyard as Mary and Perce watched.

Perce was relieved and very happy to see the horrible looking man leave.

Mary was ambivalent. She sensed that violence was a natural element of his existence. But she sensed a yearning in the man, a vulnerability that caught her in its grasp. He wanted something from her but apparently was unable to ask. Why? What was it?

Mary was bothered by Sohn's walking away silently and humbly. She liked getting answers. That was a reason she was such a good investigative journalist. Never let an opportunity to obtain useful information pass by. She'd been reticent a few times in the past and each time that happened she was angry at herself.

"We should go after him," she urged.

"Are you serious?" He saw the fire in her eyes. "I guess you are. But why?"

"I'm not really sure." She grew restless as seconds ticked by.

"Okay Mary, let's go if it's that important to you." He picked up the basket.

"Thanks," she replied.

They set off after Sohn.

He was a hundred yards ahead but his excellent hearing allowed him to hear their quick footsteps on the dirt and pebbled road. He was very surprised. Suddenly the dark cloud lifted and there was hope Mary could be more than a flash in the pan.

Sohn continued walking slowly, allowing them to catch up and pretend he didn't know they were in hot pursuit. He wanted to enjoy the moment and thought it would be better for Mary, too.

They drew together a minute later. Sohn peered down at them and smiled, Mary smiled back but Perce couldn't pretend to be happy. He made himself walk between Mary and the giant. It was the bravest act of his life. He couldn't back down in front of Mary. Hopefully she would notice his valor and reward Perce by spending more time with him.

Chapter 12

Perce had somehow fallen asleep standing in the road in broad daylight. He felt a sudden pain on his right arm. His eyes opened and saw Mary preparing to punch him again.

"What the hell!" he called out, rubbing the sore arm gently.

"I'm really sorry, Perce. I've tried to awaken you for a few minutes. You were practically catatonic," Mary said as she looked at him with real concern.

Perce yawned. He had drunk half of the wine bottle and felt it. It was a stupid thing to do, especially as he was a solid couple miles away from the boat. He had dreamed about an encounter with an enormous being on the island and defending Mary against him. He looked about but there was only the two of them. They were still near the raspberry bush.

"I think we're being watched," she whispered.

Perce started to turn his head, but was stopped by Mary.

"Keep looking at me," she added softly.

Perce started to feel nervous. "Are you sure?"

"I heard a snapping sound a couple of minutes ago. Apparently you were too much out of it to hear."

"Sorry." He paused, and then spoke again in a low tone. "Maybe we should just pick up our stuff and hit the road."

"You're probably right. Let's move slowly. We don't want to act skittish."

"Sure.'

They left the edge of the meadow and walked onto the dirt road leading back to Perce's boat. Their path was suddenly blocked by the monster in Perce's dream as it leaped out of the woods onto the roadway.

Perce grabbed Mary. They stopped abruptly, both scared out of their wits. Perce looked quickly to his left and right for an escape route.

"It's you again," Mary said after her nerves settled. "Why are you here?"

"Think about it, Mary Godwin."

Mary was perplexed. Her nerves were too rattled to think straight.

"You know him?" Perce asked in wonderment. The wine induced cobwebs inside his head were gone. He had completely forgotten about the tender arm.

"Mary?"

Sohn laughed.

"What's funny," Perce asked warily.

"You are."

"I think you are having a bad effect on her. Please leave us alone. You need to leave at once."

"And if I don't?"

Perce had no response. He had never gotten into a fight or wielded a sharp object other than the time he dissected a frog in biology class. Perce was essentially a gentle man. His intellect was his greatest asset. But in the present circumstances he was matched evenly against the interloper but severely mismatched in strength and violent aggression. What could he possibly do, he wondered, to get Mary and himself safely away from the human roadblock in front of them?

Mary was disturbed that the man was making a habit of following her. It was a weird coincidence that he appeared at the house but the present situation was unbearable. What did he want? *Do I really want to know?*

Somehow he needed to understand she had a life and it would be better if he backed off. Mary didn't enjoy being in the eerie dream with him. The God forsaken laboratory was just too creepy for words. What was the purpose of hijacking her mind? Why did he force that experience on her?

Sohn was driven by jealousy, despair and rage. He was shocked to find Mary with the fair-haired man. It never crossed his brilliant mind that she had a man. He was still naive in certain aspects after such a long life. Believing she would be amenable to a large role in his existence was apparently unrealistic.

Earlier, from his concealed position in the woods, Sohn became distraught in seeing their congeniality around each other. He felt like an intruder spying on the couple. He inadvertently stepping on a broken branch while moving his feet around. Mary and the man spoke quietly shortly after that and then hit the road.

He now knew what caused the dread he sensed earlier in the afternoon. Her union with the young man jeopardized his vague plans for her. Lyrics from a song by The Smiths made him flinch. *I'm human and I need to be loved just like everyone else does.*

Blind despair overwhelmed him. He sprinted through the woods and made a fifty foot broad jump onto the road, intending to make the two mile distance to the boatyard in four minutes. But his peripheral vision while he was in midair brought him up short in his landing.

Mary and her friend were walking quickly up the road in his direction. He was discovered.

So when they squared off, all three were fairly evenly surprised, though the young couple was more horrified than anything else.

The silence hung heavily in the air for minutes but it seemed longer.

"You haven't answered my question," Mary said.

Sohn didn't reply.

"I didn't expect to see you again, at least so soon."

Sohn nodded.

"I deserve an explanation."

"I know," Sohn agreed.

"Well?"

"I didn't know you were here until I saw you and him a few minutes ago."

"That's incredible," Perce said.

Sohn glared at his potential adversary. Perce looked away timidly.

Mary was perturbed. "You must admit it's strange to run into you here. I thought you went back to the mainland."

"I did but caught a sea taxi over here afterward."

"Why?"

"I had an urge to come over here," he admitted with a shrug.

"That's an enigma if I ever heard one," Perce said. Sohn took a small step forward. He was getting tired of the man very quickly. He was surprised when Mary inched ahead looking very determined. Perce felt embarrassed by her grit but thankful, too.

"I think you should allow us to leave," she said sharply.

"Why should I?"

"Because you don't want me angry at you, do you?"

She had him there. He didn't want to alienate her at all. He took a couple of strides to the side. The narrow road was clear. He bowed briefly.

"Thank you Sohn. Do you have transportation off the island?"

"I may have a ride waiting at the boatyard."

"Why don't you run ahead and see. If the boat's not there you can double back and meet us at the Edgerton's dock. The house is a half mile up the hill from the yard."

"Thank you. Have a nice time."

Sohn then jogged away at an easy 20 miles an hour pace. Perce gaped at the sight of the tallest man in the world running faster than he deemed possible. It seemed so effortless, too.

"Are you serious?" he asked.

Mary grinned. "You should see him chasing a full grown deer."

Perce glanced at Mary to see if she was joking with him then turned back to the road to follow Sohn but the man was already out of sight.

"He should be on television. The man's a freak of nature!" Perce exclaimed.

"That's not fair, Perce. I don't think he likes the how he looks. He's stuck with it. He reacts naturally to how we treat him, which isn't very nice."

Perce agreed. "Okay, I understand now. He's the ultimate walking nightmare."

"I think he's gotten enough of a head start," she said pointedly.

"Right, let's try to get to my boat before he does." He shuddered at the prospect of seeing the behemoth waiting for them.

They walked briskly. The romantic mood was subdued as each of them thought of the eight footer who could be lurking. Perce glanced at Mary. She seemed pensive and perplexed. He decided to leave her alone for a few minutes. But the silence grated on him.

"This walk of ours has turned into a grind," Perce said.

Mary turned her head to Perce. "Excuse me?"

"Just that the walk we had earlier was much happier than this one."

"I suppose so," she said mechanically."

"Mary, is there something I can do to help you?"

"Thanks, Perce, but I have to work it out myself, at least for now."

Perce was disappointed.

Mary touched his face briefly, saying "I appreciate that."

Perce nodded.

Woodsby sat in the boat yard's office speaking with the manager. He had decided to keep the boat docked for a while to see if his passenger would return from his mysterious mission. The captain glanced at the wall clock past the manager's right shoulder realizing he had waited long enough. He stood, thanked his acquaintance for his time and exited.

He started to walk toward the pier.

"Captain," a familiar voice called out from behind.

Woodsby congratulated himself and stopped. He turned around to scrutinize his once and future customer. The tall man's breathing seemed slightly quicker than normal. Woodsby guessed the man had been running.

What or where had he run from? He had no way of knowing without the big man voluntarily providing that information. Woodsby didn't anticipate the quiet man would chat about the island romp. He decided to wait for him to ask for a ride back to Lincolnville instead of offering it. Perhaps a little loosening of the tongue would encourage more of the same.

"I see you are still here. That is good," Sohn said.

"I just paid my respects to a friend," Woodsby replied.

"Would you be going back to Lincolnville, Captain?"

"I wasn't planning to. I dock at Grindle Point for the night."

Sohn looked at him blankly.

"That's the ferry landing on Islesboro."

Sohn looked disappointed.

"But you should be able to catch the last ferry if we get under way immediately."

"By all means, Captain. Let's be off."

A few minutes later the water taxi backed off the outer float, turned and then accelerated forward. Sohn looked back at the island, wondering where Mary was at that moment.

Perce was relieved to find his boat empty. He exhaled loudly.

"Feel better?" Mary asked.

Perce grinned at her. "It feels like dodging a bullet though I've never actually done that."

"I'm happy, too," she admitted.

"I guess he found another ride."

"I guess."

"Let's get you home."

Mary hopped nimbly onto the boat. Perce handed the picnic basket to her. He untied the bow and stern lines, stepped onto the boat and started her engine. Perce opened her up to full speed forward, needing to some exhilaration to reverse the psychological undertow that tugged at him only minutes earlier.

Mary concentrated on the here and now as well. She refused to allow the unpleasant confrontation to keep her from enjoying the speedboat. She opened her arms wide in the stern to feel the full effect of the wind blowing against her body. The wind pressure made her eyes squint and moisten. She closed her eyes, feeling the vibration of the waves skimming off the surfaces coursing through her.

"Ah," she said contentedly.

Perce watched her little performance, wishing he could leave the helm and caress her slim body. But he knew taking chances out on the water risked disaster. He sighed and turned his focus to the choppy water ahead.

Chapter 13

The pickup pulled into the driveway an hour later. Sohn parked the vehicle and sat a while. He was reluctant to get out. Going back to his lonely home was cold comfort. *Maybe it's time to adopt another pet. A German Shepard or Small Münsterländer would be appropriate as I'm basically a human mutt. I'll build a fence around the yard to give it room to run around. The fence will protect him from predators and keep him from escaping, not that he'd ever want to leave me.*

He laughed bitterly then started up the warm engine. There was a Home Depot a few miles away in Rockland. That would be a good place to buy the fencing materials. He'd go to the kennel only after completing the installation.

Sohn's somber mood lifted in knowing he now had something to look forward to. He enjoyed physical labor and building projects. Physical exertion diverted his mind from troubling thoughts. A good workout relaxed his mind and body.

The process actually started while driving to the superstore as Sohn planned out the quantity of coils of wiring and other materials to purchase. He thought about metal posts. Being somewhat of a naturalist, he decided to anchor the eight-foot tall fence with wooden posts cleaved from nearby fallen trees. He suddenly remembered where he'd seen a pine tree lying on the forest floor. It was a satisfying moment.

Sohn passed a few gas stations lined with a long line of cars waiting to fill up that stretched out to the highway. He didn't take notice as his mind was on the project.

He parked the pickup moments later still deep in thought. It took him some time to notice the urgency of shoppers pushing carts loaded with plywood, batteries, flashlights, generators and pumps to their parked vehicles.

"What's happening?" he asked. The first two people rushed past him, eyes averted. Their stress was needlessly intensified by the sight of the horrifying figure in their midst.

Sohn blocked a burly man. When the man stopped the cart and looked annoyed, Sohn popped the question again.

"Ain't you heard Mister? That hurricane that landed this morning down in New York City is storming up New England. We may be in for a doozy. It's all over the news."

"Doozy, you say?"

"Ayuh. Now if you don't mind I gotta get home to the missus. She's kind of anxious if you know what I mean."

Sohn stepped out of the way. "Thanks," he said.

The Mainer nodded. He hurriedly pushed the cart away to his parked car.

Inside the store, Sohn overheard a number of people discussing Hurricane Isabella. Apparently it made landfall in Brooklyn, New York and had since swept northward into New York and Connecticut, knocking down power lines wherever it went. The projected path of destruction was western New England of all places but mid coast Maine was still preparing for the worst. Never trust a hurricane!

Sohn passed empty shelves of emergency supplies. He was too late but that didn't concern him. He had candles, matches, well water and enough food to last a few days. The only worry was that the gas tank was hovering near 1/8 full or 7/8 empty depending on one's point of view and attitude. He could make it home easily with gallons to spare.

Thankfully there was no run on fencing rolls. He loaded up three rolls in the cargo hold and eased into the driver's seat. Traffic was congested on Route 1 making it so going. Cars backed up on the highway near the town's gas stations. Sohn didn't care to wait in line so he drove past them. He hated crowds and dawdling.

There was a gentle breeze and a cloudy sky. The clouds were streaming northward.

The prospect of gale force winds and torrential rain excited him. He loved getting lashed by the wind and soaked by the water drops. It was an invigorating and spiritual cleansing experience to be in the path of nature's fury.

He set to work as soon as the pickup was unloaded. The three rolls of four feet high galvanized zinc-coated steel were laid side by side on the left perimeter of the backyard. He then took an ax and carried it into the forest abutting the property. The tree he sought was ¼ mile from the house. He measured out twelve foot long logs with a twelve to fifteen inch diameter and started chopping the trunk with powerful blows. His years of being a lumberjack and mill worker paid off handsomely. Each cut section weighed about four hundred pounds.

The ax was propped by the logs. Sohn picked up the first log to carry back to the property. He hoisted the heavy weight on his right shoulder and stepped carefully along the undulating surface. It was a real balancing act as he had to compensate for going up and down the forest floor and moving around trees. He grunted from the strain but kept trudging along until finally dropping the log on the edge of the yard.

I'm getting old. Hell, I am old! Sohn told himself while rubbing the sore shoulder. Being a glutton for punishment, he went back for the next trunk length.

This time around he carried the weight on his left shoulder. It didn't go so well. His concentration waned briefly. He misjudged the distance between trees. The log slammed into a mammoth oak tree knocking the log off his shoulder. He lost his balance from the severe shock and fell heavily on his side.

"Aagh!" he called out in pain after landing heavily on the ground.

He lay there a few minutes to assess what part of his body was damaged the most. His left shoulder and neck were in agony from the collision with the unmovable tree. He sat up slowly, waiting for the pain to subside. After a while it was better. He stood, swaying a little from lightheartedness. But that wasn't enough of a deterrent to dissuade him from getting the second load home.

He did it backwards. Holding one end with both hands, he backed his way through the woods, looking right, a less uncomfortable direction than looking over his left shoulder. Each step was an effort but he kept moving, breathing heavily from the pain and strain.

Sohn lost track of time but finally arrived at his destination. He dropped the heavy load and stood there staring into space. His mind was a clear slate until he gradually recovered from the grueling task. He plodded back to fetch the ax, unable to carry anything heavier.

I should have used something lighter and more manageable. I guess I deserved this pain. Sohn looked up at the sky. *It's payback for the sins I've committed. Isn't it?*

He lowered his sight line and continued onward through the pine forest.

Are you angry with me God? Yes, I guess you are. You and I have never seen things eye to eye and your son and I aren't on speaking terms either. Is it too late?

He listened for a reply. The only sound was the rustling branches blown by the outer band of wind from Hurricane Isabella.

So be it. You are angry with me. I have broken a few of your sacred commandments. Thou shalt not kill is the first and foremost, isn't it? I have said your name in vain too many times to remember. And I have failed to honor my parents as they were in a past life. I only remember my Creator who little deserved to be honored by me. He cast me out from the outset. You might say he orphaned me after looking into my sorry eyes.

Sohn laughed unhappily. The ax was carried back to the house without any memory of ever picking it up. He looked thoughtfully at the two logs lying side by side. *There's another use for them, isn't there?* He looked up at the darkening sky with renewed hope.

"I will erect a cross and hang it from the ceiling rafters of my living area." He paused while trying come up with more he could do to befriend God, then added enthusiastically, "Or I can build an altar. Would that please you?"

Sohn felt like he was on the right path. It was a good feeling.

"I will try to change my evil ways."

That meant he would allow people to show their scorn without his becoming angry enough to murder them. It would be a challenge.

"How do I turn the other cheek?" he asked God. He remembered his anger against Victor for making him look like a monster. The rage from being constantly rejected turned him into the monster. He single-handedly wiped out the Frankenstein family with his wiles and enormous hands.

"It seems an impossible task to demand of myself, but I suppose it must be done," he said with doubt shrouding the euphoria from moments ago.

"Please give me strength."

"Amen."

He paused, waiting for acknowledgment. Nothing. He sighed and walked into the house.

Hurricane Isabella swept north that night, causing heavy damage to western New England, a region totally unaccustomed to tropical storms. She gradually weakened but still cast out her wind and torrential downpours over hundreds of square miles. Fifty mile an hour gusts struck the Maine coast on Sunday. The ferry services were shut down and all schooners, fishing boats and pleasure craft was safely moored or docked as white capped waves relentlessly churned through the normally calm waters of Penobscot Bay.

The pen etched evenly spaced blue colored words of varying lengths across the line of the journal. The writer continued the process on the next line and so worked on her entry of the day. She described in infinite detail each encounter with the ageless giant. Mary had seen him three times in the real world and twice in his old domain. It was a progression with an unknown future. The journal would gain more substance only with continued encounters.

The pen paused when Mary didn't know the content of the next sentence. She questioned herself. How had she trapped herself into this predicament? A terrible thought crossed her troubled mind.

He did this to me. He wants to keep seeing me and somehow expects me to write his story.

Mary shivered. Can that be possible? He is that conniving?

Mary put the pen down and closed the journal. The subject matter was too disturbing to continue. She needed to unwind. Otherwise sleep would be impossible.

She normally slept like a baby with the lights out but tonight she closed her eyes with the lamp on her night table on. She needed whatever comfort was available to wait for a fitful sleep to get her through the night. *Please let me sleep. It's not fair my mind keeps thinking of him.* Time passed. *At least I'm resting my eyes.* That was small comfort but better than nothing.

William and Jane Godwin gazed through the broad living room window at the panoramic windswept bay. The deck chairs and other outdoor furniture had been moved into a shed yesterday afternoon as a precaution. Their skiffs were doubly secured with extra knots and fenders to ride out Isabella's eastern front.

Jane looked anxiously at Summer Days, their 40 foot motor cruiser moored a hundred feet from the dock. She was bucking the mooring.

"Willy, do you think we should have put Summer Days in dry-dock?"

Godwin looked briefly at the straining boat then turned to his wife. "She'll be fine. The mooring will hold her." He admitted to himself that the heavy gusts would test the strength and durability of the mooring. He overheard that some boats had been taken ashore by cautious owners.

The beautiful yacht looked agitated as she pointed into the wind. Still, he didn't want to alarm Jane.

"She'll be fine Jane. She has weathered small craft winds before," Godwin said with a stiff smile.

"That's good." She knew the winds were expected to increase during the day to well above small craft warnings but Jane didn't want to belabor the issue. She forced herself away from the window as Mary entered the room. Willy turned around to face her.

"Good morning, Mary" he greeted.

"Hi, Mom and Dad."

"How are you dear?" her mother inquired.

"Fine thanks. It seems I haven't completely missed Isabella after all, she said cheerfully. *I didn't go to Isabella so she is coming to me.*

She stood at the window as her parents watched her.

"Will you see Perce again?" Jane asked. She wasn't sure he was a man her daughter should see. Jane heard several womanizing stories about Perce. Mary didn't deserve to be pulled down by a man with low moral fiber.

I hate it when they ask me about what man I am seeing and who I danced with at a party. She sighed. *I guess I'll do the same if I become a mother.*

"I don't know, Mother. I probably will. We had fun yesterday."

Her father remained silent. He had no advice to offer on the subject. He considered Mary to be generally sensible.

Besides, his friends rarely gossiped the way Jane's friends seemed to do. He despised gossip, despite the fact newspapers and magazines used it as the basis of articles.

"Does Shelly live in his parents place over near the old inn?" he asked conversationally.

"I haven't been there," she replied. "But the answer is yes."

He nodded and glanced at his wife, wondering if she'd pursue the subject. Mary turned from her father to her mother for the same reason. Jane didn't mind the attention.

"Just be careful dear," Jane urged.

"Don't worry about me," Mary replied wearily. "I'm going to get something to eat. Can I get either of you anything?"

"No thanks," her father said.

"No dear," he mother replied.

They watched her head toward the kitchen.

"Mary has good judgment," he said quietly.

"I don't doubt she uses common sense at the magazine but you need another set of skills in figuring out men."

"You figure me out yet?" he asked playfully.

"I'm still working on it," she replied.

"Seriously though, I think Mary's good a good judge of character. Let's let her figure out the guy on her own. If he's not more than one dimensional she'll lose interest in him."

Jane hoped her husband was right.

Chapter 14

He had a high tolerance of pain but even so lying in bed was an ordeal. Every time he put pressure on a shoulder, whether the left or right, a pulsating pain awakened him. He could only sleep on his back and sleep was sporadic. Most of the night he listened to the rustling leaves and branches as Isabella's wind strengthened.

By morning the shoulders felt a little better but the ache was enough to make him postpone the fence project. Any labor requiring upper arms and shoulders would have to wait a day or two. His mood darkened again until remembering the promise to behave himself and be a better person. He just needed to figure out a way to do it.

Constable Stone's cell phone rang. He handled a variety of enforcement matters on Islesboro including motor vehicle, criminal, marine resource and animal control. Any 911 calls deemed urgent and requiring his involvement were automatically relayed to his cell phone.

Stone looked at the Caller ID. It was the service on the line.

"Stone, what's up?"

"Hi Bert, its Verna."

"Verna, hi. What's up?"

"We got a call reporting a possible missing person out your way. Are you ready for the info?"

Stone reached for a pad on the passenger seat of his police car, a black SUV marked with huge POLICE lettering and Islesboro Public Safety in smaller font on the sides of the vehicle.

"I'm ready to copy," he said.

"Jonah Herston's been missing since Friday night. He works on the ferry."

"I know who he is, Verna. Keep going."

"He didn't show up for work yesterday. He doesn't return calls."

"Who reported him missing?"

"His friend, Jim Nebors who was listed as the only emergency contact. You need his telephone or address and Jonah's, too?"

"Sure, go ahead."

Verna gave him the data which he wrote down on a fresh page under the heading 'Herston MPR'.

After ending the call, Stone drove over to Herston's small home up island. It was a one story white cape style shingled house with a weed filled gravel driveway. No car was in the driveway and there was no garage. He got out and immediately pulled the hood of his police jacket over his head. Stone stretched and turned full circle, taking in every detail of the small property and the neighboring houses.

He was unarmed presently but carried weapons when needed, mainly to put a wounded deer out of its misery. Stone had never been forced to shoot a suspect but thought he had the grit to get it done if necessary. He stepped to the front door and rang the doorbell. The house felt empty.

The corpse of Jonah Herston lay undisturbed under the boulder about two miles away. Inside a trouser pocket was a cell phone. The battery had been fully charged shortly before Jonah had left his house for his fateful drive to the beach. The phone's GPS could act as a homing signal for another 24 to 36 hours.

Stone turned the doorknob. The door opened.

"Hello," he called out. "This is Constable Stone. Herston?"

Silence.

He stepped inside a few paces, leaving the door slightly open. There was no need for a search warrant as he was there to begin looking for the missing crewman, a person whom he personally disliked. Stone considered Herston a loudmouth, wise ass and a bully but the man's lousy personality wouldn't prevent Stone from doing his duty to locate him.

Islesboro's senior police officer thoroughly searched the house for a clue that would tell him why the resident disappeared. His mind rotated between what he saw, what could be missing and the next phase of the investigation. He located and pocketed an address book in Herston's messy bedroom. The bed was unmade and dirty clothes lay on the floor and piled on a chair.

Stone stopped in the kitchen on the way out to look in the refrigerator. He counted eight cans of chilled Budweiser. There wasn't much else. The constable looked in the garbage can. It was full of empty beer cans and a pizza box.

Okay, he may have a drinking problem, *he's a slob and likes takeout. Big deal.*

Stone closed the door behind him and scanned the immediate neighborhood. An empty potato chip bag blew past him. He smiled. The wind was still strengthening, accompanied by a steady rain. He hoped there would be no power outages, but he would handle the situation if it happened. A number of homes had generators including his own. The municipal offices had emergency power.

He would interview the neighbors and his coworkers and take it from there. If the guy had any drinking buddies, chances were he'd find them in the address book. The island didn't have a bar or even a restaurant. Stone considered whether to start with the neighbors or drive over to the ferry landing. He started with the neighbors.

While Stone went door to door trying to learn some of Herston's habits and find out the last they had seen him, Sohn Schrenk drove to the library, keeping vigil on the gas gauge hovering just above empty. The wind howled. The tree branches swayed and debris blew across the highway. The windshield wiper kept visibility decent. Traffic was light as most drivers were home glued to The Weather Channel and local advisories watching the former hurricane's path in live feeds and computer projections. Sohn didn't need to watch the TV reporting.

Observing the wind driven rain told him all he needed to know.

The library was closed. He shook his head. His disappointments continued to pile up unabated. He wondered if it was an indication that his salvation was too much to hope for. A church was a block away.

Do I dare? Will God strike me down with lightning bolts if I enter his house of worship?

Thunder and lightning were not out of the question on the stormy day. He drove the block and parked. Sohn remained seated a while, frowning at the church. He feared what could happen to him. Would he be struck dead upon entering the structure? Would the minister cast him out with a crucifix held out for protection?

Sohn forced himself out of the pickup and walked slowly on the slate walkway, taking unusually small steps. His heart thumped loudly in its chest cavity. He stopped in front of the large oak door and waited. The rain soaked him. He looked up at the gray sky waiting for the lightning to strike him dead. It would put a welcome end to a long suffering life. But there was no lightning. Instead footsteps sounded from within the church. He lowered his eyes guardedly to the door.

The door opened. He gazed at a middle aged man wearing a long white garment down to his ankles.

The minister stared at Sohn with wide eyes. His heart stopped beating for several seconds.

Has Satan himself seen fit to seek me out while hell's furies blow wind and rain? He surely looks like Satan with those yellow eyes, alabaster skin and demonic looking face. And his height. It pains me to look at him.

The minister closed his eyes in an effort to compose himself. When they reopened, the visitor somehow seemed less threatening. He saw the giant standing still, absorbing the sheets of rain, and making no threatening moves toward him.

I have sworn to open the door to all who seek sanctuary within. I must, if I can, invite, for better or worse, this man into the church.

He did the sign of the cross with his right hand, took a deep breather and smiled at the drenched giant.

"Why are you here?" the Episcopal minister asked.

"Fear not. I need your help, minister."

"Very well."

Slowly, the door opened.

Sohn ambled up three granite steps and across the threshold into a small vestibule.

"Welcome to St. John's Church. I am Reverend Horace Dudley," the minister stoically announced. Without thinking, he held out a hand to his visitor.

Sohn shook the man's hand carefully making sure he didn't apply too much pressure. He wasn't ready to provide his name.

"Did you come here to pray or would you like to talk?" Reverend Dudley asked.

"I'm not sure," Sohn said hesitantly.

"If something is troubling you, son, you may pray to the Lord at a pew or you can talk with me. Either way let's go into the nave."

Sohn followed the minister through an open interior door into the main body of the church. He stopped in mid stride, awestruck by the simple beauty of the place. He was impressed by the stained glass windows, the carefully crafted hardwood pews and a simple alter above which hung a cross.

His host was pleased by the stranger's humble reaction. It was a good sign. He strode to a pew, sat a few feet from the aisle and waited patiently for the space next to him to be occupied. He frowned briefly wondering if the pew was too small for the man to sit comfortably.

Sohn grimaced as he bent his knees deeply but the pew was too tight for them.

"I'm so sorry. Let's sit in the chancel near the altar. There's more leg room."

Sohn slid carefully from the pew and followed the minister to the front of the church. They walked past the stone altar and sat in a pew beside the left wall. As promised the padded seating was roomier.

"Now then, before we start you must tell me your name," the reverend said in a trembling voice.
"Sohn Schrenk."

"Thank you, Sohn."

Sohn looked around, try to buy time to put his thoughts into words. At last, he spoke.

"It's kind of you to allow a great sinner into your house of worship. I am not a churchgoer. I have stayed away from churches as long as I can remember. A long, long time," he said, giving his listener a meaningful expression.

"I am not welcome in many places because of how I look. I am a monstrosity in more ways than one. I have allowed uncontrollable anger and revenge control my actions in the past. Now, if it is not too late, I want to atone for my sins."
The minister cowered. He prayed for strength and God's protection.

Sohn recognized fear when he saw it. Fear was the customary emotion people displayed toward him, especially when forced into close proximity.

"I mean you no harm, reverend. Please believe me."

"Go on," Dudley said.

Sohn told the minister about his life, omitting the worst atrocities. He concluded his confession be saying that despite many years of avoiding violence, he had been forced to take another life in self-defense and now felt deep remorse.

Dudley had vast training and experience knowing when a member of the congregation and others were being honest or deceitful. He heard sincerity in Sohn's voice and read it in his eyes.

Dudley's hands were tightly clasped together as he considered the confession. He was shocked about the apparent longevity of Sohn's life causing him to briefly wonder again if the confessor was indeed sent by Satan to test him. He chastised himself for such a thought and then tried to rationalize Sohn's words.

The minister considered redemption. Was it too late? Not at all. Was this man on a wanted list? Were the police and FBI searching for him? *That is not my concern. He came to me for help and that is what I will try to give him.*

223

He looked up at the giant who waited expectantly and apparently anxiously, too.

"Sohn, thank you for coming to see me. You have shown courage in doing so. Do you know any prayers?"

"I have read both the New and Old Testament but I know of no prayer to say aloud or to myself."

"Do you know The Lord's Prayer?"

Sohn shook his head.

"Do you recall Jesus's Sermon on the Mount?

"Yes, it was Jesus telling a throng of people about his beliefs."

"That's right Sohn.

Our Father who art in in heaven,

Hallowed be your name.

Thy kingdom come.

Thy will be done,

on earth, as it is in heaven.

Give us this day our daily bread,

and forgive us our trespasses,

as we forgive those who trespass against us,

and lead us not into temptation,

but deliver us from evil.

For thine is the kingdom,

and the power, and the glory,

for ever.

Amen

"Do those immortal words sound familiar to you, my son? They are known as The Lord's Prayer. You should learn them and recite them daily. I will lend you a prayer book to take home. Learning some prayers and reciting them from your heart will make a good beginning or rebirth for you."

"Okay, I will read it."

"Please do. Now, I'm concerned about your getting home safely in the storm."

Dudley handed a prayer book to Sohn. The two men walked back down the aisle to the door. Outside, Sohn turned to the rector.

"I do have one question."

The rector raised his eyebrows.

"How did you know I was standing here before?"

Dudley laughed easily. "I saw you get out of your pickup truck. My office has a view of the parking lot."

"Reverend, I am impressed you dared to open the door and show yourself to me. You are a brave man."

Dudley smiled. "I needed strength from the Holy Spirit."

Sohn frowned. "Will God help me, too?"

"If you open your heart and mind to Him. Thanks for stopping by, Sohn Schrenk,"

"Thank you for your help," Sohn replied. He looked down at the prayer book. "I will read the book through from cover to cover."

"If you have any questions, feel free to call or we can discuss it next Sunday after the service. It's at 10am. Dress is casual."

"All right," Sohn said without conviction.

Sohn walked back to the parking lot. Reverend Dudley watched him leave. The man of God knew Sohn may never be seen as one of God's children. However he hoped that Sohn would give himself a chance to allow the prayers to heal wounds and inspire him to perform good deeds. The alternative made Dudley shiver.

He closed the door.

Chapter 15

Constable Stone's investigation hadn't come up with any leads that had panned out yet. He still had no idea where to find Jonah Herston. One neighbor had seen Herston's car backing out of the driveway Friday evening. The car braked loudly, then accelerated with a shriek. Stone wondered where Herston was going to in such a hurry. If Herston was still on the island, finding him should be simple.

I mean the island is only fourteen frigging square miles. I deserve to be fired if I can't find the bastard!

Earlier the lawman had called Jake Hawser, the captain of the Margaret Chase Smith. Stone told the ferryman about the nature of his call. Hawser told him the ferry had been short-staffed the first two runs yesterday after Herston failed to show up for work but that someone filled in the remainder of the day. The ferry was out of service today due to robust waves and a driving gale.

Stone arranged for the captain and his deckhands to assemble at Hawser's house for Stone and his part-time deputy Merle Taggart.

Stone picked up Taggart at the deputy's house. Taggart, unlike, Stone, was a native of Islesboro and knew everybody on the island.

"Now Merle, I'll ask the questions. I'll mainly need you to monitor the tape recorder and help identify each man before they speak. Got it?"

"Ayuh."

Stone looked at him sharply. He was forever trying to get the deputy to speak real English, not local jargon.

"Yes, Captain."

Stone frowned. Taggart liked calling him that even though that wasn't his rank. He let it pass.

They motored on until arriving at a split Colonial. Four vehicles were parked in the driveway. He parked at the end closest to the road to block anybody from leaving.

Stone wasn't thrilled with interviewing some many in a single session but he sensed it was prudent to get as much information as possible quickly. He was starting to have a bad feeling.

Captain Hawser let them in. "Can I offer you both coffee and something else?"

"Thanks, if it's already made," Stone replied.

Taggart grinned and nodded. "Light and sweet'll hit the spot," he said.

"Just black for me," Stone requested.

A few moments later Hawser escorted both men, each carrying a steaming mug, to the dining room. The constable recognized the six men who clammed up as the lawmen and ferry captain entered. Stone turned to his deputy.

"Please set it up in the middle of the table at high volume."

The crewmen watched as a sleek black tape recorder was placed on the rectangular hardwood table. There were three empty chairs. Taggart sat in a chair in the middle near the recording device. Hawser extended an arm to the remaining places.

"Thanks, Captain but I'll stand for now. Please by all means sit down."

Hawser took a seat. Everyone looked at Stone expectantly. He gave Taggart a significant look. Taggart nodded. He pressed Record.

"Now then, everybody. Everything being said from this point on is being recorded. I want short and direct answers. As we need each speaker identified on the tape, please provide your name when you have something to say. Now some of you may have guessed why we are all here."

"It's about Jonah Herston, isn't it?" a heavyset man with a goatee inquired.

"Please identify yourself starting with your position," Stone requested.

"Seaman Ralph Carter. It's true, isn't it?"

Stone looked at an official list of the ship's crew. He put a check mark next to Carter's name before looking at the man.

"Yes, it is true. When did you last see him?"

"Friday, after we secured the ferry for the night."

"Did he tell you his plans for the night?"

"No, but he could have told Danny over there?" he said pointing his head at a muscular man, mid 30s with the tannest face the law officer could recall. Everyone turned to the bronzed man.

"Please introduce yourself for the record and tell us about your relationship with Herston."

"I'm Danny Bender, engineer" he said with attitude. Me and Jonah have known each other about five years. We don't date, if that's what you mean by relationship but we hang out sometimes. Have a beer and talk, if you know what I mean."

"When did you see him last?"

"After work Friday. I dropped him off at his place. We had a beer. Then I left."

"What was on his mind Friday night?"

Danny's eyes flickered a second then went back to normal. "Not much."

Stone noticed. Bender knew something.

"Did he have anything planned that night or Saturday?"

"Well, he was supposed to work Saturday."

"And Friday night?" Stone repeated.

"I told you I don't know, didn't I!" Bender exclaimed. His eyes narrowed while watching Stone jot something down in his notebook. He glared at the constable.

Stone looked at him then. "Something else?"

The engineer shook his head. Stone turned to Captain Hawser.

"I apologize, Captain Hawser, for not starting the session with you as the senior man."

"That's fine, Constable. What else you want to know?"

"That's the sixty-four dollar question all right. Let me just put the question on the table to everyone here. Did anybody else see Herston Friday night?"

He looked everyone in the eye for a few seconds. Only Bender seemed to know what was on the missing man's agenda that night and he wasn't ready to discuss it.

"If anybody here is shy about talking about this in front of others, here's my card." He handed his business card to everyone except his deputy.

"Okay. Now, Captain." Stone stopped. He had jumped the gun, realizing he should have had a preliminary with the captain earlier. He turned to Deputy Taggart. "Please stop the recording and come with us. "Turning to Hawser, he said "I want to speak with you in another room privately."

Hawser contemplated the matter. "Let's adjourn to my study. If you'll follow me, Constable."

Stone and his deputy followed their host out of the dining room, down a hall and into a small study furnished with a desk, nautical paintings, photographs of the ferry and Hawser's certification. He closed the door after them and pointed the two men to visitors' chairs near the desk.

"Thank you, Captain Hawser. I want to ask you a couple of questions, for the record. Out of earshot of your crew in the other room."

"Fair enough. I understand, Constable. "

Stone nodded to his deputy. They watched him activate the recorder.

"Ready," he said.

"Captain Hawser, how long have you operated The Margaret Chase Smith?"

"It'll be eight years in January."

"What are your primary duties and responsibilities as master of the vessel?"

"Well, I have several. Of course, I must make sure the ship makes it between the Islesboro and Lincolnville berths safely. I make sure she arrives and departs according to schedule. Also, I supervise my crew to make sure they do their jobs properly. There are other more tedious aspects of the job."

"I see. Tell me about your supervision of the crew. If there is an infraction, is it written up?"

Hawser nodded in understanding as he was seeing why this interview had to be private.

"Why, yes. I have a file for each crew member. Is there a particular file you want to discuss?"

"I guess you know the answer to that, Captain. What can you tell me about Jonah Herston? Is he an exemplary employee or does he have performance issues?"

"Jonah is a decent worker. Or was," he said sheepishly. "He knows his job. The problem with him is his personality."

"How so?"

"He can get rather moody. If he doesn't like you, he shows it. What you see is what you get. I've had to reprimand him a couple of times on being disrespectful to passengers. Frankly, one more incident will end his employment. He knows it. He lets his mouth run and will say some nasty stuff."

"When was the most recent incident?"

"The last official one was a week ago but I heard one of the men talking about something that happened last Friday."

"Tell me about it, Captain. What happened on Friday?"

Hawser looked at Stone uncertainly. He didn't have the facts and wasn't the type of ship's officer to speculate. Still, he wanted to tell Stone everything he knew that was useful.

"I heard he had a little problem with a passenger."

"Do you know the passenger's name?"

"No, sir. He was a stranger."

That figures! It would have been a great lead if we could find the passenger.

"I don't suppose you saw the passenger," Stone offered without much hope.

"No, I didn't. I have to put all of my attention on maintaining the ship's course and avoiding other boats out there." He paused thoughtfully. "You should question Bender. They don't keep much from each other. Perhaps Bender or one of the seamen witnessed the altercation."

"Thanks, Captain for the suggestion. It's worth following up. Do you know of anyone else on Islesboro or the mainland who's close to Herston? Family, girlfriend or whatever?"

"No, he isn't the type of person to be liked that much or get close to."

"Yet your engineer is an exception."

"True, but Bender's no angel either."

Stone turned to his deputy. "Do you have anything to add?"

"I've seen Bender and Herston around during my patrols," Taggart offered.

"Any place in particular?"

"Let me think a minute, Captain."

Hawser looked at Stone quizzically. Stone shook his head as Taggart tried to jog his memory.

"Now I remember. I've seen them drinking and cooking hot dogs at a couple of the beaches," he said brightly. He was happy to have been asked to participate and happier still to make a contribution.

"Thanks, Deputy." He looked at Hawser and Taggart. "Let's get back to your crew."

The crew was collectively restless. A couple of the guys talked about leaving. There was some murmuring and stewing as they didn't appreciate being there on their own time and away from family during the storm. At last they looked up as their captain and both lawmen returned to the dining room. After the recorder was turned on again, Stone took over.

He looked at each man and spoke as he focused on Bender. "So tell me about Herston's altercation with the passenger on Friday."

Bender stared back, then blinked. "What are you talking about?"

"Anyone?" Stone asked, looking around the room. "If we identify the passenger, it could help us locate your crew mate."

He watched and waited patiently.

"I've got all night. Nobody is going nowhere until one of you tells me what I need to know. I suspect Herston talked about the incident during the trip over and one or more of you saw who it was."

The constable patiently folded his arms and half closed his eyes, but kept looking at the engineer. Benton seemed incapable of intimidation. Stone calculated someone could be worried about saying too much in front of Bender.

Stone waited to see what seaman would receive a dirty look or cold stare from the engineer. The seconds ticked by. Nobody except the constable knew what was going on. Some of those at the table looked dumbfounded.

He heard whispering.

"That's damn rude to just nap out like that," said a man.

"He doesn't give a shit about nothing but himself," another man said.

"Let's get out of here," a third man suggested. He heard a chair move and opened his eyes.

"I heard that. You don't want to piss me off. Nobody's going nowhere until somebody tells me about the mysterious passenger. So let's start with the basic description. Was it a man or woman?"

He looked at Hawser's crew expectantly. Perhaps an insult would be helpful to loosen a tongue.

"It's not a difficult question, is it?"

"I think I saw him," a sandy haired man offered, carefully avoiding Bender's glare.

Stone smiled. "That's great. Please give your name for the record."

"Sam Pickens."

"Well then, Sam Pickens, please tell me what you can about the man."

"Um, he was a big guy. Real scary looking. He sat in his pickup the entire crossing."

"What makes you think it's the man Jonah had a quarrel with?"

"Jonah pointed him out to all of us."

"How could you tell he was a big man if he was in the vehicle?"

"His head looked like it almost touched the cab ceiling."

"What made him scary beside his size?"

"His eyes for one thing. They seemed yellow like."

"Yellow?"

"Real pale," another man suggested.

"That's impossible. People don't have eyes like that," the constable announced.

"Well that man surely did," Bender piped in.

"What else?" Stone inquired.

"His skin seemed real thin, like it barely covered his face."

"Was he wearing a mask?" he suggested.

"The bastard's face was a real-life mask if you want to know," Bender replied belligerently.

Did anyone get the license plate numbers?"

Nobody spoke. Stone shrugged.

"So he's still over here?"

"No sir, he was on the first ferry Saturday morning," Pickens replied.

"Interesting."

"Anybody here see the guy on the island Friday night?"

Stone saw some heads shake. *I got something to go on anyway.*

He leaned forward. "Tell me, Mr. Bender, what did Jonah have planned after you both had some beers?"

"How would I know?" he answered coldly.

"Was he going after the man in the pickup truck?" Bender shrugged and smirked.

"That's good enough for me." He scribbled some notes then looked at Pickens.

"What color was the pickup?"

"Jet black, sir."

Stone stood. "Alright gentlemen. That's good enough for now. If any of you have anything else, please call me any hour of the day or night. The sooner your crew mate is found the better."

"Do you think something happened to him? Hawser asked.

"I don't know. I can't rule out anything right now." Looking at Bender, he added, "That's why nobody should hold back on me."

Bender turned his head away.

"Meeting adjourned!"

Chapter 16

The remnants of Hurricane Isabella passed through eastern Maine. By Monday morning it was a memory. There were scattered power outages and cleanup work to do. But life returned to near normalcy in the mid-coast region. People were thankful that the brunt of the storm missed them.

The next week leading up through Labor Day Weekend was a transitional time for the coastal communities such as Islesboro. Summer residents such as the Godwins and many others closed up their cottages and returned to their regular homes in New York, Boston, Philadelphia and other cities. The week marked the end of peak time for the tourist industry. The schooners would remain active a while longer, hauling passengers on day sails and overnight voyages around Penobscot Bay and the fringes of the nearby Atlantic Ocean.

Mary was ambivalent about the last week of August. She was sad that the summer had flown by. The time renewed her appreciation of living a leisurely life. She enjoyed the slow pace but also thrived in the rat race of the big city. She needed to spend time in both environments to feel balanced.

Her parents planned to leave midweek but Mary wanted to stay a few more days. She wasn't sure if she a full time position at the magazine or to look for something else. Her indecisiveness troubled her as until a week or two ago she had been devoted 100% to the magazine. What had eroded the commitment?

The battery in Jonah's cellular phone was low. There was perhaps another twenty four hours before it would be as dead as its owner.

Constable Stone sat in his office listening to the tape. He transcribed it onto a computer screen. His fingers moved quickly, keeping pace with the words coming out of the tinny sounding speaker. He figured another hour would complete the task. Then he intended to listen and read simultaneously to see what new insight could be attained.

A telephone rang in an outer office. It disrupted his concentration. He turned from the computer screen and keyboard and put the recorder on pause. He yawned and stretched. The uniformed policeman reached for a mug of coffee as he heard a knock on the office door.

"Come in," he said, holding the mug in both hands. He took a sip to test the temperature. It was tepid. He swallowed the rest of energizing beverage and put the cup on the desk.

The door opened. Deputy Taggart entered the room carrying a note pad. He stood a few feet from Stone. He smiled broadly.

"Merle, you look like the cat that swallowed the canary."

"Excuse me, Captain?"

"Never mind. What do you have for me?"

"I called the ticket office in Lincolnville like you told me to and spoke to Lorraine over there. She remembers a giant of a man buying a ticket Friday. She said he was a walking nightmare."

"That sounds like our man. Good work. How'd he pay?"

"Excuse me?"

"We need to know if he paid by cash or credit card. If he charged the ferry ride then we'll learn his identity. Got it?"

"That's sharp, Captain. I'll call Lorraine back right now."

Deputy Taggart started to leave the room.

"Wait up, Merle. Let me think a moment."

Taggart waited expectantly as his superior pondered calling the ticket office. *I'll get more info than Merle for sure but it's good for his morale to give it another effort.*

Stone decided to allow Taggart to call again. If more information was required he'd do the follow up. The constable wanted to get an accurate description of the mysterious ferry passenger who may be connected to Herston's disappearance.

"Go ahead and let me know what she says," Stone told his deputy.

Taggart nodded and exited the office to make the telephone call.

He returned a few minutes later looking subdued. Stone immediately guessed the reason.

"Lorraine said he paid with cash. She said he gave her the willies. Couldn't wait for him to leave."

"Did he say why he was going to Islesboro?"

"I don't know. Do you want me to call back?"

Stone smiled. He didn't want the deputy to feel bad. "No need, Merle. Thanks. That will be all. Please close the door on your way out."

After Taggart left, he looked up the phone number for the Lincolnville ticket office and dialed the number.

Lorraine watched as a two roundtrip tickets printed. The phone rang. She handed the tickets to a customer who thanked her and stepped away from the counter. Lorraine stared at the phone as it continued ringing. Three calls in ten minutes was a hectic pace for her. *I hope it's not that deputy again.* She sighed then answered on the third ring.

"Islesboro terminal, Lorraine speaking."

"Lorraine, this is Constable Stone."

"Constable Stone. I was just taking to your deputy. Did he tell you?"

"Yes he did but I have some questions for you." She sighed again. "What do you want to know? Is it about that awful man?"

"Tell me everything you recall about him. I need a description. You must tell me everything he said." Lorraine shuddered. Her heart started to beat faster. The seconds passed while she tried to collect herself.

"Lorraine, are you there?" Stone asked. He was getting impatient. Every second counted in locating Herston.

"Yes, don't go on a high horse. This ain't no picnic. I've tried to forget all about that monstrous man."

"I appreciate what you're going through but this is important."

"You think it has something to do with Jonah, don't ya."

Loose tongues and faint hearts is a poor combination.

"Just tell me everything and you can go back to your work, please."

And she did.

"So you don't have his name?"

"No."

"Did he say why he was coming over here?"

"No."

"Lorraine, I may arrange for a police artist to stop by. Would you work with him or her so we can get a good likeness?"

"Is that really necessary? I mean how many eight footers live around here?"

Stone thought the man's height was over exaggerated by a foot or more. He took a few seconds to look up the height of the tallest humans in recorded history and discovered Lorraine could be right.

"You have a good point, but a good sketch of this guy would do wonders."

Lorraine sighed again. It seemed she'd be unable to forget about the horrible man for some time.

"Okay, I'll do it," she said reluctantly.

"Thanks, Lorraine. Either myself of someone from the sheriff's office will be touch."

"Right," Lorraine replied. She felt a little dizzy. Stone hung up.

Lorraine held the phone to her ear. She was in shock.

Stone shook his head. He had to call in the Waldo County sheriff's office to augment the investigation. Increased manpower and resources were needed at this time to track down two men.

He got Sheriff Hank Benoit on the line.

"Hank, how's it going on the mean streets of Belfast?"

"Funny you should ask, Bert, as I'm investigating a collision involving a tourist going the wrong way on a one way street. What's up?"

"We have a missing person situation. Nobody's seen one of the ferry crew members since Friday evening. It seems he had some quarrel with an eight-foot tall passenger."

"Eight foot, you say? You're pulling my leg."

"No, I'm absolutely serious, incredible as it sounds. The fellow scared the living daylights out of Lorraine in the Lincolnville ticket office. The description she provided of him sounds like stuff from a horror movie."

"Sounds like it. What can I do to help, Bert?"

"I was thinking a good sketch of the passenger would help identify him. He stayed over here Friday night and caught the first ferry back Saturday morning. Someone over there must know him."

"I'd remember someone like that forever. I'll ask around and call some other counties, perhaps the staties, too. I'll make arrangements for an artist. Good idea."

"Thanks, Hank."

"Okay, give me whatever description you have for the guy."

"Eight foot tall, pale skin, yellowish eyes, short black hair."

"You sure you're not trying to pull a fast one on me Bert?"

"I'm dead serious, Hank. Really!"

"Lovely. Have you searched the entire island yet?"

"There's only two of us over here, I'm afraid."

"Bert, the staties have a K9 unit that could help with the search." He paused then added "If you think something happened to your citizen I should make the call immediately."

"I agree. Go ahead then. I can use all the help you can provide."

"Talk to you later, Constable Stone."

"Thanks, Sheriff Benoit."

They severed the connection.

Benoit assigned a deputy to take his place writing the report at the scene of the car accident. The missing person's incident on Islesboro with extenuating circumstances took priority.

He drove back to the Waldo County Sheriff building and parked in his assigned space.

Once back behind his desk Benoit sat back considering who to call first. He contemplated reporting the incident to the homicide unit of The Maine State Police in Augusta. On the other hand he could hold off until questioning nearby police departments about the mysterious eight foot all man. He needed some verification that the ferry passenger existed before he dared tell them about the man. The sheriff didn't want the elite Staties to think of himself as a lightweight and become the butt of their jokes.

Benoit made an assumption that the man most likely lived within twenty miles of Lincolnville. So he made calls to the police units in Searsport, Bucksport, Thomaston, Camden and Rockland. He followed protocol in asking to speak to the senior officer at each location. He gave each police officer the same physical description. Not surprisingly, every time he was asked if this was a practical joke. He pushed his growing exasperation into submission while firmly telling them what he knew.

He struck out on every call. His final one was to Captain Davis Radley in Rockland. After listening, the police captain had something to say about it.

"Sheriff, I may have something for you."

"That would be good. What can you tell me, Captain?"

"There's a man who fits the description in this area. He keeps a low profile despite his height," Radley offered with a chuckle. "He continued promptly after hearing no acknowledgment of his witticism. "Anyways, we have his name and address here even though he lives several miles outside the city. Do you want him brought in for questioning?"

"I don't want to scare him off but at the same time the missing man, if he's alive, needs to be found ASAP. I've a mind to call the Staties now."

"Why give them the credit, Sheriff. We can get it done together. Why don't you have me check and see if the man's at home?"

"What's his name and address?"

"Give me a moment. I'll put you on hold."

Radley didn't allow Benoit to respond. He wasn't the type to dwell on manners. He was a hard man who'd gotten promoted up through the ranks by interfacing regularly with the city's selectmen and being a tough policeman. Thanks to his approach, crime was at an historic low. Radley encouraged greater visibility by increasing foot and bicycle patrols. He occasionally patrolled the city with his police officers.

The captain had an excellent memory. He recalled the names of people he'd met only once. His subordinates were proud to serve under him.

Radley used the firing range almost every day. It paid off. He was the best sharpshooter on the force and planned to maintain that position until taking early retirement in a few years. The man and women who protected and served the citizens of Rockland were well served.

He stepped over to a walnut cabinet and unlocked it. He looked in section marked "Persons of Interest" and pulled the file for Sohn Schrenk. He took it back to the desk and placed in front of him. He picked up the phone receiver.

"Are you there, Sheriff?"

Benoit was getting a bit peeved with the brusque phone manners of the Rockland man. Benoit had an edge when replying, "Yes, I am."

"I'll have the information you need in a minute."

He put the sheriff on hold again with a smile as he opened the thin folder. It contained a copy of Sohn's driver's license including an image of the man looking sourly at him. The police captain wasn't afraid of much, but the man he beheld looked lethal. He'd need more than one squad car to handle the resident. Radley glanced at the date of birth. It read 03-30-33. He moved his attention to something else then looked at the DOB again.

"Those DMV people can't get it fucking right," Radley muttered. He looked at the face carefully trying to determine Schrenk's age. Perhaps 48? Definitely not 80!

The photocopy showed the motor vehicle operator's height as 7'11 ½', weight as 369 pounds and eyes as YL which he suspected meant yellow. Radley assumed that the Department of Motor Vehicles in Maine or any state for that matter had never previously specified yellow as a driver's eye color. It was an aberration of the extreme kind.

There was little else in the folder other than his last known address and a remark Schrenk was employed by Pine Tree Lumber. There was no known phone number for the man.

He picked up the phone again. "Sorry, Sheriff. It took longer to locate the file than I intended but here's what you need. Ready to copy?"

I've been ready for half the friggin' mornin'!

Benoit, pencil in hand, replied. "Go ahead."

He wrote down Sohn's name and address. "What's his phone number?"

"We don't have it, Sheriff. Would you like me to send a patrol car over to Schrenk's house?"

"Not right now. I'll get back to you, Captain. Thanks for your assistance."

"If Schrenk turns out to be a real suspect, I'm going to be sorry to wait too long. You understand me?"

"Of course, Captain. Talk to you soon."

The sheriff ended the call without waiting for the Rockland police captain's reply. *Do unto others as they do unto you.*

The case was getting too creepy for Sheriff Benoit's liking. He thought there could be a real chance that the missing crewman was dead. The probability of homicide escalated the longer the man was missing. The State Police had a Major Crimes Unit (CID) in Belfast. Their detectives were trained to identify, track down and apprehend killers.

Let them solve this missing persons or suspected homicide case. They should check out this Sohn Schrenk. Better them than that Rockland captain!

He picked up the receiver and auto dialed CID in Augusta. They had facilities also in Belfast but the point or origin should be to their headquarters.

A person answered after the second ring.

"CID, Trooper Jack Olsen speaking. How may I direct your call?"

"This is Sheriff Benoit over in Waldo County."

"How may I help you, Sheriff?"

"I need to discuss a potential homicide with one of your detectives in Belfast, Islesboro and Rockland."

"I'll put you right through to Detective Pounds."

"Thank you, trooper."

"You're welcome, sir."

There was silence while the call was transferred.

"Hello, Sheriff Benoit. This is Detective John Pounds. How can I help you today?"

"Detective, we have a missing crewman from the Islesboro – Lincolnville ferry named Jonah Herston who's been missing since Friday evening."

"Sheriff, give me everything you know, then I'll have some questions for you."

Benoit looked carefully at his notes while speaking. "Okay, Friday some giant of a man, an eight-footer named Sohn Schrenk was on the ferry going over to Islesboro. The now missing man, Seaman Jonah Herston, had some choice words with the passenger for an unknown reason. The passenger's name is Sohn Schrenk and he lives outside Rockland city limits according to Captain Radley. Anyway, after work, Herston had some beers at his house with a buddy from the ferry. That's the last Herston was seen."

"Tell me about this Sohn Schrenk," said the 27 year old man as he scratched an itch under his crew cut length hair.

"He spent the night on Islesboro. We don't know where. Then he caught the first ferry back to the mainland Saturday morning. Constable Stone could find nothing on the man and no sign of Herston. It's like he dropped off the face of the Earth. I spoke a while ago to Captain Radley in Rockland who has a copy of Schrenk's driver license. It lists the guy's height as 7'11 ½ inches in height. He has, get this, yellow eyes and black hair and is alabaster colored skin."

"That's no description I've heard in my life. You being serious with me, sheriff?"

"Yes, I'm deadly serious."

"Give me a minute, sheriff."

"Sure."

The detective pulled up the Maine DMV data base. After entering his search criteria, Sohn's driver's license appeared on his computer screen. Pounds couldn't believe his eyes as he stared at the image. The face made Freddy Krueger almost seem handsome.

"Wow! He's one for the record book, isn't he," Pounds said. *Have I seen that face before?* It seemed vaguely familiar to the young detective. He couldn't remember where.

"I'd say so from what I've heard. The ticket lady in Lincolnville was terrified from her close encounter with him on Friday. I told her a police artist may be in to do a sketch of the man. She almost had a fit about it. She'd sooner forget anything about this Schrenk fellow."

"You know we don't automatically get involved in missing person's investigations."

"I know that. I'm hoping there's a 'but' after that statement."

"But if this Sohn Schrenk is involved, it may worthwhile for us to interview him."

"Thank you," Benoit said with audible relief."

"There may be only a slim window of opportunity to locate Herston alive. Who did you say called in the missing person incident to you?"

"That would be Bert Stone, the Islesboro constable. He's a good man. Detective, do you want his phone number?"

"Yes, I do. I'll take his office and cell numbers if you have them."

Benoit gave Detective Pounds both telephone numbers.

"Detective, I have Captain Radley's phone number if you want it."

"No need, sheriff. I know how to reach him," Pounds replied tersely. The police captain was not a personal favorite of his. The young detective had crossed swords with the Rockland man a year ago. He thought Radley was too self-serving and arrogant.

"I'd appreciate if you email me everything you know about the disappearance and Schrenk. I'll call Stone now."

Pounds gave the sheriff his email address. They spoke a couple of minutes more before ending the conversation. The detective printed the driver's license and took the printed image with him to report to his superior Sergeant Trent's.

He stood outside the open door to Trent's office waiting for the man to get end a phone conversation. When at last that happened, Pounds cleared his throat to announce his presence.

"Come in, Pounds."

Pounds entered and sat down in a chair facing his superior.

"What do you have there?" Trent asked, eying the paper.

"This is the possible suspect in a missing person's case over in Islesboro," Pounds said, handing the photocopied page to Trent.

"This is the worst looking operator's license photo I've seen," Trent said, frowning at the image and Pounds. "And I thought all Mainers are good looking! What has this man allegedly done, detective?"

Pounds told the Sergeant Trent everything he knew about the case. Trent listened attentively. He sat thinking it over after Pounds finished speaking. Pounds waited patiently, knowing his superior was deciding whether or not the unit would take responsibility for the outcome.

"Without this photo ID, you probably know it would be iffy at best we would accept Sheriff's request. But looking at the picture of this Sohn Schrenk causes me to believe we must add this to our case load. He definitely looks capable of violence. I suppose you already checked to see if he has a police record."

"No, sir! I was in too much a hurry to approach you to do that."

Trent looked at his subordinate narrowly. He expected more from his junior detective.

"Well, get on that as soon as you get back to your desk. I want you to make a nationwide search for any alleged or convicted crimes for our suspect here. I'll call Captain Radley to tell him we'll bring Schrenk in for questioning. You can let Benoit know we're on the case and contact Constable Stone. Get an update from him and have him contact you 24/7 with any new developments. Any questions?"

"I want to get Herston's cell phone number. Perhaps we can track it, assuming of course, the battery hasn't died."

"Good idea. Have it done, sooner the better. Maybe we'll get lucky. Anything else, Detective?"

"No sir. I'll keep you posted."

"Alright then, get cracking."

The battery of the missing, murdered crewman's cell phone was almost dead. It had only a few hours left before the GPS chip became useless. People picnicked on the beach, completely unaware about the nearby corpse. A boy sat on the boulder doing his required summer reading. His nostrils unintentionally caught an unpleasant whiff. "Gross!"

The boy looked around for a dead seagull. He couldn't locate the cause of the foul odor. He hopped off the rock and walked down the beach to join his family where the air was fresher.

"Bingo!"

Constable Stone had given Pounds the phone number of the missing man. He was tempted to call the number but that would only drain the battery. Instead, he made urgent arrangements to track it. His efforts panned out.

"I need to fly to Islesboro," he told Sergeant Trent excitedly. Herston's phone is located on a beach on the southern tip of the island. I called Constable Stone a minute ago. I gave him the coordinates. He's on his way there. I want to be there, too, sir."

"What about Schrenk?"

"If we find the phone, we'll find Herston. Then I'll concentrate on Schrenk."

Hopefully alive, Trent thought.

"Okay, I'll make the call. A chopper will be waiting on the helipad for you. Good luck, detective."

"Thank you, sir."

Pounds exited Trent's office.

Chapter 17

Sohn once again felt a strong foreboding. Something was happening not very far away that could endanger him. *What's going on? Is it Mary?* No, he didn't think so. *Who's after me and for what?* He thought about the last terrible act of his.

The ferry worker who came after me? It was kill or be killed. There were no witnesses to attest to that. Sohn truly believed he had no choice other than taking a life. *Justifiable homicide? Absolutely!*

He wondered if it was time to pack up and leave, now that he felt the body was either exhumed or about to be located.

How did they locate the body? I thought I hid it well by the boulder.

He deduced that his physical description could have been passed along to the police by Herston's coworkers and others.

Sohn tried to keep a low profile wherever he lived, but he stuck out like a sore thumb because of his immense height and horrific face. He found himself sitting behind the steering wheel but couldn't remember getting into the pickup. *Am I losing my mind? Am I insane in the membrane?*

There was nobody to offer guidance or comfort. He relied on his own judgment for an extremely long time. It served him well most of the time. His decision to visit Islesboro worked against Sohn. He was too eager to see Mary for his own good.

Did Sohn deserve to live alone forever? Was it the penalty for killing off the Frankenstein family? A life sentence. He knew some mass murderers were sentenced to several hundred years in prison without parole. Sohn would do everything possible to prevent that from happening as centuries in prison on top of the centuries he had already endured would ultimately drive him crazy.

Sohn sat motionless until he could figure out what to do and where to go. He knew the answer would come to him sooner or later.

Mary looked up at the sky as soon as she heard a helicopter approaching the island from the mainland. It flew eastward over Warren Island. She picked up a pair of binoculars and looked at the aircraft. It was still too far away to see sharply but she thought there were decals. She trained the binoculars as the craft flew closer. The letters sharpened until she read MAINE STATE POLICE. She wondered what brought the state police to Islesboro. Hopefully it was only a drill. But it could be something more. Was a serious crime committed on the sleeping island?

Mary decided to follow the chopper in her car. At the very least the exciting occurrence broke up the monotony of the day. She welcomed an opportunity to hone her investigating skills.

The intrepid journalist ran into the house, grabbed the keys from a table in the foyer and ran out to the front drive. She couldn't see the helicopter at the moment but heard its rotors ricocheting overhead.

Mary started the car and drove to the end of the driveway. She lowered all the windows to get a better sense of the direction to take. It seemed to be flying toward the southern part of the island. She turned right out of the driveway and pushed down hard on the accelerator with her right foot. The posted speed limit was 30 miles per hour. Mary eased off at 45 mph. She tried to listen to the helicopter and watch out for it simultaneously while driving on the narrow two lane road. It was a challenge. Her eyes alternated their focus between the trees overhead and the road every few seconds.

She slammed on the brakes a few yards from a stop sign. The car screeched, tires burning rubber, before stopping completely. Mary craned her head out of the car, trying to determine where the helicopter had gone. She barely heard the chopper's engine and spinning rotors.

"Where is it?" she asked herself. She decided the police aircraft was still heading in a southerly direction. She drove the car onto Pendleton Point Road at a reasonable speed to prevent an accident that could cause her to miss seeing where the police aircraft landed.

She drove through the small village of Dark Harbor in pursuit.

Constable Stone stood, hands on hips, looking at the boulder. He turned as soon as he heard the distant growl of a helicopter. It sounded a little like a machine gun to him.

He was astounded by the day's events. Sheriff Benoit called first to warn him that the state police may be taking over the search for Jonah Herston and to expect a call from Detective Pounds of their Major Crimes Unit.

"Why Major Crimes?" he asked surprised.

"Well, the state thinks your resident may not only missing but killed, too. You didn't hear that from me. Stone, do you understand me?"

"Yes, I do. Sheriff, does that mean Herston had a confrontation with that big fellow on Friday evening?"

"Maybe. I better sign off in case Pounds tries calling you. Call me with any developments."

"Okay, sheriff."

True to Benoit's word, Detective Pounds called thirty minutes later to introduce himself and inform him that Herston's cell phone still had a signal, though a very weak one. It was coming from Pendleton Point on the southern tip of the island.

Stone was instructed to drive to Pendleton Point and call the state detective when he got there. The signal from Stone's cell phone would be monitored as a location beacon. That's what Stone did.

"Thanks, constable. Now if you could stay on the line and get out of your vehicle."

"I am, sir."

"Now start walking in any direction. I'll let you know if you're getting closer to the target."

"Yes, detective. I'm walking now."

Stone stepped along a rutted dirt path that ran parallel to the beach. It was just wide enough for a car. He walked about one hundred feet

"Turn around," Pounds called out.

Stone stopped. "Okay."

"Go for it."

He walked back. "I'm back where I started."

"You're closer."

"I have three choices. I can keep going in the same direction, or go left into a wooded area or take a right onto the beach."

"It is your choice, constable. Just do it as we only have minutes left before losing the signal."

Stone walked straight ahead.

"You passed the location. Please turn around. When you get back to the spot we last spoke, make a left or right."

"Okay." Stone stopped a short time later and made a right into the woods. It didn't feel right but he plodded forward a hundred feet before stopping.

"Well?" he inquired.

"I think you are farther away."

"That means it's on the beach." He turned around and navigated his way around trees, continued through the dirt road and then strode down a slight embankment onto the beach. He noticed there was more seaweed than normal due to yesterday's heavy winds. He stopped above the rotting black and green algae.

"I'm on the beach."

"You're getting real close."

Stone looked to his right and started walking in the direction, just along the high tide line strewn with smelly black and green seaweed.

"Turn around."

"I'm going back the other way now," Stone commented after making a sharp U-turn.

"Getting there."

"Almost there now," he heard a short time later. "What's ahead of you?" the detective asked.

"A picnic area. There's a boulder beyond that and a rocky point at the end of the beach. I'm about even with the picnic area now."

"You're almost dead on," Pounds said excitedly.

"Should I stop or keep moving?"

"Go a few more steps. . ."

Stone walked beyond the boulder a ways.

"Damn! Turn around."

Stone turned around and trod on the sand, pebbles, and seaweed up to the boulder.

"That's it! You're there! Can you mark the location with a big X in the sand?"

"That's interesting. I'm right next to a boulder."

"Can you move it?"

Stone tried to with all of his strength. It wouldn't budge. "Not a chance. It would take heavy equipment," he said, out of breath from the exertion."

"Okay. Do you see any sign that a person was there recently?"

Stone looked around the rock, alert to any possible evidence. He saw small footsteps only.

"It looks like a kid was here recently. The storm apparently erased any signs of anyone else."

"I'm on my way. I'll be coming by chopper. Give me 30 or 40 minutes. Make sure nobody gets near that stone."

"Okay. Anything else?"

"Yeah. Is there a bulldozer you can get your hands on?"

"You want to move the boulder and see what's beneath it, detective?"

"Do you have a better idea, constable?"

"I can have a shovel delivered and start digging around carefully until you arrive."

"Do it then. I'm signing off until shortly before landing."

"Roger," Stone replied.

He heard a click as Pounds disconnected.

Stone then made a couple of calls to arrange for a bulldozer to be transported to the site on a flatbed trailer. The equipment arrived a little while later. It was delivered by a local builder several minutes before the helicopter's arrival. The constable ordered the bulldozer driver to park the heavy equipment some fifty feet from the boulder.

Stone was fascinated by the operation of the bulldozer. He owned a toy one as a boy. He had a hell of a good time playing with the dozer in the dirt and sand. Stone guessed he would still have fun playing with it on the beach. He watched the larger than life yellow machine ease down onto the upper beach, its rubber and metal belt-like feet churning up sand. Its tread left a significant trail. The heavy serrated blade would be lowered when necessary to push the heavy boulder out of the way.

At first Stone couldn't hear the approaching chopper due to the racket the bulldozer made. But when the operator turned off the diesel engine, Stone immediately heard the aircraft. He looked up, seeing it was less than a quarter of a mile away and crossing over the distant shoreline toward him.

Deputy Taggart drove up in his patrol car out of idle curiosity. He wanted to be where the action was. He was excited by the unexpected action. Merle looked at his boss to see if it was okay to be there. Stone nodded at him before turning away to see where the helicopter would land.

Landing on the beach would create a sandstorm. The pilot selected a parking area a hundred yards away. Stone headed that way to meet and greet the state detective. He arrived in the paved lot as the helicopter set down gently.

Pounds stepped onto the ground carrying a leather bag. His head was bent down a little bit to put as much distance as possible from the rotors. He stepped forward, head up now, smiling at Stone.

"John Pounds," he said with his right arm stretched out.

"Bert Stone," the constable replied, shaking hands with the young detective. "Welcome to Islesboro."

"It sure looked beautiful from the air," Pounds said.

"Hard to beat the views," said Stone.

"So, any luck on getting a bulldozer?"

"Yes. It's ready to go."

"Okay, lead on."

The two lawmen walked side by side over to the beach.

"By the way, shortly before landing I caught a reflection of something metallic in the woods near here. It was too bright to make out."

"Whereabouts?" Stone inquired.

Pounds stopped and pointed into the woods. "About fifty feet in that direction. Behind that growth."

"I'll check it out. After the boulder is moved?"

"Fine with me," Pounds said with a shrug.

They walked onto the beach. Taggart was next to the bulldozer chatting with the operator. He turned to watch them stride over. Stone made the introductions moments later.

Pounds then moved closer to the colossal rock and scanned the sand, shells and pebbles around it. He put the bag down on the ground and un- zipped it open. Stone walked over to peer inside. Pounds removed a sifter and a spade.

"You planning to do some surfacing mining?" Stone asked half seriously.

"If it'll get me a cell phone. I'll need some space to myself."

"Sure." Stone backed a few feet then stood watching the detective start a laborious process of spooning surface material onto the sieve, shaking it, until only pebbles were left. Then he quickly dumped them on the ground and started over again. It took about twenty minutes to cover thirty feet around the rock. Stone grew grimmer by the minute as he squatted and moved around. Finally, he stood and wiped sweat from around his eyes. He looked at the construction worker. "Start 'er up."

The man nodded and climbed into the high seat. He turned over the ignition and a puff of smoke wafted up. Pounds walked to the bulldozer and spoke loudly to the driver so he could be heard over the engine.

"I want you to move the boulder about fifty feet in any direction that's easy."

The man nodded. The others got out of the way as the bulldozer moved forward. The blade was raised about two feet off the ground as the equipment closed in on its target. It stopped just before hitting the boulder. Then, it continued at a crawl until the blade tapped the boulder.

The operator put the powerful machine in forward gear. The bulldozer strained a bit but managed to gradually push the three ton boulder down the beach. Until a few days ago, the boulder hadn't budged an inch since the last Ice Age. Now it had been moved twice in four days!
Moving the heavy weight created a long furrow more than a foot deep.

"Everyone should now step to where the boulder sat and look closely for the cell phone or a body," Pounds ordered.

"A body?" Deputy Taggart asked with surprise. That made no sense at all.

"Yes, why do you ask that, deputy?"

"Well, how could a body have been buried under that heavy stone? I mean it took that frigging bulldozer to move it, didn't it?"

Stone agreed but kept quiet. He waited for an answer.

"Good point. I didn't mean anything or anyone is buried directly under where the boulder sat, but possibly somebody dug a hole next to the boulder."

"Oh, okay," Taggart replied, a little embarrassed.

"So now we need to make haste and start the widening and deepening. The only tool I have is the spade. One of you can use the sieve and the other will have to use your hands."

Stone took the sieve, bent down and started pushing surface material backward between his feet. Taggart did the same with his hands while Pounds used the spade. They worked hard while the bulldozer operator watched fifty feet away.

I ain't being paid to do that shit! He sunk lower in the seat to feel less visible.

The depression in the sand gradually deepened and widened. Taggart was tuckered out and had a bleeding finger. He paused in mid stroke and looked at the detective derisively. Stone and Pounds noticed their cohort had stopped working. They looked at him questioningly.

"Okay, what is it now? You need a break?"

"Why can't the bulldozer do the job for us? I mean it would save time, wouldn't it?"

Stone smiled and nodded at his deputy and turned his eyes to the detective.

"I like a man who thinks on his feet. Constable Stone, you have a good man."

"I know."

Taggart's face reddened. He grinned.

Pounds looked over at the bulldozer. The driver looked away quickly. "Hey," he shouted. "Don't think I didn't see that."

The bulldozer operator looked back somewhat sheepishly.

"Bring it over ASAP. You're need here now," Ponds said hotly.

The three men stood as Pounds directed the one way traffic with one hand. The hole was now two feet deep and six feet across. Nothing had been excavated out of the ordinary other than a couple of empty beer bottles.

The bulldozer stopped in front of the dig site. The operator looked sullenly at Pounds.

Smiling encouragingly, the young man in charge told him to shave small layers a few inches at a time.

"Let's keep our eyes peeled. It's now or never." He nodded at the driver.

Chapter 18

Moments earlier, Mary Godwin parked her car across the parking area from the helicopter. A micro recorder was tucked into her pocket. She smiled at the pilot while walking past the aircraft toward the beach and picnic areas. He smiled back, enjoying the view until she disappeared from view.

Mary heard the bulldozer before seeing it. She stood next to a tree above the beach taking in the scene. Then she stepped onto the beach.

The bulldozer's blade gradually deepened the pit. All eyes keenly watched every sweep of the sharp metal on the ground as it shaved off another layer. The men hadn't noticed that Mary stood beside them, transfixed at the bottom of the pit.

"Whoa!" Stone shouted. What's that?"

Something brown and red was mixed in with the beach sand, stones and pebbles. The bulldozer operator either didn't hear him or didn't care as the blade moved forward.

"Stop now!" Pounds screamed with waving hands.

The blade stopped in mid motion.

"Is that blood?" Mary asked. Mary moved a hand over her mouth as she stared at what looked like red paint. She desperately wanted to look away but couldn't.

The men were startled. "This is a crime scene, ma'am. You should leave." To Stone, he instructed "Take her away immediately." Stone nodded at his deputy. Taggart grabbed Mary's arm but she didn't budge.

Pounds jumped down into the pit, landing with feet apart and arms out to stay balanced. He squatted, looking carefully at droplets of blood that clung to clumps of sand and thin strands of brown hair. He duck walked to where the mixture started. He looked up at Stone. "Give me that spade, damn it!"

Stone looked around, located the detective's bag and retrieved it. He dropped the small hand shovel into the open crypt. Pounds reached to his right, picked it up and started systematically spooning fractions of inches of sand from the precise spot where the blood appeared. He gradually uncovered the back of a man's head. The detective suddenly stopped. He shook his head. His eyes stung from the foul odor. Breathing the air was difficult.

"What's the matter?" Stone asked.

Pounds stood. His back was sore but he ignored the dull ache for the time being. He said wearily, "This should be done correctly. I'll have to call in the CSI unit to take over from here. They'll uncover the body properly and tell us exactly how this man died. My ass'll be on the line if I continue this operation like an amateur. Now give me some space so I can make the call," he said irritably, pulling out his phone.

"You got it," Stone said warily. "Let's take a walk", he said to Taggart and Mary. "Miss Stone, you shouldn't be here anyway."

They moved away from the excavation site to give Pounds some privacy. The detective decided to climb out and head in the opposite direction to get some fresh air. Then he called Sergeant Trent.

Mary felt a little nauseous. She tolerated a slow walk down the beach for a minute. Then she stopped and bent forward a little, trying not to think about the blood and the dead body.

"You okay?" Taggart asked kindly.

Mary was afraid she'd puke if forced to talk. She nodded slightly.

Stone realized what had made her sick. "Take it from me. The first time you see something like that is the worst. You're lucky the detective stopped when he did. I don't envy those forensics guys that'll come over."

Mary straightened up. She looked back at to see the state policeman talking animatedly on the phone near the far end of the beach. *I'd love to know both ends of that conversation.* That reminded her the micro recorder was still on. She decided to put it to good use.

"So Constable Stone, who is buried back there?" Stone was reluctant to tell her without getting permission from the young detective.

Mary noticed and quickly asked deputy Taggart.

"I believe that's Jonah Herston, the man we been looking for, right, Captain?"

Stone looked sharply at Taggart, ready to admonish him, but doing so in front of a witness was unprofessional. He blew out some air in frustration, refusing to admit or deny.

"Jonah from the ferry?" she asked, looking from one to the other.

Taggart saw he had said the wrong thing so he looked out at the bay instead.

"Wow! I can't believe someone's been killed and buried on Islesboro of all places. She was both excited and scared. "There's a killer on the island. My God!"

Stone stepped in, saying, "Easy does it, Miss Godwin. We can't say for sure the killer is here or not." He hesitated, then continued adamantly, "You know, that detective over there was right. You should have left the beach when you were told to do so. Now you're a risk. You must keep quiet. This is a police investigation and we can't have you scaring the populace. Do you understand?"

"Of course I do. I won't tell a soul," Mary said, her eyes locked on Stone's eyes until he nodded.

"Let's see what Pounds has to say about that. It looks like he's done with his call."

They watched him walk over to the bulldozer. Stone started heading over there. Mary and Merle followed suit. She put a hand on the deputy's arm, stopping him. She waited for Stone to move away a few more seconds as she didn't want him to overhear them.

"Merle, who do you suspect killed Jonah Herston?" she asked softly.

Merle, licked his lips, looking uncomfortable. He glanced at his boss then at Mary. "I can't say, Miss Godwin."

"But you know don't you?"

"Yes, well, maybe but I can't say who it is. You don't want to know either. If it's who we think it is, you don't want to mess with that giant."

Oh no! She suddenly felt dizzy. Her heart pounded. The news was too much to bear!

Merle was aghast as he saw her face turn ashen. Mary put a hand over her heart and fell onto the beach unconscious. "Help!" he shouted.

Stone stopped and turned. He raced back, followed by Pounds.

* * *

Mary lay on her back. She looked tormented and that, she was. While Stone tried to resuscitate her, Mary unwillingly fell deep into another time and place she hoped never to visit again. When the unconscious young woman reluctantly opened her eyes, she was back in Frankenstein's laboratory with the bane of her existence.

He looked down at her as she lay on an operating table. Sohn, sensing something was wrong with Mary, had taken it upon himself to hijack her back to the laboratory.

Mary cringed at the sight of him, knowing him now as a killer and a monster.

"I will step back as I see now what you think of me," he said despondently.

Mary looked up at the ceiling, noticing cobwebs and cracked plaster. She counted the cracks as a way to forget who stood nearby.

Sohn waited patiently, waiting for Mary to recover. Then he would find out what had happened to her on the island. He watched her eyes looking upward and her mouth silently counting numbers.

Mary stopped counting. She felt disconnected from reality. *Am I going insane? He's done this to me!* Anger built up inside and quickly consumed her. She was too agitated to lay down a second longer. She sat up then swung her legs to the side and stood facing him. Sohn was momentarily startled and even a little frightened of her. Her reaction was unexpected and unwanted. He had to pacify her. Otherwise there was a very real possibility she'd never recover; not here nor in Maine.

He called out to her as she glowered at him.

* * *

Detective Pound ordered that the unconscious Mary to be taken by helicopter to Pen Bay Medical Center in Rockport escorted by Stone or Taggart.

Trent ordered him to guard the excavated body until the team arrived from Augusta.

Stone and Taggart carefully carried Mary on a stretcher to the waiting helicopter.

Mary murmured, "I want to leave." Her eyelids flickered.

"I wonder who she was talking to. It doesn't sound like it's a good place," Pounds Stone commented."

* * *

Mary cooled down enough to begin conversing with her host. Sohn was greatly relieved. It was much healthier than keeping all her anger to herself. He had done that countless times, especially in the early days, with violence being the end result every time.

"Why am I in this God forsaken place again?" Mary inquired crossly.

"This is where we can exchange ideas and help each other without interruption from the future. You can actually go back any time you wish, Mary." He added quickly, "Tell me what has happened."

"You killed that ferry worker, didn't you?"

Sohn sighed deeply. "Yes," he said despairingly.

"You're a killer."

"Yes, Mary, I've killed."

284

Mary looked about her for a weapon and a safe hiding place. She forgot all she had to do was wish to return to Maine and it would happen.

"I will never harm you," Sohn said softly.

Mary looked him in the eye and somehow believed him.

Sohn decided it was best to tell her about his altercation with the ferryman on the ship and later that night on the beach. He left nothing out, ending his story. "He had murder in his eyes. I couldn't just let him shoot me, could I?"

"I'd be too frightened to do anything. I'm not a killer."

"But I am?"

She didn't reply.

"Would you let someone kill you or would you try to prevent that from happening?" Sohn said, trying to make a point.

"I suppose I'd do whatever it takes to live," she admitted.

"If you saw the person intended to pull a trigger or kill you by other means, and there was no way to escape other than disabling or killing, what would you do?"

"I'd prefer disabling by far."

"Okay, point taken. That man the other night had it in for me. I saw it in his eyes. He would have probably reported me to the authorities for harming him or threatening him. And if you're a cop, who would you believe? Me, a scary looking stranger? Or him, a man who's been in the public eye on Islesboro every working day?"

Mary smirked. She realized he was right. She hoped never to be put into an intolerable situation like that. Perhaps cutting this man some slack was prudent.

"You should know his body will be examined by the state police. They'll determine his cause of death. And there's something else."

"What is it?" Sohn said, reluctant to ask.

"At some point someone will wonder how a body was buried under that boulder. I mean it took a bulldozer to move it."

Sohn looked from Mary to the floor. He never guessed the body would be discovered. How had it been located? "How did the cops know where to find it?"

"What are you thinking?" she asked.

"How did they know where to look?"

"I don't know. Maybe there was a witness who just came forward?" she guessed.

"Perhaps but I don't think so."

"Why not?"

"I would have known. I would have sensed it," he said knowingly.

She nodded. Sohn previously proved he possessed some extrasensory perception in tracking her down at her home. She looked at him with a different perspective. Here was an extraordinary man. But even a man of his size, intellect and other abilities couldn't be expected to remain free from capture forever, let alone much longer.

Sohn watched her evaluate him. What would it mean? Would it change anything? He waited patiently.

"Stating the obvious, and pardon my rudeness but you stand out like a sore thumb everywhere."

He grimaced. "Go on."

"You were seen on the ferry going to Islesboro. Perhaps someone knew Herston disliked you and the cops know that, too? I'm only guessing."

Sohn's heat began to pump harder as he grew anxious about his well- being in Mid Coastal Maine. He started pacing. Mary watched him tap into his nervous energy. He stopped in front of her after two minutes.

"I must leave Maine immediately. It makes me sad because I will never see you again."

Mary was touched by his apparent attachment to her.

"Where will you go?"

"I won't know until I leave the house. Do you even care?"

"I want you to be safe. When you leave, does that mean we'll never see each other here again?"

"This place," sweeping a hand, "will be here for us to meet anytime you choose to do so."

"How is that possible?"

"All you need to know is if you ever feel a need to see me or think of me, I'll be here for you."

"You almost make it seem romantic," she said, blushing slightly.

Sohn felt heartsick.

"How can I be here and on the Maine beach at the same time?" she asked.

"Your body is there and you are here."

"Sohn, you make it sound so simple. So if you are here, where is your body?"

"It is home."

"What if it was, say, sitting on a park bench and a cop started asking you questions?"

"I wouldn't be able to answer him as I'm here. He'd see a man who is unable to respond to any stimuli."

"If somebody hurt your body, would you know it from here?"

"Yes."

"Okay, that's good. So there's some connection, right?"

"That's right, Mary."

They were silent for a short time. It was a comfortable silence. Both were thinking about something about the other person.

"Mary?"

Mary looked up at Sohn. "Yes?"

"Tell me what you want from life."

"Well, I am something of a journalist. I have a job at my father's magazine. I write articles about Manhattan. New York City."

"I know where Manhattan is."

"Of course you do. I'm concerned about the rising ocean and what it will do to the city. I'm trying, in my small way, to warn the city it should raise barriers, move boiler rooms from basements to higher floors and other things to help the city adapt."

"That is very commendable. I have seen many changes in my lifetime. When I first emigrated to this country, this area was in a mini Ice Age. It's much warmer now."

"Wow! I can't imagine. I wish I knew more," Mary replied. She was curious about his life.

"What do you know about me?"

"I know you are very old, but don't show it. You have some type of ESP. I know some more. What are you getting at?"

"Would you be interested in learning something more of my life?"

"Are you serious? That would be fantastic! But you will be leaving Maine very soon. Right?"

"That's true enough. There are two ways it can be done. I can let you interview me here or we can take a road trip."

Mary was speechless. If she accepted either offer her life would change forever. Every second here meant she'd be absent from her 21st Century life. Would her body decay? Did she need to eat here?

She wondered what was happening to her body. She had collapsed on the beach. Detective Pounds, Constable Stone and his deputy would eventually believe she was in a coma and would take her to the hospital.

"My poor parents," she blurted. "They must be with my unconscious body now and worried sick about me."

Sohn had not foreseen that complication, in part because he was essentially born an orphan. He was sympathetic to Mary's grief.

"You should go back to the future.. You need to open your eyes and show them you are all right."

"And then?"

"That is entirely up to you, Mary."

"Okay, I'll go back and make up my mind about what I'm going to do. Learning about your life and writing it down would be really interesting. Thank you for making the offer."

She meant it, too.

Chapter 19

Mary's eyes opened. She lay in a hospital room hooked up to an IV. She felt fine except where the hollow needle punctured her skin pumping fluid into a vein above her right wrist. The prone patient regarded it bemusedly.

Detective Pounds stood at a nearby nurses' station getting an update. He just arrived from Islesboro. The corpse was totally uncovered by the CSI Unit. A telemetry unit at nurses' station abruptly beeped. A nurse looked at the monitor. It showed a spike in the heart rate of the patient in room 132.

"I think she's awake," she told Pounds and the senior nurse on duty.

The detective's phone rang. He excused himself and stepped outside.

"Darling, you're awake!"

Mary turned to the euphoric voice. She smiled at her mother who sat next to the raised bed.

"Hi, Mother."

"Your father and I have been so worried about you. Thank God you're awake. How are you feeling?"

William Godwin entered the private room in Pen Bay Medical Center at that moment. Godwin smiled as he beheld his daughter and wife talking. He walked to the other side of the bed and lent over to kiss Mary on the cheek.

"You're a sight for sore eyes," he ventured.

"Thanks, father. It's good to see you both. How long was I, um, out?" she asked.

"A little over four hours."

"I'm sorry to put you through this."

"We're relieved you're awake. What do you remember? Constable Stone was rather vague," he said.

Warning bells sounded in Mary's head. If the constable had stonewalled her father, then . . . ?

"Ah, Miss Godwin, I heard you had come back to us," Detective Pounds said as he joined them. He made his way to the foot of the bed. "I hope you haven't taxed yourself by saying too much," he said meaningfully.

"No, not at all. My father just asked me what I remember. I must admit", she said, playing along, "my memory is hazy at the moment."

Pounds barely nodded, much relieved she had not told her parents anything about the investigation. The helicopter had picked them up on their flat front lawn after Stone called the house. The beach was now an official crime scene and sealed off from the islanders. Jonah Herston's body was flown off the island and taken back to the medical lab to be autopsied.

The detective just got off the telephone with Stone. The constable provided him with some good news. Herston's derelict car was located in the woods near the beach. The interior of the vehicle was littered with empty beer cans. More interestingly was the discovery of a box of shotgun shells.

But that development was nowhere near as fascinating as the unearthing of the shotgun itself, found below the dead ferryman. Did the ammunition prove the gun belonged to the man or was it planted in the car by the killer to deceive him?

"Constable, tell me you didn't put your fingerprints on the shell box."

"I may seem like a second rate cop, but I've never forgotten my training in Boston PD. The only prints will belong to whoever put the ammo in the car and possibly earlier latent prints from whoever sold him the ammo. Needless to say the box is safely in a plastic evidence bag."

"Good to hear, Constable Stone. Sorry if I offended you."

"No problem. Naturally you'll want to match the prints to those on the gun."

"Naturally," Pounds replied.

"Do you want me to drive the box to Augusta?"

"I'm in Rockport now."

"Is she still unconscious?"

"No."

"Anyway, I'll have preliminary results on the prints when I get back to the shop later. Should take a little longer to run the nationwide search. If you want to swing by later that'll be cool. I can give you the tour."

"Fair enough."

They concluded the conversation a short time later.

Now, he had to make sure Mary refrained from saying anything relating to what she saw at the crime scene.

"I need to speak to your daughter in private," he told her parents.

"Is Mary in trouble?" her father inquired.

"Not at all, Mr. Godwin."

"Come on," he beckoned to his wife. She looked at Mary and Pounds anxiously then left the room. Pounds stepped to the door, closed it, and returned to the bedside.

Mary watched him attentively and apprehensively. She knew the killer and should cooperate completely with the cop. However, she wanted to protect Sohn as long as possible.

"All right then. Can you tell me what upset you so much?"

"I think it was the shock of that dreadful bloody head and that nauseating stench more than anything else," Mary said quickly, trying to look sincere. She was partly telling the truth anyway.

"Is that right?" Pounds thought there was more to it than Mary admitted. Back on Islesboro, he had questioned Stone and Taggart closely about what they were discussing before she blacked out. He insisted on every word being repeated verbatim to get the most precise determination of her point of view.

"Put yourself in my position, Detective Pounds. Today was my first time ever I've seen a corpse, let alone one that's been dug up." She shuddered involuntarily. Pounds observed her sympathetically and analytically.

"I understand, Miss Godwin. Thanks for your honesty. Now you must keep what you saw to yourself or if you need to discuss anything, call Constable Stone. Forget about speaking to Deputy Taggart. Do you understand me?" he asked a little sharply. He was impatient about getting back to Augusta.

Mary was perturbed by his abruptness. She wondered what had annoyed him. The worst case scenario was that the detective knew about Sohn.

"Do you have any suspects yet?" she asked. Her palms were turning clammy and the room seemed to have warmed.

"Not yet."

"Are you all right, Miss Godwin?"

"Yes, thanks. Call me Mary. We seem close in age." She looked around, searching for something.

"You lose something, Mary?"

"My recorder. I always have it with me."

"It must be with your belongings." Pounds stepped over to a bedside table and opened a drawer. "Bingo! Here it is," he said lifting a clear plastic bag containing the recorder and her clothing." He smiled triumphantly at her, thinking he'd done a credible job at detecting.

Mary looked down at herself, noticing for the first time she wore a hospital gown then looked at him red faced.

"Stop staring at my bra and panties. Give me that bag now!"

"Yes, ma'am!"

She grabbed the bag from him and put it under the thin bed covers.

"There's no reason to 'ma'am' me. I'm not an old woman."

"Sorry. So what are your plans with the recorder?"

"Can we talk on the record?"

"Perhaps another time. I should run. But I'll allow you one free question off the record."

"How was that ferry guy buried under a boulder?"

"Excellent question. It's one that has been bothering me."

"And what is your conclusion?" she asked as calmly as possible.

"That's two questions." He winked, then added somberly, "There's an unidentified suspect out there not far from here. That's all I can tell you."

Pounds noticed a cloud pass over her face and wondered why. A nurse walked into the room.

"You look well considering," she said. "Your pulse has returned to normal but your blood pressure is elevated. How are you feeling?

"I'm ready to go home. I feel great!"

"We'll see about that. You'll have to wait for Dr. Prescott. He should be by a little later."

The nurse held out a digital thermometer. "Say ah." Mary reluctantly opened her mouth and allowed the thermometer to be placed under her tongue. Less than a minute later the nurse announced the result. "99.2."

"That's normal enough for me," Mary said.

The nurse smiled wearily. "Can I get you ginger ale and a snack?"

"I guess so. Can you tell the doctor I'm ready to see him?"

"Dr. Prescott is a woman, Mary."

"Okay, sorry."

"I'll let her know,"

The nurse exited the room.

"I guess that's my cue to leave, too. Have you gotten all this recorded?" Pounds asked.

"Yes, I'll do some editing later. I have nothing else to do here," she said.

He handed her his business card. "Perhaps we'll talk again. Will you stay on Islesboro much longer or do you intend to return to the big city?"

"I don't know. I might stay until Labor Day. Why?"

"Just curious. Give me your home and cell numbers in case I need some more answers."

"Answers to what?" she asked quickly.

"Never mind that now. We'll talk after you're discharged. See you."

He left. Mary wondered if Sohn was going to be arrested. *Why should I care what happens to him? If he's apprehended, he'll likely go to prison for a very long time and I'll never see him again. Justice will be served and the world will be safer with him behind bars. Right?* Part of Mary never wanted to see Sohn again but another part cared about him.

Sohn sorted through his belongings. There was no sign that anybody had been in the small house while he was gone. Any visitor would have seen his body seemingly asleep in his bed and a rather deep sleep at that.

Sohn didn't know how much time he had left before the police's arrival. It could be minutes, hours or days. While deciding what to take on his unwanted exodus his mind bitterly turned back to the ferryman. *That bastard ruined my chance of staying here. Why couldn't he mind his own business and leave me alone? Just because he didn't like me?*

Sohn stopped packing, too upset to continue. He was miserable.

Perhaps it's for the best. I'd have to move on sooner or later before people around here take notice I never age. But who's going to notice? I haven't any friends here. Just the store clerks, gas station attendant.... Nobody would say anything to me.

Sohn lay down again, depressed. *Let the police come and take me.*

He stared at the ceiling until his eyes couldn't stay open and fell asleep.

Chapter 20

The Jaguar crawled through the heavy fog enveloping Route 1. William Godwin drove cautiously, peering at the road illuminated by the headlights while Jane sat tensely in the front passenger seat. Mary, tired and weak, but happy to be released from the hospital, dozed in the back seat.

"I can't see more than twenty feet," William complained.

"Please slow down," Jane replied, her eyes glued to the rotating windshield wipers that removed the tiny droplets of moisture from the glass.

"Jane, I'll miss the damn ferry if I go any slower. Close your eyes if you don't like what you see."

She stared ahead at the twin white beams of light that pierced the grey fog. Then she screamed upon seeing the monstrous being that suddenly blocked them. Mary's eyes opened.

William was momentarily overcome with anger and for an instant wanted to step on the accelerator. But rationality prevailed. He slammed on the brakes. The vehicle skidded a few feet, stopping inches from Sohn.

Mary's unfocused eyes witnessed what had just happened. Her mind was convinced it was a nightmare, not reality. Then she beheld Sohn looking calmly at her, stepping around the passenger side of the car and opening the door beside her. He stepped aside and beckoned for her to get out.

"Don't!" William warned, turning his upper body and face as much as the dual seat belt permitted.

"I need to tell you something. Then you can continue your journey with your parents," Sohn muttered.

Mary removed her seat belt and stepped onto the side of the road.

"Father, you better move the car onto the shoulder or else there'll be an accident. I'll only be a minute."

She walked with Sohn about thirty feet. The car was invisible in the pea soup fog but she could make out the headlights.

Mary stopped and waited for Sohn to explain his actions.

"I killed the ferryman after he tried to shoot me." Sohn stopped speaking, looking sadly down at Mary.

"Go on," she said, arms crossed over her chest.

"The man hated me the moment he saw me. The hate drove him to take extreme action. Mary, I don't want to look like this forever. I need to have my face altered. Perhaps people will accept how I look with a new face. Perhaps nobody will scorn me anymore. Perhaps surgery will improve my quality of life."

Sohn stood expectantly, regarding Mary's face and body language.

Mary's arms slowly dropped to her sides and her face softened.

"Wow! That's really huge!"

Sohn frowned, clearly not understanding her. Cars passed on the nearby highway every so often.

Mary laughed softly. "I'm not making fun of you. I'm just saying that you've perhaps made the most important decision of your life."

"It is. Do you agree?"

Mary blew out air. "You have to do what you think is best."

"If I proceed, who should I see?"

Mary glanced back at the car headlights. The fog wasn't as heavy. The car was now clearly visible. "I know my mother's used Doctor Millard Strange. He's on East 72nd Street in Manhattan."

"Doctor Strange," Sohn repeated to himself.

"Do you want to ask my mother about him now?"

"No, I think not. She can't stand the sight of me."

Mary turned her face away from Sohn causing him to look anxiously at the back of her head.

"What's wrong?"

She whipped her face around, suddenly angry. "How did you know to wait by the road for me? That I'd be passing by here?"

Sohn stared from her to the ground.

"Well!"

"I know where to find you," he replied with a hand over his heart.

Mary gaped at him. Then she turned away and headed toward the car.

"You wouldn't react like that with your friend."

Mary stopped and spun around. She approached him slowly and angrily.

"What? Who?" she exclaimed angrily.

"Your man friend from the other day," Sohn said a little hesitantly.

"Perce is none of your business. You have a problem with that?"

Sohn stared at her a little timidly, surprised by her boldness. He wasn't used to be treated like that.

Mary nodded defiantly before walking back to the car.

Sohn stood there forlornly, watching Mary get in.

The vehicle sped away.

Chapter 21

That night, still disturbed by the way Mary ended their encounter, Sohn had a surrealistic dream that took him back to Victor's laboratory in 1792. Here is his dream.

My yellow eyes flutter open. Like all newborns I do not speak or understand any languages. I sit up and look around a dim laboratory. Then I stand. I take a stiff step, then another, trying not to fall.

I wander through the dark, shadowy laboratory feeling scared and alone until entering a small chamber. A man sleeps on a small bed.

I am not alone! Do I know this man? Somehow, he looks familiar.

I take a few halting strides closer, then stop to look down at the man. Watching his chest gently rise and fall with each breath fascinates me. I don't notice that his eyes are staring at me.

Victor is horrified by the apparition towering over him. *Please let this just be a nightmare. God help me! No, He has forsaken me to allow this monstrous being to come alive. See how he looks at me. There is something childlike and naive that almost draws me to him. I must overcome my revulsion. He must never know that he looks like an unholy fiend from hell.*

Victor Frankenstein shivers.

Their eyes meet and lock.

I mustn't look away as the first impression would be indelibly imprinted forever. It could make a difference on what he does and how he sees the world and himself. Look, he seems to be smiling down at me. It's rather hideous, but it's a smile.

"Hello," Victor mutters. His mouth feels parched.

I don't know what to make of the sounds from the man. He points to himself, saying "Victor."

I try to say the word, but can only manage "Iter." My pathetic attempt makes him smile. He seems deep in thought.

Then he speaks again, pointing at me. "Sohn," he says slowly and clearly. "It is German for son. Sohn.

"Sohn," I say.

"Very good, Sohn." Placing a finger on his chest, he says "I am Victor. Victor."

I say "Victor."

Victor smiles. He sits up slowly. I take a small step back as Victor rises to his feet. We take the measure of the other. I am surprised how short he is. The top of his head barely reaches my heart. I learn later he is 5'9", an above average height for the 1790s.

Victor rarely leaves the facility during the next several weeks. He spends many hours a day teaching me German. Victor seems astonished by the rapid speed that I pick up words. I am content to have his full attention and especially happy that he is so pleased with me. Then, after observing me thumb through an anatomy book, he teaches me to read and write.

One day, when he's gone out on errands, I discover a hand written journal sitting on a table by his bed. The script is difficult to understand as I am not yet a proficient reader and the handwriting isn't neat.

It is Victor's diary. A large part of the book is about me. I learn Victor is a 22 year old scientist. He brought me to life. He wants to introduce me to the scientific community at the university after my language skills are more advanced. He wants to travel with me to

Europe's finest universities and give lectures. He says he will be admired for making me. It is the greatest accomplishment ever.

Then I read something bad. Father says he is concerned about how I look. Do I look like a demon? He wonders if the world can tolerate somebody with gigantic height, yellow eyes, black lips, and almost transparent skin. Is that how I look? I have no way of knowing how I look. I close the book, too upset to read anymore. Why would Father, who is so kind to me, write something so upsetting? I want to ask him, but a voice inside me tells me not to.

I enjoy looking at the view of the world through an open window. People of all ages scurry about purposely on the street. Where do they go? I want to go outside and follow them around. But Father says not yet. Later? My mind is preoccupied when I hear a scream below on the street. I look down and see a frightened crowd, peering anxiously up at me. It confirms what Father wrote. I close the window and cover my face. Am I so terrible to look at?

The incident prompts a visit from a constable. For some reason Victor explains I am a cousin visiting from Geneva. The policeman asks me how long I'm staying in Ingolstadt. Father quickly replies, saying only a few more days. That's news to me. Our visitor seems relieved.

The next two days pass quickly as Father prepares for the trip home to the Frankenstein home in Geneva. He hasn't seen his family in two years. I learn about his father Alphonse, brothers William and Ernst and his cousin Elizabeth. Victor's mother died from scarlet fever some time ago. Victor doesn't know when he'll return to the laboratory. I don't know if I'll ever see my birthplace again.

I watch Father rummaging through a closet. A two by four foot object covered by an old blanket leans against a wall.

"What is that, Father?"

Victor frowns. "It's nothing that concerns you."

"I want to see what it is."

"You may not like it, Sohn."

"Please."

Victor reluctantly carries it out of the closet, sets it down and removes the blanket. He sighs for good reason. I wail at the repulsive reflection staring back at me in the mirror. Victor looks away.

"Why?" I moan. "Why do I look like this, Father?"

"I'm sorry."

"You're sorry!" I reply angrily.

"Sohn, please listen to me for a moment," he says, raising a hand before I can interrupt him. "You are a magnificent specimen of a man. Nobody has your height, strength and brilliant mind and you have all three features. It's true you are not handsome by any means but you have everything else, don't you think?"

"I don't know, Father. Tell me why you gave me this face."

"I didn't give it any real consideration. It's what's inside the head that matters the most."

"No small wonder people hate my face so. It will be my downfall, won't it?"

"That is not true, Sohn. You shouldn't be overly concerned about your face or how others react to it. There will be people who are attracted to your intelligent intellect. I am not a romantic by nature but I think David Hume wrote 'Beauty in things exists merely in the mind which contemplates them.'"

"Is that supposed to make me feel better?"

A private coach takes us away the next evening. I'm too tall to fit inside with Victor. I sit up top next to Otto. He avoids looking at me. I'm both sad and excited about leaving my first home but look forward to this adventure.

I ask Otto a million questions about the team of horses and everything we see on the trip. I want to take a turn driving. Otto says maybe tomorrow.

In the morning I see distant snowcapped mountains and tell Otto they're breathtaking.

"What, you've never seen them mountains? Where you been, Sohn, if you don't mind my asking?"

"I can't remember much of anything."

"Maybe you lost your memory?"

"Maybe, I don't remember."

Otto looks at me doubtingly. "Perhaps you banged your head hard. Makes you forget stuff."

I don't pursue the subject anymore. *I'll ask Father what he knows about losing a memory though I know it has nothing to do with me. What a beautiful world!*

The coach passes hundreds of people on the road. Everybody casts unfriendly and terrified looks at me. Some cross themselves to ward off evil spirits. I want to hide somewhere safe.

Otto glances at me. "Forget about those peasants. They don't know better."

"Thanks." I can't believe Otto tried to comfort me. He is a real friend.

We arrive at the Frankenstein villa on the outskirts of Geneva. The city is situated on the shore of Lake Geneva. Both the Alps and Jura Mountains tower majestically in the distance. There are ice caves up there.

I stand nervously as Victor is welcomed home by his father, brothers and Cousin Elizabeth. Victor introduces me as his "philosophical friend."

The library is my favorite room in the stately house. The tall walls of the spacious room are arrayed with thousands of leather bound books.

Time flies by as I spend most of my time pouring through them. Victor sees no harm in the reading Shakespeare, Homer, Swift, Ovid and Dante. I learn much about the ways of the world and man's imperfections. I begin to believe there are some people who are more monstrous than me.

One day Victor and Elizabeth enter the library together. Victor watches me remove a book from an upper shelf.

"You've finished *Gulliver's Travels* already?"

"Yes, Victor. It was quite illuminating."

Victor's frowns at me. Was it because I didn't call him Father?

"It is fiction, you know," Elizabeth comments.

"I know that. But there is much in the book that gives me a perspective on how people react to somebody much larger or smaller than themselves. I was quite disturbing while reading the book and thinking about peoples' reactions to me."

"That is rather severe, Sohn. What book have you selected next?" Victor asked.

"*Paradise Lost.*"

"Ah, Milton. I don't know if that is a wise selection."

"Why not?"

"Milton is more depressing than Defoe. Why not pick something lighter like Chaucer?"

I glance at the book in his hands and then study Victor's face. *What's in this book that he doesn't want me to read? What's he afraid of?* I put the book down on a nearby table and scan the bookcase for another book.

"What about Aeschylus? Should that be avoided, also?"

"He might like reading about Prometheus," Elizabeth suggests.

"Read what you want Sohn," Victor says wearily. "Please let me know if you have any questions about the contents. There is a lot of thought provoking material in these books that deserves discussion. That is why the books are here."

"I shall try to read them with an open mind and engage you in a lively discussion."

"I look forward to that," Victor replies without enthusiasm. "Some of these beautiful volumes are studied in schools of high learning and can only be appreciated by advanced students. So feel free to write down anything you either don't understand or disagree with."

I glance at Elizabeth. "I need to speak with you privately," I whisper to Victor.

Elizabeth curtsies, turns, and leaves the library. Victor steps closer to me and waits expectantly for me to speak.

"Victor, you are a great man to have created life. I need you to do something that should be relatively easy for you."

Victor's eyebrows arch perceptively. "What is it you want me to do?"

"I need you to alter my face so people don't tremble and turn away. I have seen more than a few give me the sign of the devil. I cannot tolerate much more without doing something we'll both regret."

"What would you do?"

"I've recently discovered the seed of a temper flickers within me. I need to control it."

Victor looks deeply into my eyes. "Do you want to tell me what happened to trigger it?"

"No, father. Altering my face will resolve the issue."

"Sohn, I wish I could make your face look better. I can't help you with that. I am very sorry."

"You can't or won't."

I feel my anger flare. I try to think happy thoughts but couldn't as my need to have a more amenable face is paramount. "Then I'll see a surgeon who will!"

"Sohn, please."

"Please? What does that mean exactly?"

"Perhaps you could wear a hood."

I'm too shocked by Victor's comment to reply. At that moment Elizabeth, who may have been eavesdropping, reappears.

"I may have a solution," she says.

She has my full attention. I watch and listen to Elizabeth approach. Her clothing rustles as she moves closer. I am unnerved by her perfume. It muddles my brain.

"Perhaps a bit of makeup could be applied," she says lightly, standing a few feet away.

"Makeup? What do you mean?"

"You really don't know?" she asks.

"Elizabeth, just tell Sohn what you can do for him."

Elizabeth nods. "There are powders that can change your complexion. It would add more color to your cheeks. There are creams, too that would further improve your face. You would need to apply them once a day."

I stare at her blankly, unable to know how to reply as I can't comprehend this makeup thing.

"All right. Thank you, Elizabeth," Victor says.

Elizabeth smiles at me. "When would you like the first treatment?"

I avert my eyes away from her intense gaze. It helps me think.

"Now, please."

"Fine. Let's go upstairs to my bedroom."

"Your bedroom?" I can't imagine entering her private space. I look at Victor for guidance.

Victor laughs. He places a hand on my arm. "It's all right, Sohn. I trust you both."

A short time later, I find myself seated in front of a mirror in Elizabeth's bedroom. The door to the hall is wide open. I've never been alone with a woman. It's scary, especially because she's so pretty. She moves so gracefully. I forget to breathe. My face turns crimson. Elizabeth laughs kindly. "It's all right. I won't harm you."

I close my eyes and tell myself to relax. It will be over soon. I think about the library. I can't wait to return to that favorite sanctuary. But a part of me treasures being so close to Elizabeth.

When Elizabeth clears her throat, my eyes dart open. I look at her adoringly.

"Look at the mirror," she commands.

I do. And see a face that isn't too unpleasant to behold. My cheeks have a little brown and pinkish flesh tone. I grin at myself. Then the mood is shattered.

Six year old William Frankenstein stands several feet away. He snickers.

"You look so pretty now," William taunts.

I look down. I feel my skin burn hot.

"That's enough, William," Elizabeth says. "It is rude to sneak around and talk like that. Say you're sorry to Sohn."

"I will not." The boy laughs and runs out of the bedroom.

"He's only a boy. It's to be expected I guess," she tells me.

I look at her and nod, but I cannot dismiss William's behavior. I hate being ridiculed. It's intolerable. I'm angry the little brat ruined a sweet happy moment. Elizabeth looks nervously at me. She must know how I feel. But I can't help it. She shivers.

"Are you all right?" I ask, trying to keep my anger at bay.

"Yes", she replies, crossing her arms over her breasts. "I'm just a little cold."

"Can I get you a blanket?"

"No thank you, Sohn. I bet Victor is looking forward to seeing what I've done for you. Why don't you go downstairs and find out?"

I look at her a moment, not understanding that she really is only trying to get me to leave the room as soon as possible.

"Very well. Thank you for the improvements. I hope Victor doesn't copy his little brother and find my face amusing. That would cause a rift in our relationship."

"Sohn, Victor's not like that."

"I will find out soon enough."

I rise from the chair and silently leave. Elizabeth silently follows me to the door and closes it. She leans against it as though her slight weight will prevent me from opening the door. I've somehow managed to make her want me out of the house.

Chapter 22

Sohn's dream about a better beginning of his life continued. He desperately wanted the dream to have a happy ending. But he couldn't control the direction his mind took. He tossed and turned as the dream edged closer to a nightmare.

"Look Victor, look what Elizabeth did," William exclaims as I walk toward them in the library.

Victor sees something in my grim expression he doesn't like. "That's enough William. Go and play outside. Maybe Ernst is around."

William grins as he runs past me and out of the room. For a second or two I am sorely tempted to grab the boy and slam him against a wall.

"I'm sorry about William. Is it because of him or Elizabeth you're out of sorts?"

"He taunted me."

"Children are like that, Sohn. You shouldn't let them upset you. Otherwise they'll consider it a game and play it over and over. You don't want that. I sure don't,"

Victor said pointedly. "Do you understand me, my friend?"

"No I don't."

"Anyway, I think Elizabeth did a fine job on your face."

"Do you?"

"Absolutely!" He extends his right arm as far as possible and pats my shoulder.

I dismiss William from my mind. He's only a child. I'll remember to tell him that the next time he treats me with disrespect.

I place Paradise Lost on the bookshelf. Perhaps father was right. I shouldn't have read that book.

I'm disturbed by Adam's fall from grace and his being tempted by Satan. In the book, Adam told Eve that as she was made from his flesh she would die if he died. I wonder if I would die if Victor died.

I should not think about something so terrible. Why does my mind do that? Am I cursed by Satan or loved by God? Which?

I lie on my bed on the floor. It is actually a carpet with window drapes over it to serve as a heavy sheet. There is no bed large enough to accommodate my humungous frame.

I thought about the lustful relationship of Adam and Eve and their evolving relationship with each other. Adam was a lucky man to have such a woman beside him during perilous times. Who is my Eve? Will I have one? Will she be born out of my limbs like Eve was from Adam? I must ask Victor about finding a woman for me. After all, he did urge me to discuss the book with him.

The next morning I join the Frankensteins at breakfast in the formal dining room. I am famished. I sit in a reinforced armchair. The chair I used the other day cracked and crashed to the floor. It was very embarrassing.

"Do you care to go for a ride this morning?" Victor asks me.

I like horses but have never ridden on one. I hope I won't break its back. I catch William eying me. I scowl at him, before turning my eyes on Victor.

"That would be good, Victor."

Suddenly Justine, the house servant, appears beside me with a platter of food.

"Thank you, Justine," I murmur.

Justine curtsies as I help myself to a heaping serving of warm, freshly baked rolls with steaming bratwurst and fried potato. As I fill my mouth with the delicious food, I think about falling off a horse. Why do I punish myself with such a disturbing thought? The food no longer looks that appetizing. I push the full plate away and look across the table.

William, Ernst, Victor and their father Alphonse seem fascinated by me. I wish they'd stop looking at me. It's getting annoying. Perhaps they'll stop if I eat. So I pull the plate back and force feed myself. I've temporarily forgotten my table manners. Victor had taught me how and when to use a knife, fork and spoon but now I don't care. Using my hands as utensils gives me a perverse pleasure.

Alphonse pretends not to notice when William and Ernst copy my rude behavior. They giggle. Then Alphonse clears his throat and glares at them. The boys promptly clean their hands with a linen cloth and obediently started using their utensils. I revert to doing so, too.

"How's the book?"

Spittle sprays from my full mouth as I reply "I finished it last night."

"You did?" Victor asked, seemingly astonished.

I stop chewing and sourly regard him. Does he doubt me?

"You are turning into quite the prolific reader."

"Which book?" Alphonse inquires, looking at Sohn and Victor with interest.

"Paradise Lost," I reply.

"That's a serious undertaking. What are your thoughts about the book, Sohn?" Alphonse asks me.

I scan the faces around the table. I have everybody's undivided attention. Then Elizabeth strides gracefully into the room. Alphonse stands politely, nodding at his sons. They stand, too. Elizabeth sits to Victor's right, and the Frankensteins sit down again.

"You don't need to stand every time I enter," she tells her adopted father.

"It's proper manners, Elizabeth. Please don't discourage it." He calls out 'Justine!'"

The young servant peeks her head from the adjoining kitchen, sees that Elizabeth has arrived, and brings out a light breakfast with steeped tea a few minutes later.

Alphonse turns again to me. "Please tell us about Paradise Lost, if you would. I'm curious to hear your thoughts."

I'm wondering if Elizabeth is Victor's Eve while I'm supposed to be providing my thoughts about the book. As I open my mouth to speak, William stands and addresses his father.

"May I be excused, Father?"

Alphonse give his consent. William fast walks from the room.

As soon as the ill-behaved child is gone, I finally begin. "The book illuminates the struggle between God and Son of God vs Satan. Both forces sought to control the destinies of Adam and Eve."

"Who was the right choice?"

"I haven't made up my mind about that."

Elizabeth covers her mouth, shocked how anybody could be undecided on choosing between Heaven and Hell. She glances at Victor.

He has a hand pressed against his forehead.

"Are you an atheist or an agnostic?" Alphonse asked.

My vocabulary is about five thousand words at that time. I somehow know that eventually I'll master more than twenty thousand words in three languages. I rack my memory for the meanings of "atheist" and "agnostic" but cannot define either of them. I look at Alphonse and shrug.

"I do not know the answer, Herr Frankenstein. I am not a religious man in any shape or form, though some think I am Satanic." I pause for a reaction from the master of the house.

"Is that true? You believe in Satan?"

"No I do not but ignorant people have given me the evil sign from afar. They assume because I look like a

extended visit at a monastery. Some monasteries are known for producing scholars and even print books."

Victor nods wholeheartedly. "The clerics don't care what one looks like."

"Really, Father?" I ask Victor without thinking.

"Why do you call Victor 'father'"? Alphonse asks sharply. "He is much younger than you."

"Sohn's just practicing for when he's in a monastery. Right, Sohn?"

Frankenstein regards Victor and me suspiciously. Victor taught me that speaking the truth is important. Getting caught in a lie can get one in serious trouble. Why does he now want me to fib? Does he want his judgmental father to have a lower opinion of me than he does already?

"I'm sorry if I offended you," I tell Alphonse. "Tell me, could a godless man be welcomed in a house of God?"

"You don't believe in God?" he exclaims harshly.

"Oh no!" I hear Victor whisper.

I forge on with my self-incrimination. "I'm searching for answers. I must hear what the holy men have to say before I can know what I believe in."

"Then you must leave at once," Alphonse stands. "I mean it."

"Father, what's the urgency?" Victor asks wide eyed, rising to his feet.

"I do not want a heathen in my home, especially around my children."

"You've put up with my beliefs," Victor cries.

"You ought to have exercised better judgment, Victor, than bring this man here. Be gone by the end of the day," Frankenstein orders me. "You may return here only if you can provide written proof of being a Christian. A baptism certificate will do." He bows and storms out of the dining room.

I can't believe my misfortune as I stare at the empty space Frankenstein just passed through. I can't move. I feel a pressure in my head and can't think what to do next.

Goodbye, Victor. Goodbye, cruel world.

Then I black out.

Sohn awakened then from his dream, too depressed to open his eyes. Being spurned by Victor's father in the dream weighed heavily on him. He forced his giant's body into a sitting position. As depression consumed him, he collapsed on the bed again.

I've been spurned now by Victor and his father. The whole family hates me both in my dreams and the real world.

He slammed a fist down against his hard stomach. It hurt. But he did it again, and again, thinking that he deserved to punish himself. He'd be sore, and tattooed with bruises for days to come. But that was as it should be.

Victor, why did you create me? Why did you abandon me, father?

He lay catatonically and shut down his mind. There was only greyness, then black.

Chapter 23

When at last his eyes opened, Sohn was momentarily disoriented. He was surrounded by total darkness.

Where am I? When am I?

He felt the bed and instantly knew he was back in 21st Century Maine or Vacationland as depicted on the bottom of license plates.

His eyes adjusted to the dimness. He got up and nervously walked to the front window facing the driveway and a small parking area. He half expected to see the house bathed in bright light from a fleet of police vehicles. Sohn was relieved to stand in gloominess and see no vehicle other than the pickup.

Was it safe to remain in the house? Were the cops really onto him or was it just paranoia setting in? He sensed no immediate danger so perhaps staying through the night was alright. Not knowing how much the police knew or suspected about him was extremely frustrating.

It made keeping a step or more ahead of them difficult at best.

Was it safe to go for a drive and if so, in what direction?

He spent the rest of the night loading the pickup truck with the assorted necessities to take with him to his still unknown destination. Then, as the sky was beginning to brighten from black to gray, he got behind the steering wheel and turned over the ignition. Sohn did not look back at his home as he drove away.

Detective Pounds awakened with a splitting headache. For some reason, known only to his subconscious mind, he couldn't go back to sleep. So he got out of bed and walked into his home office. There was a bookcase with several hundred books standing upright.

His eyes and fingers scanned over various titles until he stopped on an old leather bound book titled *The Journal of Josiah Pounds*. Josiah was his great, great, great grandfather and a legendary figure in the old New England family.

Pounds was never permitted to personally leaf through the delicate old tome until he inherited it from his grandfather. He fondly remembered sitting in front of the fireplace watching the logs burn and sparks fly up the flue, listening to the old man read from the diary.

Now the book drew his attention. He carefully pulled the antique book from the shelf and sat down at his desk to read it. Pounds slowly and carefully flipped through the pages as he didn't want to loosen the binding. The minutes fell away rapidly as he read about his ancestor's maritime career culminating with the *Navigator*'s fateful voyage to The Northwest Passage.

He knew the story about the ship getting stuck in the ice and the harrowing trek southwest on foot to stave off death from the elements and starvation. But he had somehow forgotten about the giant who saved their lives from the wolf pack and helped keep them alive with hunting forays.

Did grandfather leave out that part so I wouldn't get scared? Or did I block it out?

Pounds yawned. The book was fascinating but he couldn't keep his eyes open. He needed to be fresh in the morning and hoped to get close to resolving the Islesboro murder case.

The detective moved the ribbon page marker and cautiously put the book back in its position on the bookcase. He returned to the bedroom and fell asleep.

His mind, apparently disturbed, awakened him a few minutes later. The giant! Was it coincidental both he and Josiah had a giant to deal with?

The man Josiah befriended was described as lethal but loyal. He killed the wolves single-handedly and was suspected of killing a crew member or two. But Josiah was eternally indebted to the stranger with the German accent named Sohn der Schrenken. They had bonded quickly despite the German's horrific face. Their long discussions about books, philosophy and survival kept them occupied during the arduous journey south through Canada.

The two men shared lodging in Toronto for several months where the crew recovered from the harrowing ordeal. Josiah recognized the challenges of his new friend having to cope with unfriendly glances from the citizens. He tried to comfort Sohn, telling him it was their shared problem. But the constant scrutiny was too much. Sohn told the sea captain that a move to the wilderness was necessary to keep him out of harm's way. Josiah understood. Sohn needed isolation to spare lives. Pounds got out of bed again. He had to look at the leather-bound volume for illustrations. Sure enough, there was one of the German hulk.

What a nightmare!

Dawn was an hour away.

The ferry worker's murderer was not justifiable homicide as he originally thought
Pounds had the suspect's description. It sounded eerily similar to the man who saved his forefather but that could only be a coincidence.

Nobody lives that long!

Captain Radley walked into his office in downtown Rockland followed by Sergeant Dredge, holding a sheet of paper.

"What do you have?" the captain asked as he sat behind his desk.

"I thought you should know that one of our residents may be a suspect in a homicide over on Islesboro."

"I heard about that. Who is the alleged perp?"

"That scary looking giant dude who lives on the edge of Rockport. His name is Sohn . . . ."

"Schrenk," Radley said.

Dredge look at the police captain with surprise. "Don't look like that. I should know something about the citizens in our jurisdiction." He stood.

"Let's get him."

"But the Staties said locals will be used as support only. It's their case, sir."

Radley looked sharply at his subordinate. "Do they know where he lives?"

"No, sir. I wanted to tell you first."

"Good. Keep it that way. I'll make the arrest then let Augusta know after the fact. Understand, sergeant?"

"Yes, sir. They won't like it, you know."

"I don't give a rat's ass! Let's go. I want three squad cars now!"

Sohn stopped the pickup on an unused logging road a mile from the house. He purposefully and wisely parked under a heavy canopy of trees in case a police helicopter happened to fly overhead in search of him. He walked through the forest toward his home carrying water and a few sandwiches. His mind was active.

Am I an idiot to be doing this? I should be back in the truck heading north or west out of the area. But I need to see who I'm up against.

When the house came in view, Sohn stood within the shadows of the great trees.

The Rockland PD cars' sirens and flashing lights showcased the highway until they were within a mile of their destination. Radley didn't want to announce their approach to the target. He didn't exactly know what to expect and decided vigilance and caution was a prudent combination.

Radley stepped out of the car. He was too restless to wait for the State Police. He needed to check out the house for any sign of Sohn Schrenk. If Trent didn't like it, tough luck! He didn't get to be chief of police by sitting on his ass. No, sir!

He carried an assault rifle. The safety was still on. Radley went down a small incline and then stepped into the woods. He clicked the safety off just in case. It took a minute for his eyes to adjust to the dimmer light created by nature's sunscreen. His right boot stumbled over a root. He fought to stay on his feet as he lurched a few feet. When concentrating on his legs, a finger inadvertently pressed down on the trigger.

There was a loud blast which ricocheted through the woods.

He stopped. *There goes the element of surprise!*

Sohn turned toward the sound of the gunshot. It was close. Perhaps near the road.

He moved to his right, staying in the tree screen, veering closer to where he thought the blast occurred.

The cops quickly climbed out of the vehicles after the gunshot. They ran, bodies bent to make themselves smaller targets. They ran right up to where their chief stood.

"What happened? You okay, captain?"

"Yeah, I'm fine. Thought I saw something."

They looked around but saw only trees.

"Which direction, sir?"

"Tough to tell with all these damn trees. Well, men, our cover's blown. No point waiting for the Staties. Spread out. We'll have to take him down ourselves."

They fanned out and started moving slowly toward the house, still invisible several hundred yards from them.

Sohn continued moving slowly from tree to tree, his eyes and ears acutely sensitive to any movement or sound.

The distance gradually lessened between the cops and him.

"Time to call in for an update," Pounds said as the cars sped east on Route 17.

"This is Detective Pounds. Patch me through to Captain Radley."

Radley's phone rang.

Damn, I should have remembered to put it on vibrate. That damned Pounds!

His men clearly heard it and who knows who else did, too. He yanked it out of his pants pocket and glared at the phone.

He spoke lowly and urgently. "This better be important."

"Captain, what's going on? ."

"There was a shot. We have no choice now."

"Schrenk shot at you?"

"Not exactly. I can't go into it. He's likely onto us now. We couldn't wait any longer," Radley whispered loudly.

"I'm a few miles out. Hold your positions." He hung up on Radley.

"Bastard!"

He held his hand up. His cops stood motionless, alternating their eyes from Radley to the woods around them. Now what!

Sohn heard the phone ring. He stopped moving, trying to hear a voice. *Should I move closer and increase the risk of a confrontation or run away?* Sohn considered his options quickly. *I'm sick of running away.*

He heard a man speak but couldn't discern his words. He was too far away. He crept closer silently, stopping and starting every few feet, careful not to step on a branch that would snap.

Why am I still moving closer?

Do I want to be captured?

Is that it?

Have I become a fatalist after all these years?

Is this the end of the line?

He continued his stealthy approach toward the Rockland policemen.

Chapter 24

The two Maine State Police cars parked behind the Rockland vehicles on the edge of the two lane highway. Pounds and his backup got out and looked around for Radley and his men. Radley appeared by the tree line and stood there impatiently. Pounds stepped over and geared up to confront the irritated captain.

"Thanks for waiting, captain. I appreciate it."

"I have my men spread out in a line in there," Radley said sharply, pointing briefly at the forest. "Do you have someone posted near the end of the driveway in case he makes a break for it?"

"No I don't," Radley growled. "Maybe you can have your guys cover the driveway while mine go in with you."

"No thanks, captain. I suggest two of your men be ordered over there right away, just in case." He waved over his own contingent. "After you," he told Radley. As they entered the tree line, Pounds took off his sunglasses.

His men followed his example. They strode diligently on the forest floor toward Radley's waiting men.

Sohn sat on a small moss-covered boulder on a line he anticipated the police would take. He finally decided to allow himself to be apprehended peacefully. It had been a difficult choice. He knew it would be one of the most important decisions of his life.

He listened attentively for footsteps. He didn't have to wait very long.

Radley recognized Sohn from his driver's license. *There he is, larger than life. What does he think is so funny?*

Sohn watched impassively. The approaching cops held their assault rifles aimed at his heart.

Pounds couldn't believe his eyes. The man waiting for them looked identical to the man who saved his ancestor's life.

He was too astonished to speak. His mind raced. *Can't be him! Impossible! Right?*

Pounds called out to the lawmen, "Halt now." He lowered his gun and stepped forward. Radley walked with him, but kept his target scoped. Ponds stopped and told him, "You can lower that. There're enough barrels on him to blow him to kingdom come."

Radley reluctantly complied. They stepped closer, stopping a few feet away from Sohn.

They sized each other up.

Sohn knew if he moved some trigger happy cop would shoot him. So he sat unmoving.

"You're Sohn Schrenk?" Pounds asked.

"Yes. And you?"

"Detective John Pounds of Maine State Police."

"Pounds?" Sohn repeated. "I once knew somebody by that name."

Radley didn't take to being excluded so he introduced himself. Sohn scarcely acknowledged him. That aggravated the police captain.

"What was his first name?" Pound inquired.

Sohn's grin widened. "Josiah," he replied evenly, looking intensely at the young detective.

Pounds swallowed. He nodded, too amazed to speak. He felt a strange pressure in his head.

Radley looked questioningly at both men. Was he missing something? Apparently. "What?"

"It's nothing. Just some genealogy," Pounds replied evasively. It was imperative that nobody other than Schrenk know about their new incredible connection. He knew Radley would hold it against him

and probably have him thrown off the case. If brought to
trial the judge would likely excuse him.

Detective Pounds badly wanted some time alone
with Josiah's friend. He couldn't think straight from the
shock of contemplating the age of the eight-foot tall
German immigrant. Somehow, he forced his mind back to
the situation at hand. But his perspective had changed. He
was less interested now in arresting the old man than in
hanging out with him.

Sohn was astounded to be in the presence of his
old friend's descendent. He saw recognition in the
detective's eyes and considered himself very fortunate
that they shared a common bond. Evidently young
Pounds esteemed his remarkable ancestor and knew
something about him, too.

*It must be that journal that my old friend
published. Yes, there's a drawing of me in that book. Of
course!*

"Tell me what happened on the Islesboro beach
last Friday evening," Pounds said.

"The ferryman came to the beach looking for
me."

"He was looking for you?" Radley echoed
sarcastically.

"That's right. He didn't like the sight of me. He
kept the evil eye on me during the ferry ride over from

Lincolnville. I tried to ignore him but he wouldn't leave me alone. I went to the beach that evening to enjoy the tranquility of the lovely setting. I dug up some clams and mussels and had just finished my meal by the campfire when he showed up."

"Why did you go to Islesboro?" Radley inquired.

"I had someone to see there."

"Who?" Radley asked quickly. He felt some control now as Pounds seemed preoccupied.

"That's my business," Sohn replied, looking sharply at his interrogator. He tried to look even scarier than usual.

"I asked you a question, Mr. Schrenk."

Pounds looked at Radley. "I'll ask the questions, Captain Radley, if you don't mind."

Radley glared at Pounds.

"Tell us what happened when Herston arrived at the beach."

Sohn described in detail what happened, leaving nothing out. He had nothing to hide in his self-defense. Pounds believed him; even Radley seemed to go along with the story.

The captain knew a lie when he heard it but he couldn't detect any fabrication from the big man.

When Sohn finished, Pounds looked at the Rockland police officer. He needed his fellow lawman to feel needed. "What do you think?"

"I think that scumbag Herston got more than he bargained for. It sounds like there was no choice. He would have shot you if you hadn't stabbed him in the hand. You must be a hell of a knife thrower."

"I've had time to practice."

Radley's eyebrows arched.

"I live alone. I have no television so I find other things to do to take up time," Sohn explained.

"Such as knife throwing," Pounds elaborated.

Sohn shrugged. "I much prefer reading a good book."

"Why did you bury Herston? You should have gone straight to the Islesboro constable."

"I didn't think anybody there would believe me. I was a stranger on Herston's island. Getting back to the mainland seemed the best course of action at the time."

Pounds and Radley stared narrowly at their suspect, each lawman trying to discern Sohn's innocence, guilt and flight risk.

"You didn't think Herston would ever be located, did you?" Radley asked, leaning in.

"No."

Sohn looked at Pounds. "How did you find him?"

Pounds opened his mouth to speak but was quickly stopped by Radley.

"Don't tell him, detective."

Pounds glanced at Radley and nodded. He knew Radley was correct. Providing information about police methods to a suspected felon was improper.

.

"I'll take it from here, Captain Radley. Thank you for your assistance. It'll be in my report.

"Excuse me?"

"My men and I will handle it now," Pounds said tersely.

"You want us to leave?"

"That's right. Do you have a problem, captain?"

"It's your decision."

Pounds regarded Radley stonily. "That's right, it is."

"You'll have your hands full. This man should not be underestimated."

"Don't worry. He'll be in good hands."

Radley gave Sohn a hard look.

Sohn looked away, pretending he was unnerved. He hoped the cop didn't see his bemusement.

Oh, how I'd love to give him my death stare. He'd probably lose his bowels.

When he dared look again, Radley was on his way back to the highway with his team. Pound's small contingent moved up closer, each man warily watching Sohn with guns at the ready.

"So, it's down to you and me. Is that agreeable with you?" Pounds asked.

Sohn smiled. "Very much so. Should I call you John or Detective Pounds?"

"John is fine. I assume you called my great, great grandfather Josiah instead of Captain Pounds."

"Absolutely, John. He was a great friend. I've had none since Josiah died. He was loyal and kind from when we met."

"Well, you did save his life and his crew, too."

"You read his journal," Sohn said with a smile.

"Coincidentally. I did so early this morning, in fact. I read about you. Then there was that amazing sketch. It made a huge difference when I recognized you today. If it wasn't for that journal you'd be in handcuffs now. Then again, perhaps there isn't a pair that would fit around your wrists."

Sohn laughed. He couldn't believe the chain of events of the past several days brought him an unexpected introduction with Josiah's descendant. Perhaps it was lifesaving in reverse. He looked closely at the detective, searching for any resemblance with his old friend. He couldn't detect any, but then again he hadn't seen Josiah in about two hundred years.

"Do you want to walk back to my house? It's only a few hundred yards from here. We wouldn't have to deal with your men staring at us, wondering why we're getting along so well."

Pounds looked over his shoulder.

"By all means. Do you mind if I have them park in the driveway?"

"That's fine."

Pounds walked back to his team and gave instructions. The men complied despite their better judgment. At least one of them should have accompanied Pounds and Schrenk to the house in case the giant misbehaved. Pounds wouldn't have a chance against such a monstrous looking behemoth. But Pounds refused the offer.

Sohn and Pounds talked amiably as they trod through the woods to the house. They arrived at the front door as the police cars pulled into the driveway. The two men stopped and watch the state policemen park their cars a few yards away. Pounds nodded.

"Where's your car?" Pounds asked.

"It's hidden nearby."

Pounds frowned.

Sohn held the door open. Pounds stepped inside followed by his host.

Pounds quickly surveyed the interior, noting how sparse it seemed except for one bedroom wall. He examined the bookcase and was impressed by the hundreds of classics on the shelves.

"You enjoy books, too?" Sohn inquired.

"Not like you but I'm growing into it," Pounds replied, looking up at Sohn.

"I see you have several German books. "

"It's my native language."

"That's where you came from before meeting Josiah."

"Yes."

"It must have been a hell of a journey."

"Yes, that's an apt description," Sohn said, momentarily thinking of Victor's pursuit of him northward from Europe into the Arctic.

Pounds glanced at the book titles a little more before turning back to Sohn. "Do you something with caffeine to drink? I didn't get much sleep."

"Follow me."

They walked to the kitchen.

"John, I'll brew some coffee. Why don't you sit on the rocking chair in the living room? I'll be in shortly."

"Thanks."

Pounds sat in the oversized rocking chair. His feet barely reached the floor making it a challenge to use his feet to push off. *This must be a perfect size for him. I didn't know they come this large.*

When Sohn returned, Pounds was fast asleep. The chair still rocked gently. Sohn put a mug down on a table beside the chair. He wanted to be sure the troopers weren't about to break into the house. He peeked out a window. They stood by the vehicles, frowning back at him.

Sohn opened the door and walked outside. "Coffee, anyone?"

He took four orders and returned to the kitchen. A few minutes later everybody was cheerfully getting their caffeine fix and feeling a bit more comfortable around the giant.

Chapter 25

"Does anybody else know you are centuries old?"

Do I tell him about Mary?

"There is one other. She's on Islesboro.

"Are her initials MG?" Pounds asked.

Sohn nodded. He was surprised at first before recalling the circumstances of Mary's fainting on the beach.

"She's a special person," Sohn admitted. He wasn't sure it was a careful or careless remark.

Either way, Pounds learned there was something between the unlikely pair. "Do you wish to quantify that?"

Sohn sipped the still warm coffee and peered into the liquid. He willed Mary's face to the surface. He saw her for an instant.

Pounds looked at him, wondering what he was missing. He glanced at his watch. He wanted to tell his team to return back to Augusta in one car and leave the second car in the driveway for him. The detective had a

353

multitude of questions to ask Sohn but at the same time he was accountable for his own time and that of the men stationed outside. He didn't want to waste their day.

"Sohn, do you mind if I send my team back to headquarters. I'd really like to spend some time catching up with you."

"That's fine. Does that mean I don't have to worry about being arrested?

"You should be okay. I'll require a sworn statement. You'll need to come in to headquarters for that. My report will be favorable, showing it was self-defense. The only problem I foresee involves what you did afterward. Trying to cover it up, I mean, burying the man was not right."

"Will there be a trial?" Sohn asked uneasily.

"I'll speak to my sergeant and the district attorney."

"A trial could go very badly. Just look at me, John. I don't look like an innocent, decent man, do I?"

He put the coffee on the table and covered his terrible face with his huge pale hands. *I should have made a run for it while I could.*

Pounds felt a pang of sympathy as he saw the torment that consumed Sohn. "I'll do everything possible to get the matter settled. But you'll have to write and sign your statement at troop headquarters and possibly go with me to the DA. It shouldn't be too bad, Sohn."

Sohn put his hands down and looked over at Pounds. He saw a man he could trust and was thankful for that.

Pounds stood up and went outside to speak to the troopers. Sohn heard an engine start up as the detective returned.

"What do you want to know?" Sohn asked.

"Everything," John replied, grinning.

Not likely.

Turning serious, John said, "Josiah didn't say much about your past, I mean about your life before he met you. The big question, though, is how it is possible you have lived so long?"

"I prefer not to talk about my earlier life. Let's just say it was a bitter time better left forgotten. I can't explain why I'm still alive. I can't say if it is a curse or a blessing."

"Sohn, you haven't answered either question."

"I know."

"You don't like discussing yourself, do you?"

"No. It makes me uncomfortable. I am alone here much of the time."

"I can understand that. Look, we just met, and I'm asking away just like our friend Mary."

355

Sohn arched his eyebrows.

"She's a journalist, you know."

Sohn nodded.

"It's amazing is what it is! You've lived to see so much change in the world. I mean, there was no electricity when you were born, no cars, no television no technology, period. Living conditions must be much better now than your early years. Right?"

"Not much has really changed for me. I keep it simple. You won't find a television or a computer in my house. I do carry a cell phone with internet access. I'll give you that. I drive an old black pickup that's in tip top condition. Of course there's electricity. I'd be a fool not to be on the grid and I'm no fool, John."

"It seems you know how to use a knife and move a boulder."

Sohn looked intently at the detective. "And I know that you are a good detective. So where does all this knowing put us, John?"

"I don't know. But I suppose it is a start."

"To what?"

"A friendship."

It was Sohn's turn to grin. He had made two friends in as many days for the first time in his life.

Ironically they had met each other due to his latest killing. Would it be the last?]

John held out his partially full coffee cup. "To friendship."

Sohn reciprocated. "Friendship!"

Sohn clicked John's cup too enthusiastically and knocked it out of Pounds' hand and to the floor. Sohn felt suddenly depressed and Pounds somewhat surprised.

"I am very sorry," Sohn said, staring at the small puddle of coffee on the hardwood floor.

"Don't be, Sohn." Pounds stood and walked into the kitchen. Sohn watched him return with paper towels.

"I'll do it, John," Sohn said, forcing himself to move. Despair froze him solid sometimes. He reached for the paper towel and Pounds handed it to him and stood watching him dry the floor.

Mary went with her parents to the ferry landing. They were returning to New York. She sat in the crowded back seat next to suitcases and bags.

"If you need a ride, call someone," her mother urged. She didn't approve of Mary's plan to walk three miles back to the house a day after being hospitalized.

"I'll be fine, Mother."

"We'll be happy to stay another day to be with you will you recover from that episode."

"Mother, we've already discuss this. Case closed."
Mary's mother nodded. "Verna will be at the house
periodically. She can do whatever you need done," she
said

"She has chores to do before the house is closed
for the winter," her father added.

"I understand, Dad. It'll be nice having her in the
house. I'll be in the office Monday morning."

"On Labor Day?"

"Tuesday then."

The car was parked behind twenty vehicles
waiting to board the ferry. There was space for a few cars
after theirs.

Mary noticed the Quicksilver approach the dock.
*Perhaps I'll see if I can get a ride on the boat instead of
hiking back to the house.* This was as good a time as ever
to say her farewells.

"Okay, Mom and Dad. It's that time. I'm going to
ask Samuel Woodsby about catching a ride back on the
Quicksilver."

She hopped out of the car and stepped over to the
open window by her father. She reached in and kissed
him on the cheek.

"Have a safe trip, Dad."

"Thanks, Mary. You, too."

Mary then exchanged kisses with her mother, whose eyes moistened. She always sobbed whenever parting for days or longer with her only child.

"Love you, "Mary said before walking toward the motor boat.

Both parents somberly watched Mary walk alone into the distance.

The Quicksilver sliced through the small waves. Captain Woodsby stood by the helm holding the wheel firmly with both callused hands. The boat's powerful engine vibrated slightly through the wheel, enabling the skipper to get a sense of the boat's power.

Mary stood in the stern gazing at the breathtaking view. She tried to memorize the scene around her. In the weeks or months ahead, when finding herself staring at rats creeping between the tracks at a subway station, she'd retrieve this fresh memory.

Mary decided to socialize a bit with Woodsby and walked into the wheelhouse. They exchanged pleasant smiles.

"Captain, do you ever tire of the beauty of this place?"

"Never! I appreciate it every month of the year. Whenever the fog clears, I renew my enjoyment of the bay. How about you?"

"I agree with you. I'll miss it."

"You leaving us again?"

"I'm afraid so. I have a job to go back to in New York City."

"Why not get one up here? There's jobs around, you know."

"Perhaps. I haven't thought about it. But my focus is on what's happening to the city."

"What do you mean?"

"Well, you know the ocean is rising."

"And the bay, too."

"I suppose you're right, captain. Of course! Anyway, I write about how the city is dealing with the situation and what measures the mayor, city council and the business community should take to prevent calamity. They need to work together you know, to get maximum results."

"I guess so. Pretty much the entire city is only a few feet above sea level, right?"

"Yes, it is. So a rise in the ocean an inch a year from the melting ice in the Arctic and Antarctic will have a tremendous impact. All you need are hurricane winds to drive more and more salt water into the subways and low-level streets to make those areas impassable. Eventually it'll become too expensive to keep replacing utilities and whole sections of city blocks may have to be abandoned to the creeping sea."

"That sounds too morbid for my taste. I suppose you'll say that the same thing will happen to Long Island and Florida." He looked at her expectantly.

She decided to drop the subject. It could get depressing thinking about the future. Instead she watched the sparkling water skim by the white hull of the sleek boat. The Godwin's dock was only minutes away. Without thinking, she looked right toward Seven Hundred Acre Island and thought of her day there with Perce and the unsettling appearance of their intruder.

Woodsby had been scanning the water ahead for any obstructions. He saw her troubled expression as she looked at the island.

"You ever go over there, Mary?"

"I was there only a couple of days ago."

"Me too."

"You were?"

Woodsby nodded. "It was one of my more memorable experiences since I started the sea taxi."

"How so?" Mary tried to ask casually.

"I shouldn't talk about it really. It's poor taste, like violating a doctor patient confidentiality, I suppose."

"I promise not to tell anybody, captain."

Woodsby looked at the water deep in thought then back at Mary.

"He was very unusual in certain respects. By far the tallest man I've ever seen. Are you okay?"

Mary grimaced. Her heart started racing again. She had to sit down in a nearby chair.

The captain powered down the engine and put the boat in neutral so he could attend to his passenger. He stepped over to her and squatted in front of Mary. Her face was a little blotchy.

"How are you feeling?"

Mary looked at Woodsby and smiled. She was just a bit unsettled, like something had shifted. She couldn't put a finger on it.

"I feel better, thank you. I feel silly to be like this."

"You shouldn't. What do you think it was? Seasickness?"

"I've never been seasick. No, it was something else. I can't really say what it was, Captain Woodsby."

He watched her carefully. There was a first aid kit on board but Woodsby didn't think it was needed. Was it the boat's motion? He shrugged and stood up. She would tell him if she wanted to. Otherwise it was not his concern as long as his passenger made it off the boat on her own two feet.

Mary sat wondering why she either saw Sohn every day or heard something about him. What did it mean? It was frightening in a way, considering what he looked like and that he had killed someone. The idea of being with him every day was overwhelming. Knowing he wanted to spend so much time with her was extremely unsettling.

The sooner I put some distance between us the better. Should I go to New York today?

Her thoughts were interrupted by Woodsby. "Are you ready?"

Mary looked at him questioningly.

"We're docked at your house."

Mary stood and saw he was right. *Where has the time gone?*

"So we have. Thank you."

She handed him the agreed fare.

"Mary, is there anything I can do since your parents have left?"

"No thanks. I think I'll be leaving today, after all."

"Then I wish you farewell and look forward to seeing you next summer."

They shook hands. Mary refused the captain's hand to help her off the boat. She turned and waved as the Quicksilver moved away from the float. Woodsby didn't acknowledge her gesture as he looked out on the water ahead, pondering Mary's disquieting behavior.

Chapter 26

Mary walked inside the house, closed the door, and stood listening. If her parents' housekeeper had heard the door, perhaps she would come see for herself who'd just entered the house. "Listen and learn" worked just as well as "look and learn" In the country. Mary heard approaching footsteps.

"Ah, you're home," Verna greeted her with a smile as she entered the front hall. But the smile faltered as Verna took in Mary's pale, dejected face. She strode over to the forlorn young woman and put a hand on her shoulder.

"Mary, what's wrong?"

I don't know where to start! But should I? If I tell Verna about Sohn, will I be sorry later? Will she rat on me and tell the whole island, even call my parents? Should I trust her?

The housekeeper waited patiently for Mary to make her decision. She hated to see her so defenseless.

"Verna, I just have to leave. Go back to the city. Summer's done." Mary barely looked at her. She needed to hold herself together and if she looked too long at the older woman she might cry or say too much.

Verna opened her arms wide. Mary accepted the invitation. They embraced in a hug that comforted them both.

"You sure, honey, you have to leave right away? I thought you were staying a couple more days."

Mary's head was better and her stress had abated. But she still wanted to leave that day. The last thing she wanted was to spend a night alone in the spacious house.

"I'm sorry, Verna, but I must leave today."

"Can I help you pack your things?"

"No."

Mary ran upstairs leaving the surprised, disappointed and perplexed Verna behind.

Upstairs, Mary retrieved three suitcases from her bedroom closet and set to work filling them. She felt bad about leaving Verna alone so suddenly. The woman wanted to help her.

Mary carried the full suitcases downstairs in two trips and left them by the front door. Then she went looking for Verna. They said their farewell in the kitchen.

"I have to warn you about somebody," Mary started. "There's a very tall man who may come here looking for me." If somebody knocks on the door, make sure you know who it is before opening it."

"Is it that awful looking man who was out in the driveway the other day?"

"You saw him? Of course you did."

"Why would he come back?"

"He likes me and asked me to spend time with him. I can't seem to avoid him. To be honest, that's why I'm leaving all of a sudden. I'm sorry, Verna."

"Should I call the constable's office?" Verna asked nervously.

"That's a good idea. Better yet, just don't let him see you. I doubt he'll come here anyway."

"I made you a sandwich," Verna said holding out a paper bag.

Mary smiled sweetly and took the bag. "You shouldn't have. I'll miss you."

They embraced.

"I'll miss you, too." Verna's eyes misted.

They separated.

"Don't be a stranger," Verna said.

"I won't. I'll call. We can Skype, if you remember how I taught you to do that."

Verna glanced at her watch. "We'll see about that. Anyway, you have a ferry to catch. It leaves in twenty minutes."

They hugged again quickly, then Mary gave her a kiss on the cheek and went to the front door. She carried two suitcases to her car and Verna carried the other.

Before Verna knew it, she was waving at Mary as her car disappeared from sight.

"That's incredible. It really is. I mean, talking to a living survivor of the Battle of Gettysburg is incredible. And you're still going strong."

"That I am, John. I cannot gauge how much longer I'll live but I can state categorically I have not slowed down mentally or physically. Do you think that is good news or bad news?"

"I would consider it good news for people who like you and perhaps bad news to the others."

"Then it is probably bad news to practically the entire human race!" Sohn exclaimed ruefully.

I can see that, Pounds thought. *He is somebody to avoid and fear unless you're his friend.*

"You think it's that bad?" Pounds asked carefully.

"I've been shunned by thousands. It is extremely depressing at times. It's no picnic to be feared and scorned by so many. John, how would you feel if you looked like me?" Sohn asked emotionally.

Pounds looked at Sohn sympathetically. What could he do or say to say the man feel better about himself? He had an idea.

"Sohn, don't take this the wrong way." He looked at Sohn expectantly.

"What is it?" Sohn asked reluctantly.

"Plastic surgery works wonders. It would change your face. You can tell the plastic surgeon how you want your face to look. Have you ever considered it?"

Sohn chuckled. "Plastic surgery, eh? Do you think I can be turned into a model and strut down a runway in the latest fashion?

John laughed nervously.

"It's something to consider, Sohn. It could make your life more pleasant. You'd still have your distinctive height. That's nothing to sneer at. More importantly, with a more pleasing face, people wouldn't turn away from you. In fact you'd have the opportunity to become a celebrity."

"But how do I explain my age? There would be too many probing questions. Do you understand, my friend?"

"Thanks for calling me your friend. I appreciate it. Anyway, I guess I overlooked the need to safeguard your age. But your life would be the ideal subject of books, movies and the like. You'd be wealthy."

"I don't care about wealth. I'm used to a simple life. You think being rich would be good?"

"I wouldn't mind it at all. But I like my job and am in no hurry to quit."

"That's good. I enjoy being something of a lumberjack and carpenter. You mentioned books would be written about me."

"That's right. Maybe you could write one. Or commission someone to write it with you, putting in only what you want."

"Perhaps," Sohn said, engrossed by the possibility.

Isn't Mary a journalist? Mary! What are you doing? What is wrong? Where are you going?

Sohn, agitated suddenly, stood.

Pounds was alarmed but remained seated, He didn't want to aggravate the giant.

"What is it?" he inquired cautiously. "She's leaving," Sohn replied unhappily.

"Who?"

"Mary Godwin. I must intercept her."

"Isn't that extreme?"

"Is that how a friend talks to another?" Sohn said, staring hotly at the state trooper.

"Yes, Sohn it is. Friends are honest with one another and say what is on their minds. I'm sorry if I offended you."

Sohn stood in place not knowing how to respond. He didn't want to alienate his friend but he needed to get to Mary, somehow. He was momentarily stumped how to accomplish both without harming or deserting his guest. Finally, his strong mind rewarded him with the perfect solution.

"John, would you accompany me?"

Pounds looked up at Sohn guardedly. Sohn reached out a large hand. As Pounds said a prayer to himself, he held out his hand and immediately was yanked up like a rag doll. Thankfully, his arm wasn't pulled out of its socket. He found himself standing a little unsteadily.

"You want me to go with you to see her now?"

"I do indeed."

"And then what?"

"We'll see."

"I won't permit you to cause her any harm, or worse," Pounds warned.

"I would never hurt dear Mary. I just need to talk to her. Let's go. Time is passing."

Mary was melancholy whenever leaving Islesboro at the end of the summer. From the ferry, she kept her eyes locked on the island. She wondered how her life would change over the next ten months before beholding Islesboro once again.

Whatever happens I'll always return to you. You are an essential part of me and will be until I die. You are my Shangri-La, sweet, sweet Islesboro.

Pounds agreed to drive his official state vehicle to save time. Sohn sat on the passenger side with the seat as back as far as it could go. Even then, it was a tight squeeze.

"How do you know she's leaving?" Pounds inquired, glancing at Sohn

"I have what you call a gift, an ability if you will, to sense danger and with Mary I am able to know where she is and can even rendezvous at a specific location."

John looked fleetingly at Sohn. "You're serious?"

Sohn turned to John. "Yes, I am. I know it sounds incredulous, but it's the truth."

"You meet up somewhere?"

372

fiend I am one. Looks can be deceiving." I glance at Victor, then look down at the table.

Alphonse looks closely at Victor. Victor avoids his scrutinizing gaze.

"I could identify, at least fleetingly, with each of the major characters in the book, even Eve."

Ernst snickers. His father, though surprised, too, reprimands his teenage son.

"How so?" Elizabeth asks bemusedly.

"Well, she, like myself was created." I hesitate to continue, not wanting to divulge my origins. I desperately want to gauge Victor's reaction. I barely have enough willpower not to look his way. I can hear his heart racing, a telltale sign he is concerned what I will say. .

"Aren't we all created?" Elizabeth asks.

I nod, wanting to change the subject away from this sensitive issue. "I relate to Eve's thirst for knowledge. I understand why she went off by herself, why she left Adam until she was ready to be with him as an equal."

Victor stares at me in disbelief. "Are you planning to emulate Eve? Go off by yourself?" Victor asks in a slightly shaking voice.

"Victor, the books have made me want to experience life to the fullest. I have much to see. There will be great libraries throughout Europe to explore. Perhaps concerts? I want to see Ludwig van Beethoven."

"I see."

"What? You disagree with me?"

"Yes I do. Think how people have treated you on the road here. The great cities are densely populated with thousands of people with similar attitudes as those who have already reacted to you so poorly."

"So I must stay here in this house like a hermit until I die? Is that it?"

"I don't know. I'll have to give it much thought."

I shake my head despondently. Does Victor only see disappointment and unhappiness in my future? He believes he is responsibility for my welfare. I'll be ready soon to go out on my own whether he wants me to or not. If I'm mistreated, then I'll act accordingly.

"We have been through much together these past months. I understand why you wish to travel. I was like that when I was young."

"When you were young?" his father says. "Victor, you are still a young man."

Victor shakes his head. "Time is slipping away."

Alphonse looks at me pensively. "Listen, Sohn, I have a suggestion for you." He pauses until all eyes are focused on the magistrate. "You should consider an

"Yes, it's a special place that she and I have. But I can find her anywhere."

"Huh. You're not going to tell me where it is, are you?"

"That's right, John. At least not until I know you longer. I've already shared more privileged information with you than I should have."

"You can trust me, at least with anything not of a criminal nature."

The Maine State Police car sped along until the junction with Route 90. The vehicle turned onto the county road and sped along the highway. A few miles later Sohn had Pounds pull onto the side of the road.

"Why here?" Pounds asked.

"This is where Mary first saw me. It seems as a good a place as any. She'll have to pass her on her way south."

"What if she stays on Route 1 all the way?"

"She won't."

"You sound pretty sure about that."

"I know she'll pass by here. Call it a gut feeling. You get those too, don't you?"

"Sure, Sohn. Everyone does."

"Does it generally pay off when it happens?"

"Most of the time. Sometimes I second-guess myself and it doesn't work out too well."

"You should listen to yourself," Sohn said knowingly.

"Good advice."

"You want me to stay in the car when she gets here?"

"No, you're welcome to join us."

Pounds smiled and nodded.

A few minutes passed. Then Sohn opened the door as he felt her presence. She was getting closer.

Mary felt a pit in her stomach as she drove southwest on Route 90. She tensed up as her car crested an incline, realizing the place where it all started would be seen in a few seconds. She took a breath and held it, seeing the State Trooper car less than a mile ahead

Mary exhaled as she rationalized why the car was there. *Must be waiting to ticket speeders!*

She slowed down to a few miles per hour. Her eyes widened when she saw Sohn step out of the passenger side. *Can't be! What's he doing with the police? Was he arrested?*

Sohn stood facing down Mary's car. He tried not to look too severe. He was very concerned about Mary's effort to leave Maine without saying farewell to him.

Seeing no alternative, Mary slowed until she stopped on the shoulder behind the cruiser. She sat behind the wheel, unwilling and unable to move. She recognized Detective Pounds as he got out of the police car and stood beside Sohn watching her curiously.

Sohn was disappointed with Mary's reluctance to get out of the car and be with him. *What did I expect? Did I think she'd run over and embrace me?*

He shook his head miserably and tore his sad eyes away from hers. His shoulders sagged. He started to turn back to the police car.

"Sohn, wait a minute. I'm going to talk to her," Pounds offered after seeing the effect Mary had on Sohn.

Sohn stopped and watched as Pounds stepped over to Mary's car.

Mary sighed, lowered the window. Pounds squatted beside the window so they were level.

"Nice to see you again Mary."

"Detective."

"What is your destination?"

"New York City." She stole a peek at Sohn. The giant stood forlornly, his yellow eyes switching from the ground to her.

"I think Sohn here was hoping you would have a few words before departing."

"I don't know if I'm up to it, Detective Pounds."

"That's up to you."

"I know. Did Sohn force you to pull me over here?"

"I saw no harm in it, Miss Godwin."

Mary stared intently at the steering wheel. She made a concentrated effort not to look at Sohn because, if she did, her resistance would falter. She turned to Pounds. "I'll make this quick, then I have to get back on the road. I have a long drive down to New York City. I'm curious. Have you wrapped up your murder investigation?"

Sohn looked sharply at Mary, shocked she asked the question. Was she really just curious or was there an ulterior motive?

Pounds glanced furtively at Sohn before looking at Mary again with a raised eyebrow.

"I really shouldn't say anything, ongoing police investigation and all. You should know, being an investigative reporter."

Mary nodded. "I know. Thanks for reminding me, detective. If you can move out of the way now, I'd appreciate it."

Pounds glanced up the highway to make sure it was safe. Then he stepped back. Mary nodded again at Pounds and without thinking glanced at Sohn. He gazed imploringly at her, looking deeply hurt. Mary sighed as she stepped on the accelerator, driving southward.

She dared not look in the rearview mirror, knowing full well Sohn would be watching. She did not want to see the expression on his face.

It was just as well that Mary had kept her eyes on the road ahead. Sohn looked up at the sky and screamed.

Pounds jumped, hand on the trigger as he stared up at the frightening sight. He took a few careful steps back, witnessing Sohn's reversion to the monster. The detective's mind raced. He visualized Sohn killing the wolf pack in the 1790s and killing Herston much more recently. Self-defense or not, the detective recognized a killing machine when he saw one.

The primal scream purged Sohn's emotional pain and distress. He stood, chest heaving, feeling good about himself. He smiled benevolently down at Pounds. He was momentarily confused about the fear on the detective's face and the drawn pistol aimed at Sohn's heart.

"Sorry, John."

Pounds stood frozen, unsure if it was safe to holster the firearm.

"Perhaps I'll walk back to the house," Sohn said. "Or better yet, I'll run. It'll do me good."

Pounds imperceptibly nodded his head and then watched Sohn speed away at thirty miles an hour. The detective then turned away. He had refrained from telling Sohn that Herston's attempt on his life was categorized as a hate crime driven by his hatred of Sohn's fearsome face and gargantuan size. That determination was based on the tapes Pounds had heard from Herston's crew mates. The Statie expected that finding could determine if Sohn would remain a free man or not.

Chapter 27

Sohn considered his predicament while he sprinted at 30 mph toward his house.

I've probably lost John Pounds now as a potential friend and ally. That embarrassing display of emotion alienated him. I'll be arrested and hauled into the state police headquarters. They'll try to coerce me into a confession even though it was self-defense. It's because of Victor that I look like a stone cold killer. I won't let anybody lock me up! Goodbye Maine!

Sohn navigated a maze of dirt roads and paths back to the pickup truck. He grabbed a loaded backpack containing essentials from the front passenger seat, strapped it on, and continued the flight to safety. His exceptional hearing and eyesight allowed him to hide in the woods before a car got too close.

Sohn hopped a southbound freight train in the safe darkness of night. He didn't know the destination and didn't care as long as the train got him out of the state.

He knew why Herston targeted him. He wondered if the slain man would have felt the need to commit violence if he had a less unpleasing face.

While he sat in a freight car, listening to the sound of the train tearing along the tracks, Sohn had plenty of time to consider his future. Perhaps it would include seeing a plastic surgeon. But that drastic action depended in part on where the train stopped.

The next morning, the snakelike seventy-five car train pulled into a large metropolitan rail yard. Sohn anxiously slid open the car door and carefully scanned the vista to determine if there were any rail workers in sight. He relaxed after seeing that nobody was around. Then he scrutinized what he did in fact see.

Hundreds of freight cars sat motionless on several parallel rails. A substantial number of cars had a CSX logo. A wide highway overpass with heavy traffic was situated a few hundred yards away. He saw what appeared to be warehouses and other commercial buildings in the distance. His heart beat faster when he regarded the skyscrapers on the horizon.

I'm in New York City!

He shivered. Seeing the mammoth towers overwhelmed him. He knew Mary probably was in the sea of humanity somewhere. He'd read New York and

Hollywood were prime locations to get work done on a face. So Sohn promised he'd not leave the city until after the operation.

Is this where my life ends or I achieve salvation? Should I hop on another train away from here?

Without thinking, Sohn leapt down onto the gray gravel surface. He walked cautiously on the crunchy surface.

When a pair of rail workers stepped in view a couple of hundred yards away, Sohn ducked under the nearest freight car. He remained hidden until the coast was clear.

Sohn realized that getting from the Bronx into the center of Manhattan without being seen was impossible thanks to his height.

A wind gust blew a newspaper page past him. Sohn quickly grabbed it out of the air. He thought about crumpling up the weatherworn writing but something told him not to. He shrugged and glanced at what was written. There was good news. He learned there were three ongoing underground projects under the city, including the Second Avenue subway, a new water tunnel, and a new connection linking Grand Central Terminal with the Long Island Railroad.

When he'd finished reading, Sohn smashed the paper in his huge hands and tossed it on the ground.

He decided to travel underground, navigating the network of commuter rails and subway lines beneath the city. When passing through restricted construction zones, he intended to hide when crews worked. Once made his way to midtown Manhattan, he intended to show his face to Doctor Millard Strange.

What about Mary? As she obviously didn't want to see him again, he'd do his damnedest to avoid her. His stress level spiked when he thought of her. *Don't think about her! It's that simple.*

He trudged along the tracks toward his destiny.

Hours later, Sohn stood in a cavernous construction tunnel that lay one hundred and twenty feet beneath the Manhattan streets. He was awed by the volcanic rock walls and the immense size of the unfinished railway extension. The immense space made him feel small for once in his life.

Sohn wore a hard hat and an orange MTA construction vest he discovered hanging on racks in a makeshift dressing room by the tunnel entrance. Both items were too small for him. But he felt safer and less conspicuous wearing them

Earlier, Sohn had hidden out of sight in a deep crevice half way up the rough-cut wall. He'd gotten cramps and was anxious to stretch his long legs but that was too risky. The cool and damp air didn't ease the discomfort. Finally, after a long and tedious eight hours of watching construction activity, a work train transported the crew to the end of the tunnel at the end of the day.

He was finally alone in the subterranean chamber. He climbed down to the flat, hard packed dirt surface and stretched his aching long legs. Rocks were strewn about on either side of the rail track. Visibility was decent near the ceiling lights that were spaced every hundred feet, but the tunnel was cast in shadows midway between the fixtures.

Sohn walked beside the tracks in search of an exit.

"Hey, what're ya doing?" a distant voice called out from behind Sohn.

Sohn tried to walk with a purpose, like he belonged there. He was undecided about stopping and facing the approaching man or continuing.

"Hey mac, stop!"

That did it. Sohn burst forward in a blur of speed.

The red faced MTA construction engineer couldn't believe his eyes. He blinked rapidly.

Sohn sprinted. His mind was too focused on finding an exit to avoid all of the rocks. He tripped over an irregular cut bedrock. "AAGH!" His body soared and crashed hard on the ground. The impact knocked the wind out of him and cracked open the hard hat. He remained motionless.

The engineer heard the distressed scream. He turned on his walkie-talkie and requested a security team. Then the man cautiously moved forward.

Sohn moaned. He lay prone on his stomach. After a short time he slowly rolled onto his back. His head hurt like hell. He gently probed his face. There was something sticky just above the scalp line. Blood.

Footsteps echoed not too far away. Sighing, Sohn rose to his feet then immediately regretted doing so. The tunnel spun around and around. Sohn closed his eyes and doubled over. He felt a little better after a few seconds had passed. He gritted his teeth, stood erect gingerly, and turned to face the man chasing him.

The transit official stopped about one hundred feet from the giant. He dared not get closer in case the colossus decided to attack. He held up the walkie-talkie, saying "Just so you know, MTA police are on their way. Who are you and why are you here now?"

Sohn couldn't validate his presence there. "I forgot where the exit is."

"How's that possible? Are you bleeding?"

"Yeah, I hit my head. I got dizzy, sir. It hurts real bad." Sohn was being honest. He hoped the man believed him and would cut him some slack.

The transit guy stepped closer, tempting Sohn to grab him. He would have if it wasn't for a slight case of reality. *I got hurt because I ran. Perhaps I should face the music. I should let the cops arrest me and go to prison. Death row would be perfect but with my luck they'll sentence me to a life sentence. That's funny.* Sohn laughed loudly, the sound ricocheting up and down the tunnel for a quarter of a mile.

The MTA man stood frozen, afraid to move. The giant was one scary wacko.

Sohn's head cleared. He noticed multiple flashlights throwing out beams in different directions. The cops will be there within minutes. His strong freedom of movement mode kicked in. "Sorry guy, but I've got to leave."

He blocked out the pain and blood droplets that seeped down his forehead while running carefully, looking at the ground as much as potential exits. For an instant Sohn heard shouts but he moved out of range quickly. There had to be emergency exits up to the surface in case a train exploded or caught on fire. And indeed there was.

The elevator wasn't in operation yet but the long narrow stairs were. He was totally wiped out when he used his superhuman strength to force open a locked metal door and stepped into the night air. He checked out his surroundings. He stood in a park lined with skyscrapers.

Central Park.

He closed the door behind him quickly and jogged away expecting transit cops would soon stream out.

Chapter 28

Victor Frankenstein's orphan walked westward as he had done over two hundred years ago. Instead of the desolate frozen Arctic tundra he was walking in the concrete and granite canyons of Manhattan.

Sohn preferred the former environment. Nobody judged him there. The cold Arctic air was much cleaner and the peace and quiet offered solace. The breathtaking combination of snow and ice and cerulean blue sky was awesome. Knowing that the Arctic was melting saddened him. He wanted to hike across the polar region again before it turned to water.

The minutes slipped by as Sohn wandered through the seemingly empty park. He was agitated. The distant city sounds aliened him. He glanced furtively at the buildings that surrounded the urban park like a wall. The skyscrapers almost seemed near enough to reach out and touch.

Sohn needed to find space to run. Physical exertion would help alleviate the stress and open his mind. A few minutes later, he strode into the huge lawn known as the Sheep's Meadow. Sohn accelerated beyond the legal speed limit. It felt good.

While allowing his efficient eight-foot tall body to move on auto pilot, his mind devised a plan. *I'll head over to East 72nd Street, locate Dr. Strange's office and make him see me first thing in the morning. He'd be a fool not to accept me as a patient. After all, I'm one of a kind.*

Sohn, feeling relaxed and tired, lay down in the center of the mowed field and closed his eyes. He needed a few hours of sleep before dawn. Thankfully he didn't dream. So when his eyes opened three hours later he felt refreshed and ready to face whatever obstacles the city would throw at him.

The morning had just broken as Sohn exited the park. He stopped on the sidewalk and peered at a two adjoining street signs that read E 72 ST and 5 AVE respectively. Encouraged by being in the right neighborhood, he looked up and down the cobblestone sidewalk that ran along the three-lane avenue.

He observed several joggers trotting toward and away from him. When the closest runner, a woman, saw

Sohn lurking less than a hundred paces away, she sprinted across the street, watching Sohn fearfully.

"Does she actually think I'm going to attack her?" Sohn muttered. "Hopefully that'll change today when I look more pleasing to the eye."

Sohn crossed Fifth Avenue after the jogger was several blocks away. He didn't want her reporting him to the police.

Dozens of doctors maintained offices on prestigious 72nd Street. Sohn carefully examined the names outside the doctors' offices as he walked eastward from Fifth Avenue toward the distant East River.

Sohn was too focused on his search to notice an NYPD patrol car do a U-turn and pull up parallel to him, siren blasting. Two cops sat in the front seat watching him. Neither seemed to be in a hurry to get out of the vehicle and confront the monstrous looking giant.

Sohn faced them reluctantly.

"Sir, step over to the vehicle," said the police officer in the passenger seat."

Sohn blew out some air, stepped onto the street and bent down severely to gaze at the policemen.

"Where are you going?" the cop demanded.

"To the doctor. Is there a problem?"

"Easy now. I'm the one asking the questions. Understand, sir?"

Sohn turned his head away from them sullenly. He'd done nothing wrong yet other than not show the required degree of respect. Then he turned his head quickly back to the cops, saying "I'm going to the doctor now."

"Are you ill?"

"That's my business. Be seeing you."

Sohn stood up and walked away slowly and purposely, forcing himself not to look back at the cops. The cop in the driver's seat persuaded his partner to remain seated and not go after the disrespectful giant. Instead, the car moved forward slowly, keeping him in sight while checking NYPD data banks for any information on Sohn. Nothing turned up.

Just before reaching Park Avenue Sohn found what he'd been looking for. He studied an ornate brass sign with etched lettering on the exterior door that read MILLARD STRANGE, M.D. F.A.C.S.

Sohn gripped the door knob, turned it right and the door opened. He stood there, surprised that the office was not closed at that early hour. His stomach knotted up. He was tempted to close the door and flee the scene. Instead, he sighed, ducked his head and stepped inside.

The police car double parked in front of the medical office.

Sohn entered a sumptuous waiting room decorated with carpeted hardwood flooring, ornate chairs, and a wide couch. Tables stacked with fashion and business magazines including Godwin's *Manhattan*. Sohn stared at framed photographs of beautiful people that adorned the walls. Sohn assumed they were patients of Doctor Strange. He wondered if his picture would eventually join the photo gallery.

"Hello there," a man said.

Sohn, startled, spun around. His head barely touched the ceiling.

"My, my," the man said, looking wide-eyed at Sohn. He extended his left hand. "I'm Doctor Strange."

Sohn shook the doctor's hand. "Sohn Schenk."

The doctor appeared to be around 60, medium height, and trim. His tanned face as handsome with intelligent eyes.

"Mr. Schrenk, you are fortunate I came in an hour early this morning. You're here for a consultation?"

Sohn glanced at the wall clock. Strange noticed.

"What can you do for me, doctor?"

"Are you in a hurry?"

"I don't like being in the city."

"You think it's because of how you look, how people perceive you?"

"Of course." Sohn added, "Aren't they one and the same?"

"Not necessarily. How one behaves really counts more than anything."

"And you're a plastic surgeon! I suspect you'd lose potential patients if you tell them that."

Strange smiled. "I am busy enough. Now listen, before we decide about facial alteration, you will need to tell me about yourself. Let's go back to my office."

The entrance door opened as Doctor Strange and Sohn started to move. They stayed put as one of the two cops Sohn recently encountered stepped inside.

The cop carefully looked at both men. "You okay, Doctor"

"Yes, why?"

"I saw this perp, I mean man, enter the premises. Just checking if he's a patient of yours or not."

"He is, officer. I appreciate your concern but all is well."

The cop stood, thumbs under his belt. He smirked at Sohn, nodded at Strange, turned briskly and exited.

Strange sat at his mahogany desk in a well-appointed wood paneled office. Sohn, too big to handle a chair, sat on a couch.

After some prompting, he told the doctor about his life in Maine, going back no further than twenty years. He didn't want Strange to know his age. Revealing that secret would greatly alter the good doctor's perception of him. Sohn feared becoming the poster boy of modern medicine. His blood could be used to find an antidote to aging and disease.

Strange jotted on a pad while Sohn spoke. Learning as much as possible about a patient could affect details in facial features. He wanted to believe his newest patient was not the evil, malicious monster that he resembled. So far, the giant had been polite and reserved, even shy.

When Sohn finished speaking, the doctor clenched a fist and pressed it gently over his mouth as he stared at the reflection of Sohn in a wall mirror.

"How quickly do you want me to work on your face?"

"This morning. Right now."

Strange's eyebrows shot up. "That's highly irregular."

"Listen doctor, I can't stay in the city. I have no place to stay and nobody I can visit. I can't tolerate the noise and crowds."

"Because of how you look to people?"

"Yes, that and because I've lived far from the madding crowd for so long. I fear the city will be the death of me."

"Due to the urgency, I'll agree. My assistant will revise my schedule." Strange smiled at Sohn.

"Thank you."

"First, I need some of your medical history. Allergies, hospitalization, illnesses, etcetera. I'll take your height, weight and a blood sample."

Sohn's large hands covered his face which had suddenly turned whiter than normal. *God help me! I have to lie to this good man, don't I? But why does he want my blood?*

"What is it?"

Slowly, Sohn lowed his hands and clasped them. He looked sharply at Strange. "Why do you have to have my blood?"

"It's a necessity for every patient. A blood work is mandatory, especially as you'll be anesthetized before the procedure."

"No I won't."

"Listen here. There will be substantial pain."

"I will handle it, Doctor Strange. I have a very high tolerance."

Strange shook his head slightly. "If you were younger than 30, I would relent about the blood work. Are you in your twenties?"

It was Sohn's turn to smile.

"The test will show me if you have anemia and many other things pertinent for the procedure."

Sohn sighed. "Who else will see my blood besides you?"

"My nurse will draw the blood. I'll analyze it myself. That's everyone."

Sohn had been sorely tempted to threaten the doctor with bodily harm if the doctor lied. He recalled issuing a threat eons earlier in a Swiss ice cave that had backfired and resulted in death and mayhem. Although he barely knew Strange, he felt that the man had more ethics than Victor Frankenstein.

Sohn decided to trust Strange. "Okay, do it."

Chapter 29

Doctor Strange was astonished that his newest patient had no spare body fat, prohibiting him from using liposuction to transplant any harvested fat on the lean and severe looking face. The observant doctor had the distinct impression that Sohn was much older than he divulged. He recognized age in the eyes and considerable scarring. But he kept his opinion to himself, respecting the giant's privacy.

Sohn was no stranger to pain and suffering. He'd been bitten by wolves, impaled by tree branches, and sustained substantial job related cuts and bruises at lumber mills. His pain threshold was high. Sohn could block out pain, forcing it deep within the recesses of his extraordinary mind.

He lay on an extended operating table. His jaw was opened wide. A long needle was inserted inside his mouth. Material to soften the appearance of his face was injected in different areas of the lining of the inside of his mouth. Sohn closed his eyes. He forced himself to ignore the severe discomfort by silently recited *Great Expectation*s, one of many books he knew by heart.

Again and again he withstood probes into the soft tissue and nerve centers of his gums and other regions of his facial cavity. He couldn't stop pain induced tears from seeping from his closed eyelids. After a nurse gently dried them, his eyes opened and beheld her compassionate smile.

"We're nearly done," Strange said.

Sohn, unable to speak, blinked before closing his eyes again. Son's mind drifted to his discussion with Doctor Strange about paying for the facial enhancement. The doctor agreed to do the work pro bono in exchange for the privilege of writing an exclusive article in The New England Journal of Medicine. The story would include before and after pictures, background information on the extraordinary patient and a description of the work performed.

Sohn had reluctantly posed for the first batch of photographs. He would have to brace himself for the second photo shoot showing his bruised and battered face. Sohn made an appointment to return for a follow up in a few weeks that would include the final picture taking.

Sohn was in a deep sleep and snoring loudly when the clamps were removed from his mouth. He was wheeled down a bright corridor by a nurse and Doctor Strange. The motion awakened him. He was disoriented. *Where am I?*

He raised himself on his elbows.

"Lay down please," Strange said firmly.

Sohn scowled but lay down, peering up at the doctor.

"Doctor, where are you taking me?"

"Your recovery room."

"I want to leave."

"Wait a moment please," Strange replied as the bed on wheels veered into a cheerfully decorated room. A private bathroom was situated just inside the doorway. The bed was parked alongside a tray table stocked with a hand mirror, cup of water and a straw.

The doctor nodded to the nurse. She walked out of the room and turned down the hall.

Strange studied Sohn's black and blue face. Sohn watched him closely.

"Let me see."

Strange picked up the mirror, saying "I have to warn you. You won't like what you see. But in a few days, you'll start to see a remarkable improvement, I can assure you."

Sohn reached for the mirror. Strange handed it to him.

Sohn grimaced at himself. "I look worse than when Victor first beheld me."

"Who?"

"My first doctor," Sohn quickly replied, eyes flickering from the mirror and Strange.

Strange nodded. "The bruising will slowly disappear. You'll also experience swelling. Your face will be as good as new within two weeks."

Sohn couldn't stop examining himself.

Strange stood by patiently.

After a few minutes, Sohn set the mirror down on the portable table. "Can I leave now?"

"Sohn, you really shouldn't. You need to rest at least 24 hours. Where will you go?"

"I'm not sure. Out of the city. I'll find a place."

"You're not returning to Maine right away?"

"No. Later."

Strange sighed. "Well, I can't stop you from leaving, can I?

"No, you can't."

"I must warn you that the paparazzi are down the street. If they see you, Sohn, a number of them will likely follow you."

"People usually turn tail when they see me."

"Not the paparazzi."

"I'm no movie star."

"No, but your extraordinary stature and, um, your face will attract them to you. Beware."

Sohn left shortly after the photo session. He thanked Doctor Strange for his fast work and courtesy and made an appointment to see him in two weeks. He wasn't so sure that he'd be able to fill his commitment though.

When he stepped outside, he glanced to his right and noticed the crowd of bored yet expectant photographers and other onlookers gathered one hundred feet down the block.

More than one casually met Sohn's gaze. They did double takes, turning around wide-eyed and agape, apparently forgetting about the celebrity they'd been waiting for. The paparazzi were frightened, yet unable to turn away from the giant with the terrible face.

Sohn glared at the growing number of people watching him. He turned away from them as cameras flashed away. Sohn fled.

Dr. Strange peered outside through a window as six photographers chased after their new quarry. He frowned, shook his head sadly, and closed the blind.

Sohn sprinted in the traffic lanes, passing taxis, trucks, private cars and city buses. Startled drivers slammed on the brakes, causing a multitude of accidents. Sohn kept running, losing his pursuit. It didn't cross his mind that images of him would be seen on television news programs and published in tomorrow's newspapers.

All he cared about was finding someplace to rest his painful face.

Chapter 30

Over the years Sohn had read news stories about muggings, burglaries and murders in Central Park. He figured it would be the perfect place to recover from the procedure, especially at night when the urban oasis was practically deserted.

He felt safe enough. Nobody would dare accost him there. And he didn't think anything bad would happen to him unless the paparazzi somehow discovered his whereabouts

He stopped, listened and tapped his uncanny ability to sense danger. All was well at the moment.

Thunder rumbled in the distance. Sohn glanced in the direction of the sonic sound and saw lightning flash in the night sky several miles to the north. He smiled.

Sohn stood near the East 72nd Street entrance to the park, basking under an overhead light. His shadow extended almost fifty feet from his long and lean body.

He noticed a woman standing beside a hydrant waiting for her dog to do his business.

She abruptly looked at him, overwhelmed with shock and terror.

Sohn smiled at the woman.

She wet her pants. She was too terrified to notice. *A monster is after me!*

The woman abruptly hauled her unhappy dog away by the leash, anxiously looking over her shoulder. The monster had disappeared from view. She scurried a block to her apartment building and dialed 911 as an attentive doorman opened the door for her. She made a complaint to an incredulous operator.

A patrol car was dispatched just to be on the safe side.

Sohn sulked. He was annoyed by the latest example of fear and scorn. He walked on a paved roadway, unsure where to go. The park would be full of people the next morning. He needed to find a hiding place in the park or go underground again. His eyes were drawn again to the tall buildings around him. *I shouldn't be here.*

He was bone weary from the strain of the operation but too stressed to sleep. He wondered if Mary was asleep. He looked up. The moon's position in the sky would tell him what time it was. But the sky was clouded over.

Another blast of thunder detonated, slightly louder than before, followed by a flash of lightning. The storm was getting closer.

"Please don't," a woman cried in the distance. Sohn squinted in the direction of the distant voice. It was too dark to see much of anything. He didn't want to get involved with whatever was happening. He just wanted to locate a safe route out of Central Park.

"Give it to me now, bitch!" an unseen man demanded.

"Don't hurt me. I'll give you money," the woman pleaded.

That set in motion a chain of events which would alter Sohn's life forever. He turned and ran toward the voices, determined to save the woman and punish her assailant.

The voices came from the Conservatory Water, a small pond used for sailing model boats. Sohn moved stealthily closer. The pond and boat rental building were still screened from view by shrubs and trees.

A gun toting mugger, face covered with a ski mask, stood over a slender woman in a jogger's outfit. She lay on the edge of the pond.

"Hand over everything you have on you or I'll drown you," the mugger growled, aiming the pistol at her chest.

"Please don't hurt me."

"Cut the blabbering. Gimme your phone, wallet, jewelry. Now!"

"I need to sit up."

"Do it, bitch!"

Thunder peeled almost over them followed by blinding lightning. A breeze struck up.

A siren wailed far away. It gradually got louder.

The trembling woman propped herself up. She reached inside the pocket of a fleece. She dropped her phone, ID and cash in a plastic bag held out by the mugger as he quickly scanned the area. Old fashioned lamps along the paths and walkways would enable him to see anybody nearby. He saw nobody.

"Can I go now?" she asked.

"Wait a minute. Is that everything?" he asked with a raised brow.

The woman nodded.

"Let's see about that."

He reached out and grabbed her neck with his free hand. She screamed silently as the assailant pushed her head over the lip of the pond into the water. Her arms waved fustily.

The siren sounded much closer.

Heavy feet stampeded through the brush.

The mugger, one hand on the woman's head and the other on his pistol, abruptly turned his head toward the sound.

His dropped his jaw and stared wide-eyed at a huge apparition hurtling toward him. He completely forgot about the woman.

She freed herself from the mugger's grasp and raised her soaked head. She breathed deeply, then stopped in mid breathe upon seeing a terrifying sight.

Sohn reached down and effortlessly raised the mugger over his head, ready to hurl him into the pond.

Flashlights blinded his eyes.

"This is the police. Put that man down and step away from the woman."

Sohn lowered the man to a level parallel to his face to block out the light beams. He could hold the one hundred and forty pound man in that position indefinitely.

But time was not on his side. He backed up one four foot stride to demonstrate he was at least half cooperating.

There were two cops. One man, one woman. They were with the Central Park Precinct. The team had responded to the 911 call. They thought it was a hoax. They were wrong. The woman, with a nervous eye on Sohn, rushed over to the victim. Her partner covered her with his pistol and kept the flashlight trained on Sohn and the man in the air.

"I'm Officer Quinn. Are you injured, ma'am?"

"He tried to drown me," the victim croaked hoarsely.

"The giant," Quinn replied.

"No."

Quinn craned her neck up as far as it would go. Sohn filled her vision.

"Sergeant, the little guy's the perp."

The sergeant frowned. "Mister, put him down and stay where you are."

Sohn thought he was safe. "Okay." He abruptly released his grip.

The man landed hard and staggered.

The sergeant quickly stopped forward and cuffed the criminal in one fluid movement. He glared up at

Sohn's unreadable face. "You didn't have to drop him like that."

Sohn shrugged.

"Stand still," the sergeant told the mugger when the man began shuffling his feet. The officer nodded to Quinn, signaling for her to question the victim.

Quinn pulled out a NYPD pad from a rear pants pocket. She obtained the woman's name and address from a Driver's License provided by her.

"What happened, ma'am?"

The victim told Quinn about jogging in the park and being accosted when the mugger, who'd been hiding behind a tree, accosted her. He threatened to kill her unless she handed over her valuables. She told the cops about almost drowning and the miraculous rescue by the giant in their midst."

Quinn looked at the sergeant, nodding slightly.

Taking his cue, he interrogated Sohn. "You were at the right place at the right time. Why were you in the park?"

"I was out for a walk." Sohn observed Quinn writing on her pad.

"What's your name?"

"Sohn Schrenk."

"Address?"

"Rockland Maine." *Until the other day anyway.*

"Why are you in the city?"

Sohn didn't reply. He searched in his mind for an acceptable reply.

"Well?"

"To see a friend." He hoped the cops would recognize some truth in his statement. It wasn't a complete lie.

"Name and address?"

"I don't see how that's relevant to my saving the young woman," Sohn said as forcefully as possible. "I'm leaving."

Sohn turned around and took a step.

"Stop there, now!"

Large raindrops started to fall everywhere. A loud thunder clap blasted directly over them, followed by a bright lightning flash.

The victim shuddered.

Sohn took another step, and another.

Then he ran.

The sergeant decided fleeing a crime scene implied guilt. He knew the giant was a hero in the eyes of the young woman, but not his. He aimed the pistol and fired twice.

Chapter 31

Sohn ran southward through Central Park as the torrential rain pelted his wounded body. He'd heard both shots and felt one when it penetrated the back of his right shoulder. The wound hurt like hell. He blocked out the pain. Blood seeped slowly down his back, diluted by the rain.

His mind switched back and forth between why he had run and where he was going. He didn't have an answer for either issue.

I should have stayed. I did nothing wrong. I was a Good Samaritan. But the police could have arrested me for vagrancy. I'd sooner die than stand behind bars. This is the second time somebody's aimed a gun at me in a week.

Sohn felt his old deadly thirst for vengeance returning for the first time in centuries. He feared what he'd do if threatened again. But he soldiered on, weaving between paved roads and narrow paths, moving closer to the zoo with every long stride. Then he had an idea.

Mary. Will she see me? I have no other place to go.
Where does she live? How do I find out?

Sohn ran through two archways into the zoo. He stopped a moment to catch his breathe. He looked all around for moving lights. There was no sign of pursuit. What was NYPD doing? Would they wait out the storm?

I have to keep moving.

The rain stopped as suddenly as it started. It improved visibility remarkably, meaning he could see and be seen much better than in the deluge. Seals barked nearby.

He'd dawdled long enough. Sohn jogged around the Arsenal, a brick building resembling a medieval fort. He felt better upon seeing wide stairs leading up to Fifth Avenue.

Sohn started up the steps five at a time. Two police cars with flashing lights braked hard by the stairs. He heard shouting as men hurried out of the vehicles. Rattled, he quickly turned around and sprinted to the bottom of the stairs, desperately looking for an escape route.

The police presence by the exit meant something. *The police don't want me to leave the park. I have to find another way out.*

But first he badly needed to get out of sight of the stairs as two cops set up a blockade at the top and another pair descended to the bottom to set up another perimeter.

Sohn ran around the Arsenal and then slowed as he passed animal cages. He stopped upon hearing familiar growling. Sohn pivoted toward the sound and saw several sets of red eyes staring at him. Wolves. He visualized the savage pack attack from 1798. Sohn glared at the beasts, then quickly left them behind.

The pain worsened. He could go into shock unless it was treated. *I got to get out of here and now or else they'll get me.*

He made a loop and passed through an exit, glancing all around every few seconds. Fifth Avenue was only a hundred feet away. He could hear it, but not see it through the trees. Barking dogs were barely audible. He couldn't tell if there were in the park. Curious, Sohn climbed a rise and peered carefully at the panorama. About a quarter of a mile north of his position, he saw two dogs and a squad of uniformed cops following his trail. He sighed.

Then he jogged in a straight line for Fifth Avenue, moving branches out of the way with both hands. Before long, he stood before a long eight foot tall brown stone and mortar wall. He listened for any police presence on the other side. Nothing. The barking behind him was getting louder. He didn't have much time.

With some effort, and a lot of pain, he reached forward, grabbed the top of the wall, and sprang up. The motion carried him over the wall onto cobblestone. Feeling a bit lightheaded, he squatted. He felt a little smaller and less noticeable in that position.

The dogs and cops continued to close in, with barking and voices shouting encouragement.

Sohn surveyed the view from left to right. Light traffic drove past to his right on the wide avenue. High rise apartment buildings occupied by the moneyed and social upper classes stood across the street. As he panned the sidewalk across the avenue, he did a double take.

He waited for a break in the traffic and crossed the roadway to a street corner. A phone booth stood a few feet away. Sohn was heartened to find a worn Manhattan White Pages. He thumbed through the thick telephone directory for the listing he wanted, glancing every few seconds at the park. He feared seeing the police scaling the wall. Not yet.

The light was too poor to read the small print. Aggravated, Sohn yanked the heavy book out of its holder. Holding it under an arm, he strode quickly away, leaving a trail of blood drops behind.

Chapter 32

Sohn rounded the corner onto Madison Avenue. The lighting on the thoroughfare was much better. He scanned up and down the street for pedestrians. The sidewalk was clear at 3am. He bent down and lowered the phone book on the sidewalk beside a store. Then he rifled through the pages for the listing he wanted. He found the name, address and phone number. Calling the person was out of the question. A surprise visit seemed ideal.

He ripped out the page, folded it neatly, and stuffed it in a pocket. He nudged the phone book against the building so nobody would trip over it. Then Sohn looked at the corner street sign to get his bearings. He was less than ten blocks from where he wanted to go.

Sohn grimaced. The intensifying pain and dizziness threatened his mission.

Sohn concentrated hard, trying to determine how close the dogs were. They were barely audible. Had they lost his scent? He was fortunate that the K-9 unit was prohibited from entering the heavily populated residential district.

He felt euphoric while striding along the deserted streets of the sleeping neighborhood. There was nobody in sight. He seemingly had the city to himself, with nobody to censure him. The relative quiet and darkness almost made him feel at home. And he didn't feel any police pursuit.

That was about to change in the form of a SWAT team from the Emergency Services Unit being assembled to hunt him down. The members of the elite unit were armed with semi-automatics. Following the blood trail would be simple.

Sohn's wounded right shoulder sagged as he loped along the quiet, empty streets. He thought back to all the killing in when Victor was alive. He thought about the slaughter on the battlefield at Gettysburg. Miraculously, this was the first serious injury of his life.

Being shot makes me feel mortal. What a weird feeling that is. I'm finally experiencing something that millions have gone through. Being wounded. Needing medical attention. Facing death.

Sohn considered his last thought for a few heartbeats. Then he forced a laugh. Thinking about his own death made him feel less invincible. He had to be strong to accomplish his task.

Sohn hadn't seen nor heard the police since crossing the phone booth. But now he felt them. His pulse quickened and his stomach clenched in knots. He had to keep moving and not dawdle when he arrived at his destination.

He reached in a pocket for his knife. It comforted him to feel it there, ready to use if necessary.

Sohn stopped under a street lamp and retrieved the folded page of phone listings to make sure the address he memorized was correct. He couldn't afford to waste time going to the wrong building.

He was on the right block. He took a deep breathe, released it and stepped toward the townhouse.

Chapter 33

Sohn stood at the front door to the Godwin's townhouse on 64th Street. A million thoughts crossed through his mind.

Why was I shot after rescuing that woman? Why the hell are they after me? I should press charges against that bastard cop.

Sohn pounded his fist angrily against the oak door. He was too upset to realize what he was doing. The banging was heard at the end of the street. And it awakened the occupants of the townhouse.

Mary was startled awake for the second time that night. The violent storm was the first. Afterwards, she drifted into a disturbing dream about Sohn in which he killed her parents and kidnapped her.

The persistent pounding at the front door downstairs drew her out of the harrowing nightmare. She lay immobile, too frightened to move, listening to the commotion downstairs.

William Godwin, wearing pajamas and a bathrobe, stood in the ornate entrance hallway holding a rifle. Jane cringed a few feet behind him, wearing in a modest nightgown.

The fierce pounding on the door had stopped but their unwanted visitor hadn't departed.

"I'm calling the police unless you leave immediately," William said angrily. He adjusted the safety and aimed the rifle at the door, a finger on the trigger.

"Open the door now," said the muffled voice outside.

"Why's that monster here?" asked Jane.

William turned irritably to his wife, a finger raised over his mouth to silence her.

"Move away from the door," Sohn instructed.

Godwin narrowed his eyes but stayed put.

The front door imploded and shattered, knocking Godwin on his back. The rifle fell on the floor near him. Jane screamed as Sohn stood in the empty door jamb, filling the empty space. She fainted when he stepped forward.

Sohn bent down and lifted the broken door off Mary's unconscious father. Then he walked to the staircase and peered up. *Where is she?* He glanced at her parents. Neither were able to speak. He looked up again.

"Mary, I'm coming for you."

He trudged up the staircase, taking the stairs three at a time.

Mary snapped out of her reverie. She jumped out of bed, ran to the bedroom door and locked it. She put her head against the door. Sohn's heavy footsteps were audible. Then she put on a shirt, jeans, jacket, and boots.

"Mary, open the door. We have to go now," Sohn said from the hallway.

I'm not going anywhere with him! She put her credit cards and driver's license in a pocket just in case.

"Mary, please open up now. I won't hurt you."

Mary found her voice. "What about my parents?"

"Your mother fainted. Your father should be okay."

Mary became braver, using her concern for her parents well-being. She unlocked the door and opened it. Sohn blocked her.

"Sohn, move out of my way," she said resolutely. "I want to see for myself."

Sohn stepped aside and followed her downstairs. *Every step she takes on her own gets us closer to getting out before the police get here. .*

Mary took in the horrible scene on the ground floor as she quickly descended the stairs. Her mother kneeled over her father. He still lay on the floor. His forehead was already black and blue from the impact with the heavy door. The cracked door lay on the floor where Sohn left it.

People milled on the sidewalk, staring inside. They backed off when Sohn came in view.

Jane glanced up at her daughter with glazed eyes as Mary arrived at her side.

"Get him out," Jane murmured.

Mary turned her head to Sohn. "What happened to your face?"

"I saw Doctor Strange."

Mary started at him blankly before understanding the implication of his words. "You must leave," she said harshly.

"But I had work done on my face," Sohn reasoned.

"So?"

William's eyes opened.

"Darling," Jane said.

"Don't move. I'll call for an ambulance," Mary said, rising to her feet. She stepped away from her parents and moved to where Sohn had to turn his back on them. He blocked out her view of them.

Mary glared at Sohn. "Look what you did to my parents!"

"I didn't intend any harm. We must leave now!"

William's eyes searched desperately for his rifle. It lay on the floor, just beyond reach.

Jane followed his gaze. William peered up at her ad slightly shook his head. Jane frowned, but remained silent.

Quietly, he dragged himself closer to the weapon. His bruised forehead beaded with sweat from the exertion.

"I'm not abandoning my parents. They need me now more than ever."

William grabbed the rifle.

Sohn's belly tightened. He felt the cops. They were too close for comfort.

"What about me?" Sohn asked.

William propped himself up. He signaled Jane to lay down. After she did, he swung the barrel of the gun toward his target.

William spoke. "You should have stayed in Maine."

Sohn pivoted. He leaped to the side as the bullet exploded out of the chamber. The violent sound was deafening.

William hadn't reacted fast enough to Sohn's fast lateral movement to adjust the aim. He aimed where the giant had been until that instant.

The bullet pierced Mary's chest, missing her heart by inches. She was hurdled backwards.

Sohn landed and sprung up one knee. He cried out in despair upon seeing blood spreading across Mary's chest.

Jane screamed.

William dropped the gun and was too stunned to do more.

Sohn, moaning, gently lifted Mary. He stepped through the open door onto the street, cradling her in his arms. Something was wrong outside but he couldn't identify what it was. The wail of an approaching ambulance drowned out all other city sounds.

Police spotlights suddenly blasted him in the face. He was blinded by the light.

"Put Miss Godwin down slow and easy," a voice commanded.

"Go away," Sohn urged, shielding his eyes with one hand. "I have to take her to the hospital."

"An ambulance will take her there. Here it comes now."

The ambulance, lights flashing and siren wailing, sped down the street toward Sohn, Mary and the cops. It stopped sharply ten yards away. Medics jumped out. A stretcher was wheeled forward a few feet then stopped by the nervous medics.

"If you want her to live, allow these paramedics to do their job."

Sohn knew the cop was right. "Okay, but I'll go with Mary in the ambulance."

The blinding light was dimmed.

"Bring her over," the cop instructed without acknowledging Sohn's statement.

Sohn carried her over to the stretch. The paramedics carefully grabbed hold of the body and lowered Mary onto the stretcher as her parents cautiously stepped outside. Seeing Mary being wheeled to the open back door of the ambulance, they hurried over.

The cop who'd been speaking to Sohn stepped over to him with two other cops, effectively blocked the giant from approaching the ambulance. "You need to stay here and answer some questions.

Sohn frowned. He saw Mary's mother hop into the back of the ambulance.

"If you don't cooperate, Mister, you won't be able to see her for a long, long time. And I know you're the Good Samaritan from Central Park. So be smart."

Sohn looked from the departing ambulance to Mary's approaching father to the police officer. Using

William A. Chanler

every ounce he could muster of goodwill and restraint, he
nodded

Epilogue

Detective John Pounds drove on a bumpy logging trail in northern Maine. It was mid-autumn. All the leaves had fallen and the air was crisp and cool. The sun which flickered through pine forest, making the hard packed road difficult to see well.

His mind half focused on the road while the other half reflected on Sohn.

Sohn returned to Maine a month ago. He atoned for his disappearance by presenting himself at police headquarters in Augusta and provided the overdue written statement about the death of Jonah Herston. He explained what happened in New York City.

John contacted NYPD to verify Sohn's story about the incident in the park. The police spokesman told him the city wanted to bestow a key to the city to Sohn for being shot in Central Park but Sohn had refused the gesture.

John also spoke with Mary several times after her surgery. She was a little incoherent the first time they spoke but several days later her mind was clear. Mary repeatedly steered the conversation away from herself to Sohn. She hadn't seen nor spoken to him since being taken to the hospital. She wondered why and seemed upset Sohn hadn't answered her calls. She wanted to know if John knew where to find Sohn. The detective told her that Sohn was working for a lumber company and he intended to pay the lumberjack a visit.

John's State Police vehicle approached the loggers' yard. He passed mammoth stacks of long chorded wood be loaded on a rig. An array of parked pickup trucks and SUVs were parked in front of an RV. John parked next to Sohn's black pickup, got out and stretched. He breathed in the cool, fresh pine scented air and smiled.

He turned in the direction of the sound of a powerful engine but the heavy equipment was too far away to see it.

A bearded man wearing a bright hard hat, wool shirt, jeans and work boots exited the RV. He stopped and stared expectantly at John.

"Hi, I'm looking for Sohn Schrenk. Know where he is?"

The logger squinted his eyes and nodded. "We call him Samson. He in some trouble, Officer?"

"No, nothing like that." The logger waited a beat for an explanation of what a Statie wanted with the giant logger, then shrugged. "He's in that direction," pointing a finger toward the distant engine sound.

"Thanks," John replied. He turned around and headed in the suggested direction. The logger regarded him with curious eyes as John moved into the distance.

The noise increased as he walked toward a yellow yarder, heavy equipment used to pull freshly cut logs from the forest floor. He was fascinated by the operation. It reminded him of playing with model sized trucks and bulldozers when he was a boy.

A chainsaw roared in the nearby forest. John couldn't see the person using it.

Suddenly, the chainsaw shutoff.

John waited expectantly.

Sohn stepped out of the forest in his hard hat. He walked briskly over to John. John noticed that the bruises had disappeared. He though Sohn's face almost looked handsome.

They shook hands and walked slowly away from the yarder deep in conversation.

"How's the shoulder?" John asked.

Sohn tapped the injured shoulder. "Good as new."

"Your face is healed. It looks good."

"Thanks. I'm supposed to go back to New York for fashion week and walk the runway," Sohn deadpanned.

"Huh?"

"I'm not serious, John." He looked closely at the trooper. "Why are you smiling?"

"The grand jury has ruled in your favor. They decided you killed Herston in self-defense. You're a free man."

"Thank God!" Sohn replied, visibly relieved.

"I've told Mary."

Sohn's face darkened. "What!"

"You told me when you first returned to Maine that it was best for you not to speak with her again, that you didn't want to affect her recovery. But that didn't prevent me from calling her."

"How is she?" Sohn asked somberly.

"There was significant bleeding of one lung. She's finally home resting. You should call her." John then frowned and averted his eyes from Sohn.

"Anything else?"

"She said she's been trying to call you. She wants to talk to you."

Sohn sighed.

"She cares for you, man. Don't turn your back on her."

Sohn shook his head. "I don't know that I'm good for her. What does she want from me?"

"That's something you need to find out for herself. I think she expected you to visit her in the hospital."

"I didn't know that."

Sohn regarded him closely as John wondered if he should tell his tall friend about Perce Shelley.

"What is it?"

"It's nothing, Sohn."

"Tell me!"

"Shelley has been calling on her."

Sohn stared at John with dead eyes.

Pounds grimaced. "I shouldn't have told you, Sorry."

"I've caused her a lot of pain. She has every right to see whoever."

Pounds didn't say anything. He avoided the giant's troubled gaze.

"I'll not bother her again."

Pounds looked up at Sohn uncertainly.

"It's probably time for me to move on. I've stayed in Maine too long."

"You're wrong."

Sohn peered closely at his friend. "You think so?"

"I know you never stay in one place very long. Frankly, I see no reason for you to relocate."

"What about the paparazzi and those news reporters, John? They started harassing me after my shoulder operation. I couldn't go anywhere without them. That's why I left the city so soon." He glanced anxiously at the distant RV. "I fear they'll show up here."

John nodded. "That may happen, but moving won't stop them. Stay put."

Sohn shrugged.

They were silent for a few moments, each man deep in thought.

Pounds broke the ice. "I've got to run. See me when the season's over. If you decide to leave the area, please let me know. And call Mary."

They exchanged farewells.

Sohn frowned as he watched John return to the parking area. Then he turned away and pulled out his smartphone from a pocket. He dialed while walking toward the forest, then held the phone to an ear.

"Hi Mary."

William A. Chanler

Acknowledgements

When I set out to write a sequel to *Frankenstein*, keeping faithful to Mary Shelley's vision was paramount. So first and foremost I must acknowledge Mary Shelley, a very gifted writer with a powerful imagination. Her harrowing story has cost me many hours of sleep.

Thank you to my wife Rosalie for her proofreading and encouragements. Thank you to my sons Jamie and Michael for their honest feedback, suggestions, and support.

Thank you to Sheriff Scott Story of the Waldo County Sheriff's Department in Belfast Maine for confirming investigative procedures.